DAMSELS & DINOSAURS

Wren Jones

Damsels and Dinosaurs

Cover Illustration and Typography by Amphi Studio
https://www.amphi.studio.com/

Chapter Illustrations by Lord Mac
lordmac36@gmail.com

ISBN 979-8-9890410-5-3 (*print edition*)

ISBN 979-8-9890410-4-6 (*ebook*)

1 2 3 4 5 6 7 8 9 10

www.wrenjones.net

To the clever girls.

May you eat the faces of those who wish
to stifle you.

Author's Note

This book is cozy fantasy adjacent.
The history of the discovery of dinosaurs and
some elements of dinosaur biology is
completely fabricated. If you're a super fan of
the history of dinosaurs, please know this is all
in good fun.

However, I made sure to include all your
favorites if you requested it to appear.
(Including the turtle-- you know who you are).

There are some elements of fear here.
But please know that everything works out in
the end.

Come on this journey with Athena and Poppy –
secure in the knowledge that it's going to be
okay.

You are safe here.

CONTENTS

Chapter One

POPPY FLETCHER IS A WRITER. OF DRIVEL

The knock on the door jolted Poppy from her work at the large writing desk. She sat up straighter, eyes narrowing at the door with suspicious regard. She did her best to position herself so that whoever came in wouldn't see exactly what she was working on.

Not that it mattered.

Everyone in her family thought her writing was either absolute drivel or complete rubbish fit only for scandal-obsessed ladies anyway.

Still, the knock was her first clue that something was amiss this evening. No one in the house ever bothered her during her scheduled writing time. They may not have liked what she did in her free time, but they at least tended to leave her be.

Morbidly, she wondered if someone had died, just as the door opened.

Her sister was already mid-sentence, though she was whispering, strangely subdued from her usual nature. "The latest shipment arrived, and it has less than half the expected inventory. It can't keep going like this." Ann shut the door quickly behind her and crossed the room to Poppy's desk. She sat in an empty chair, hands clasped on her lap. "How can they keep things running there?"

"The shipment came in?" Poppy asked. "And there was no note, no explanation?"

"Nothing. You *know* how she is."

Poppy sighed and put her pen down gently. She reached for her sister's clenched fists and squeezed. "Yes, Aunt Rose is... eccentric."

Her sister pulled her hands away. "Poppy!" she hissed, louder than she expected, by her own surprised expression. She turned to the door again, then back quickly. "She is not *eccentric*. She is going to run the business into the ground. And when they run out of money, what will we all do?"

"I have already made plans to handle it." Poppy opened the top drawer of her desk quietly. She shuffled a few sheets of stationery aside, some clippings from articles about the collapse of their other Fletcher honey farms. Her heart skipped a beat, and for a moment, her head went light.

Where was it?

Her fingers dug through the drawer until she found it—the edge of a thick, but small paper. Poppy let out a small breath and lifted the single ticket. It cast a shadow across her face in the dancing light of the beeswax candles.

"You did not! I never thought you would actually do it." Ann grasped the ticket, her eyes inspecting the lettering closely. "Mother will *never* agree to let you go. Does Benedict know?"

Poppy scoffed. She waved her hand dismissively, then snatched the ticket back. "She doesn't need to know. And neither does he. At least, not until after I'm aboard."

"You have talked about this before, but... really doing it?" Ann trailed off.

"You said it yourself. The latest shipment shows that Aunt Rose is ill-equipped to deal with this. All the other bee colonies have failed. I can't let this one follow the same fate."

"But Aunt Rose. You know... with all her... well, the *experiments?*"

"Rumors and speculation." Poppy laughed.

Fear of the unknown always seemed like a motivator for people around her to freeze. That alone made Poppy all the more motivated to spring into action. She had to admit, she liked being a contrarian. When her sister would gasp at her recklessness, or someone in the household scolded her, she felt as though she was truly living. There was nothing fake about anger or shock.

No, if there was anything to fear on that island, Poppy *had* to know. If there was any strange experimentation being done, as was often the rumor surrounding the island and its mysteries, she wanted to get to the bottom of it.

But more than anything, she was not going to let her aunt's wild ways ruin her family. She was still laughing when she said, "I will get to the bottom of this."

Her sister pushed Poppy's knee with her own, trying to get her to quiet herself. "You are not a detective."

"But I *am* a writer."

A terrible one, in her sister's defense. At least, she hadn't been terribly successful. No one in the family particularly believed in her talent or hard work. But she had been proud that she had at least found herself writing about the gossip of London. After her failed serial had been met with a sad lack of interest, that is.

Ann held a hand to her mouth. "You're a *lady*! You write a *ladies'* publication!"

"And *you* are my younger sister," Poppy said. She hoped her tone was more authoritative than biting, but her face softened when she noticed her sister pull away. She let out a little breath, and her shoulder slumped slightly. "Do you want this handled or not?"

Ann looked away sheepishly. "It sounds dangerous. Traveling all alone. What if–"

"I was able to speak with a member of the crew. I will have safe passage. And I will be disguised as a young man. I even bought pantaloons!" She perked up at the word, her usual cheerful demeanor back.

Her sister smiled, letting out a small snort as she shook her head slowly.

"You need not worry about me." Poppy looked down at her desk. She fiddled with the pages she had been working on, trying to indicate that the conversation was over.

"And Giuseppe?" Ann was persistent.

Poppy shook her head. She stuffed the ticket back into the drawer and covered it with papers, hiding it from any meddling glances. "I feel bad for Seppi," she admitted. "But..." She tossed a lock of blond hair behind her shoulder and looked up at the ceiling. "He will be fine. We can postpone the wedding."

Ann's hands were back in her lap, worrying at the fabric of her dress. "I just do not want to end up like the Balfour cousins," she said at last.

Poppy rolled her eyes. The true issue finally broke free from her little sister. She was sure that some part of Ann was genuinely concerned for her safety and worried about breaking the rules. But really, at least most of Ann simply didn't want to end up like their destitute distant cousins.

And she called Poppy frivolous.

Poppy tuned her out as best she could.

Ann, graciously, didn't seem to notice that Poppy had stopped truly listening. "Did you hear they are back in France?"

Poppy looked out the window at her blurry reflection as her sister went on about the Balfour cousins, who, in her mind, had it coming to them. They always were quite rude to their housemaids.

"And they had to sell everything!" Ann went on.

Poppy hummed. A noncommittal reply. Her brows knitted as she pondered the sudden collapse of their bee colonies throughout their farms. It started small. One little bee yard stopped producing honey. Then, stopped producing new bees. Then another farm went under. Then another.

The only thing that had managed to keep the family

afloat had been her aunt's farm. The Fletcher honey business was in trouble. And it was looking bleaker with each new, small shipment from the island.

The praise for the ridiculous 'exotic' flavor of honey that could only be found on the island was shrouded in mystery. Luckily, exotic meant exorbitant pricing. Smaller shipments meant exclusivity.

But Poppy could see it for what it was. A warning sign that her aunt's farm, and thus their wealth, was coming to a collapse of its own.

"-- they can only afford the one floor—"

Poppy tried to make her ladies' journal more popular by selling more to compensate for the decline in honey sales. She tried again to get her serial off the ground, writing about a young lady who went to a remote jungle and battled pirates in their quest to plunder ancient treasure.

It hadn't worked. At all.

Derivative, dull, and directionless, the review had read.

Poppy supposed, ultimately, that this was fair criticism. She hadn't lived life, gone on incredible adventures, seen enough to write any kind of adventure other than cheap remakes of ones she'd already read...

"—and even Lady Marigold was talking about—"

Poppy took in a deep breath.

She had to get to the bottom of it. Their family had worked too hard and come too far just to let it all slip away into destitution.

She finally tore her eyes away from her own blank expression and turned back to her sister. "I will find out what's going on, Ann. I promise."

Ann let out a heavy breath; her body finally relaxed. A

long pause lingered between them. Poppy started to think that Ann had finally dropped the discussion when, at last, she said, "What will you tell mother and Benedict?"

"I'm leaving them a note," Poppy said slowly. "I'll explain it all there. I told you not to fret, but the less you know, the better equipped you will be not to give away anything."

Ann chuckled lightly. "Yes," she said, "that's probably true. I never stop talking, do I?"

Poppy smiled at her sister gently. "No, you really don't."

Chapter Two

POPPY AND THE NICE NEW PANTALOONS

"I know you said the less I know, the better, but I am determined to help you." Ann slipped back through the door like a cat, pushing in with her head first, then slinking her shoulders through the narrow gap as if Poppy was barring her from entry.

But she was still at her desk, gawking at her sister's silly entrance.

That didn't last long... Ann had been gone less than two minutes, Poppy was sure of it.

Ann closed the door behind her with a gentle *click*. She tiptoed back to the writing desk with silent but exaggerated sneakiness. "At least let me help you pack," Ann whispered. She clutched her hands at her chest, begging.

The chair scraped gently across the wood as Poppy stood quickly. "Of course," she said. She found that relief had taken root in her heart, breaking through the fear that had slowly risen.

It was an eight-day trip to get to the island. And, once she arrived, she wasn't sure how long the whole adventure would keep her away from home. But she did know, however long or short, she would miss Ann. They hadn't been apart longer than a day since Ann was born.

"Can I see the pantaloons?" Ann asked. Her head was already bobbing up and down, as if trying to spot them out in the open.

Poppy's grin widened. She hurried to her bed and ducked below to retrieve a small trunk. She flung the trunk open on her bed with a soft thud and held the trousers up for Ann to admire. Warmth and a bit of pride spread through her. "I'm leaving tonight," she whispered as she lowered the pantaloons. "And, I'm a little worried my boy disguise won't be convincing." It was a half lie. A part of her was nervous. But what she wanted was one more moment of fun with her sister. "Will you help me?"

"Absolutely!" Ann sprang forward. She grabbed the pantaloons and gave them a good shake. Her eyes moved up and down the line of them quickly, then her brow furrowed. "First, we need these to look a little more worn. You probably don't want to draw attention to yourself on a ship, and these are well crafted. You'll look too put together." She crumbled the fabric in her fists. "A little more wrinkle ought to help a bit."

"Good thinking." Poppy gathered up her hair and tied it low with a black ribbon.

Ann shook her head at her. "I don't think this is very well thought out," she said. "But, if anyone can make a half-made plan a success, it's certainly you."

"You think I look manish, then already?" Poppy teased.

"By the time I'm through with you, even Giuseppe won't recognize you."

Poppy's faraway gaze hardened. She turned to the corner of the room quickly before Ann could spot her discomfort. Seppi was a good man. A good man who could only see what was in front of him. She would be surprised if he thought of her at all if she weren't in the room.

And, she was perfectly fine with that arrangement. A marriage of convenience. A way to keep her family from poverty, if it came down to it. What exactly he was getting out of it, though, Poppy still wasn't entirely sure. Perhaps he was simply kind.

She shook her head a little, messing with the curls that fell from her bun. "I have a hat, too," she said, shoving her ugly thoughts of marriage aside.

"Do you think we ought to give you a little coal to rub on your upper lip as well?" Ann cocked a brow. She was still crinkling the fabric of the pantaloons. Suddenly, she threw them on the ground at last and began to step along the hem. "It could be quite dapper. You know, a stately mustache."

Poppy rolled her eyes, but she laughed despite herself. "I think I'll stick with the hat and pantaloons for now."

Ann inspected the seams of the pantaloons with narrowed eyes. "Hmm, if you insist." She pulled at a thread that had come loose. "But I think you're making a mistake."

"It's a short trip," Poppy said. "I just need not to talk much and keep my head down. And then the voyage will be over before I even have time to miss the comforts of home."

"It's simply, I never thought you'd actually go through with it," Ann said gently. "I'm just worried, that's all."

Poppy placed a hand on Ann's shoulder. "It's my job to worry about you. It's *your* job to help me look like some dratted boy."

Ann nodded. She squeezed Poppy's hand. "Give me your hat, then," she said. "I'm sure it's just as pristine as these pantaloons were."

"Not at all, I found it at the stables."

Ann's face paled.

"Kidding," Poppy lied with a wry grin.

Chapter Three

POPPY'S PANTALOONS ARE NOT CONVINCING

oppy Fletcher hated nothing more than when her little sister was right. As the older sister, she was accustomed to having more experience and knowledge than Ann, and she would often use that to win almost any argument.

But she had to admit, after spending hours getting ready, practicing her wider stance and deeper voice so she could board the ship bound for Isla Miel in disguise, she still did not make a very convincing man. It seemed, at least, that with her shoulders back, gruff expression, and utterly unearned confidence, she at least carried herself like a man well enough.

The journey was almost over, and she had yet to be found out. Or, at least, no one outright told her that they suspected her. It had been smooth sailing, quite literally. The crew and a few other passengers bound for Spain were kind and mostly left her alone.

Frankly, the whole journey had been surprisingly boring. Though she had gone looking for something, anything to happen, it was eventless. There were no fantastical stories told late at night over rum and candlelight. No pirate attacks, or large beasts rising from the depths. No tentacles wrapped around the ship to splinter the wood and drag them all down... Not even a single confrontation between the crew and passengers about any petty squabble.

No, if anything, she was now convinced that all the serials she had read about swashbucklers were completely fabricated, which felt like a sham and a lie.

She let out a frustrated breath. Her shoulders and arms completely slumped over the railing on the deck as her body relaxed into the ship. For a moment, she hoped maybe at least she'd get a sunburn for her troubles. Otherwise, there'd be nothing to show for it at all.

"We're almost there," a voice behind her said softly. He had a thick accent and a growling way of mumbling, so his words and sentences ran together smoothly.

The first mate.

She had come to recognize his voice after their days of travel. He always seemed to be shouting orders at the rest of the crew, making himself known wherever he was. It was odd to hear his voice soft now, low and nearly lost in the hiss of the sea waves that splashed at the ship's hull.

Poppy lifted her head, securing her hat over her forehead better as she did.

The first mate's smile lines formed deep cracks in his cheeks, splitting his sun-worn face. She noticed now, up close, that his wrinkles were all laugh lines.

She wondered, briefly, what kind of life he had lived to sound so angry but smile so much.

"We'll take you to shore when we pick up the honey," he said. "It won't be much longer."

"Thank you," she said, doing her best to make her voice deeper. It still sounded silly, all these days later.

"You're welcome, mija," he said with a slight bow of his head. He turned back and, with the strong voice she had learned to enjoy over the past few days, he barked out orders across the deck, and a half dozen men scurried to their posts.

Poppy's expression softened as her body relaxed.

Almost there.

She assumed she would be nervous when the voyage came to an end. But, instead, she found herself serene. She wanted to absorb every moment of the trip. It was boring, but there was something beautiful in the quiet.

She squinted into the vast ocean, blinded by the dark blue that stretched so far it melded with the clear sky. As she gazed into the farthest reaches of the ocean, she noticed that, in the distance, a single lone island, as if by magic, appeared on the horizon.

It looked small, at least, smaller than she expected. There couldn't be much room for farming or bees, or anything really. Most of the island seemed to be composed of tall, jagged peaks that silhouetted into the sky like fingers reaching for the fluffy white clouds that hovered above their grasp.

As the ship sailed closer, Poppy watched as the harshness of the cliffs was transformed by the lush emerald jungle that covered the mountains. It was still impressive, the cliffs completely unlike anything she had ever seen, but it looked softer now, more like what she would expect from a fantasy world, a dream she would have had as a child.

Of course, Poppy had seen green before. She had been to the countryside, away from all the gray and dreariness of London. Every time, she had been stunned by the vast openness of the sky, the massive, stretching trees that speckled the horizon. But here, now, her eyes were lost in the depths of the jungle before she even stepped foot off the ship. It was so green that her eyes stung. She held her hand over the brim of her hat and blinked a few times, trying to take it all in as they sailed closer.

With the ship safely anchored and a small rowboat lowered into the gentle waves, Poppy held the bench where she sat between two large crew members with white knuckles. Her stomach was turning, made all the more sour now that she was on the little boat, being bounced about on the waves. She craned her neck to look around one of the men and stare into the clear water.

A school of bright orange fish jetted by beneath them, their scales shimmering brightly as they caught the sunlight for a brief, quiet moment.

"Don't look down," the man said, positioning himself farther back from her. He was still doing his best to row into the waves while also seemingly attempting to provide her with plenty of space. "That'll only make you more sick. And you'll need to keep your wits about you on that island."

Poppy's hat flopped as she looked up at him. She held it tightly to the top of her head to keep it from revealing too much of her face up close, though she realized it didn't matter much now if they caught on to her ruse. They were almost there. What could they do on a short rowboat ride?

"Keep my wits? Why's that?" she asked, her voice still stuck in the lower octave.

"There's something not right about that place," the other man said. "Something unnatural there."

The stones in Poppy's stomach grew heavier. She worried she might weigh the boat down and drown them there in sight of shore. She did her best to ignore the sinking feeling and instead, she straightened her back and squared her shoulders. "I can handle myself," she said. This time, her voice quivered.

The men continued to row quickly, their oars cutting through the water with silent, practiced movements until they were upon the beach where a long, worn dock stretched far into the shallows.

They stopped at the edge of the platform, pulling the long oars aboard and readying ropes.

The dock was staged with two wooden crates with "Fletcher Farms Family Honey" painted in black and gold along the sides. They were large crates about half her size, but...

Poppy bit her lower lip. *Only two?*

From behind them, a young woman suddenly stood. A mess of wild red curls tumbled over her shoulder as she inspected the ropes she was holding in her hands. The heavy ropes looked harsh, splintering roughly throughout, though she wielded them with an effortless ease. Her expression was focused, and the tip of her tongue peeked out from the corner of her lip as she made herself busy fixing the knots that held the lids secure. She hadn't yet noticed them, or at least, hadn't noticed Poppy.

The rowboat wobbled as Poppy rose to a squat. "Cousin! Surprise!"

"Whoa, there," the first man called. He grabbed Poppy's wrist and lowered her back down. "We're not stable yet."

Willa's eyes expanded like an owl, landing on the boat with an intensity Poppy was unfamiliar with. The Willa of her childhood was quiet and kind, a little skittish most of the time, if Poppy was being honest. This look was like that of a wild creature.

But recognition quickly took its place, starting from her brows that rose in surprise and easing down to her jaw that loosened slowly. She smiled, though she cocked her head to the side as if she didn't quite understand what she was seeing. "Poppy..?" she asked.

The rowboat pulled alongside the dock, and Poppy looked to the man closest with a raised eyebrow.

"Yes, lass," he said, rising. He held a hand out to Poppy. "Let's help you up, then."

She took it quickly, glad that no one seemed to care at all about silly social norms here. He pulled her up and widened his stance to help her get free from the boat. It rocked back and forth a few times as she heaved herself up and out.

Poppy held both arms out when her feet hit the solid wood of the dock. It wasn't moving, she was sure of it, but her legs felt like smoke beneath her, her whole body unstable.

"Sea legs, lass," the man said as he and the other hopped out and onto the dock with cat-like poise. "You'll get the hang of land soon enough."

Poppy lowered her arms, she tucked one around herself, and looked down at her costume. How long had everyone known she was a woman? She shook her head. It didn't matter. What mattered now was that she was here at last.

The men hauled the crates onto the rowboat with small grunts. Poppy watched the boat sink a little under their weight, but it seemed sturdy enough. Still, her eyes narrowed as she noticed that the ship probably couldn't carry much more. They must have known how small the shipment would be...

They gave each woman a little nod as they jumped back into the boat and rowed away into the sea. One of the men called something to them, but his voice was lost in the sound of the crashing waves and Willa's shrill screech–

"What are you doing here?" she demanded as Poppy still struggled to find her footing. Willa looked her up and down quickly. "And dressed like *that*?"

Poppy stretched her arms wide again. She did a little turn, though she wobbled as she did. "Like it? I bought *pantaloons!*"

"I do not like your pantaloons," Willa said dryly. She

crossed her arms over her chest. "And again, what are you doing here?"

"I'm adventuring, of course!"

Willa rolled her eyes. "Does your mother know you're here? Does Benedict?"

Poppy's smile faded. "Well, I left a note."

"A note," Willa repeated.

"Well, I'll admit, it's not just for the adventure. I've come to see if I can assist in any way. I noticed honey sales were down, and I–"

Willa pinched her brow with her finger and thumb gently. She squeezed her eyes shut. "Mother is going to kill you," she breathed slowly.

"Aunt Rose? No, she'll be glad to see her favorite niece."

"No," Willa said with a heavy sigh. "She'll kill you." Willa looked up at the sky with a pained expression for a long while.

Poppy waited. She shifted her weight from one leg to another. She scratched her ear as she began to itch in the sun and silence.

Finally, Willa let her gaze fall back on Poppy. "Alright then," she said. "Let's get this over with."

Poppy shrugged, letting go of the feeling of uncertainty that had begun to creep up her limbs. She followed Willa down the dock and onto the white sandy beach. "Ann liked my pantaloons..." she whispered with fake solemness in her tone.

Willa glanced back at her with a half-smile. "Fine, Poppy, you win. I like your pantaloons."

Poppy skipped to catch up to Willa. She linked an arm with her cousin's and rested her head gently on Willa's shoulder. "Thank you, Willa. I promise, this is all for the best."

Willa shrugged her off, though she kept their arms crossed together at the elbows. "I'll take you to our place. But, and I hate to damage your happiness, my mother *will not* be glad you're here."

"And why is that?" Poppy asked as they continued their trek into the jungle.

Beneath the heavy shade of massive tropical leaves, the air was cooler, wetter. Poppy's skin prickled. She looked up into the branches, eyes moving over the vines that covered every limb of the tall trees. Her gaze followed the sprawling connections between each tree, the way they wrapped around the trunks like leafy blankets.

It was all so different...

"There are things on this island, Poppy. Things you just..." Willa said slowly. She stopped, her arm unhooked from Poppy's, and with warm fingers, she held Poppy's hand loosely. "Well, I think it's best if you just see for yourself."

Chapter Four

POPPY FLETCHER THINKS TIGERS CAN SURVIVE A SHIPWRECK

Willa led the way through the jungle, absolutely refusing to answer any of Poppy's questions. She dodged each one with either a frustratingly vague answer or a noncommittal hum.

Poppy liked to think she was usually calm and collected. But right now, she was fighting the urge to shake her cousin until answers poured out of her. She remembered enough from their childhood to know that it was useless. Willa was sweet as honey, and stubborn as cold molasses. If she said

Poppy would have to see for herself, Poppy would simply have to wait and see.

But it wasn't long.

Poppy jumped as a rustling in the leaves instantly ignited a primal fear within her. Her eyes widened, and she grabbed Willa's arm quickly, nails digging into her cousin's skin. "What's that?" she breathed as the leaves from the tall trees continued to move and a sound like snapping branches echoed through the jungle. "Tiger?"

Willa laughed loudly. She didn't seem at all concerned, either about whatever was hiding in the jungle or Poppy's nails forming crescent indents in her forearm. "A tiger? Off the coast of Spain?"

Poppy shrugged, her cousin's nonchalance catching her even more off guard than her sudden panic response still surging through her body. "A capsized ship bound for London carrying exotic animals?" she speculated, her voice coming out as a quiet and urgent hiss.

Willa shook her head. Her smile was sweet, but her eyes were closed in apparent annoyance.

"It could happen." Poppy's voice was still low and steady, though her heart beat rapidly beneath her shirt. She let go of Willa's arm and raised a hand to her chest, wondering for a moment if whatever lurked in the woods could hear it pounding as loudly as she did in her ears.

The rustling grew louder, a few trees shook, flexible trunks parted to make way as a giant, brown, armor-scaled beast emerged from the jungle.

Poppy gasped, head tilting up to see the face of the creature that towered over them. Her mouth hung open as she followed down to its massive, elephant-like feet, half hidden in the thick green ferns.

Her eyes swung back up quickly to the creature's face. It was wide and much, much taller than them. Its neck, thick and muscular, swept low so its black eyes could look at them more closely.

Willa only giggled and reached for Poppy's hand at her chest. She lowered Poppy's hand carefully and said, "This is Theodosia."

The creature let out a heavy breath through its slitted nose and tossed its head to one side with a low flute-like sound.

Willa leaned in a little closer, inspecting its protruding brow and the green speckles that lined its eyes like a mask. "Oh, this is Dorothea. Sorry about that, Dotty."

The creature, Dorothea, emitted another low rumble. She took a few strong steps toward them with her head lowered gently. Her body moved closer and out of the shaded jungle vines. Poppy's eyes followed up her back, taller even than she could have imagined. A long row of dark green, leaf-like spikes dotted her back in two rows. They shimmered in a beautiful iridescent as they caught the few rays of light that had managed to cut their way through the small gaps in the canopy above.

A breeze from the sea blew the leaves gently, swaying softly. The beams of light glided along the creature, illuminating every place they touched with vibrant scales like a mosaic.

Poppy's breath caught in her throat. Her heart had not slowed since she first heard the rustling in the leaves, but now it was racing with excitement. Her mouth hung open, and she realized she hadn't breathed. She took in a deep breath, and her body began to quiet. Her heart slowed, and her lips twitched up. Just a little at first, until she broke into a wide, gasping smile. "What—" she began to ask, but her voice stilled when Dorothea's head lowered, pressing her snout into Poppy's hand.

"Dinosaurs," Willa whispered, the grin evident in her voice, though Poppy's eyes were fixed on the giant in front of her, watching as Dorothea's saucer-sized eyelids closed slowly. Her skin was cold and rough as she nuzzled deeper into Poppy's hand. "My mother brought them back…"

Chapter Five

ATHENA IS A HYPOCRITE BUT SHE DOESN'T REALLY CARE

The drawing room was gaudily decorated. At least, Athena thought so. While she and her cousin were from a comfortable family, she had always hated the overdone spaces, the uncomfortable couches, and the oppressive floral smells when she entered anyone's home of her same station. She supposed, as she adjusted herself on the hard cushion, that this made her a hypocrite.

She didn't care.

She picked at a loose thread on her dress when she

realized, with slight frustration, that the old woman in front of her had finally begun to speak. She glanced at her cousin beside her and was at the edge of his seat, listening intently.

"She has been gone for two weeks. It is entirely too long to be engaged. We cannot delay her return. Especially not for some silly ladies' journal." Poppy's mother was sitting opposite them in the drawing room, looking like an ancient statue in her white empire waist dress and cold, overdone jewelry. Her rings glittered in the light from the window at the far end of the room with every minute movement. Her mouth was drawn into a hard, thin line. Her stare was even more challenging, as though she was watching for any micro expression on Athena's or her cousin's face. Any twitch that may give away something she was after.

Athena was never afraid. At least, she carried herself like nothing scared her. But here, sitting before the older woman, she felt like a child being scolded. She stopped picking at the thread, straightened her back, and took in a deep breath. She had done nothing wrong. She hadn't even *seen* her ex-girlfriend in years. But any mention of Poppy left her feeling uneasy. Especially when she was reminded that her cousin was now her betrothed.

Athena swallowed the sour taste in her mouth quickly, trying to ignore the ancient history that lingered in her mind. A history that only a few people even knew about.

She wasn't sure what the woman wanted from them. Poppy was going to do what Poppy was going to do. If she wanted something, barring tying her up and stuffing her in a wardrobe, there wasn't much anyone could do to stop her.

Everyone in the room knew that just as well.

Giuseppe stole a quick side eye at Athena, his eyes

seemed to be pleading for her to rescue him. But he played it well under Lady Elizabeth's predatory gaze. He looked away as he handed his cousin the letter that Poppy had written explaining herself.

Athena took it carefully, as though it was laced with venom and one small papercut from its sharp edges would be the death of her.

She read it over slowly, occasionally glancing upward at the hawk-like eyes of Lady Elizabeth. A chill ran down her back under the Lady's watchful stare. She tried to savor every word on the page, but the letters left her mind as quickly as they came. It was as though Poppy's words were water slipping through her fingers, leaving her only cold and clammy and gasping for air. She grimaced, unable to hide her distaste for the Lady interrupting her immersive reading.

Something about going to visit her aunt. Something about writing an article about the family's prized honey for her ladies' journal to bolster sales.

The corner of Athena's mouth ticked up a little. She hated that her own face betrayed her. She did her best to stifle it back down quickly. Poppy and her writing. Athena would be proud that she had continued to pursue her passion, if she weren't so angry.

"You wish for us to go and retrieve her?" Athena heard her cousin ask. It snapped her mind from the words on the page.

Athena cast another look at him, hoping her dark brows didn't give away the concern that his words ignited in her chest.

Giuseppe had a kind heart. And a timid one. He

couldn't retrieve anything that didn't enthusiastically want to go with him.

Poppy played at being tame, but she was wild. Realistically, neither of them would be able to *make her* come home. Still, Athena tried to keep her face neutral before she handed the letter back to Lady Elizabeth. "Poppy is on your sister's island, then?" she asked.

Lady Elizabeth nodded. "Lady Rose, you mean. And I am sure you have heard the shipments of honey have become... less frequent. However, Poppy journeying alone is dangerous. Our reputation is at stake, should anyone discover she is missing."

Athena nodded back, though she had to bite her lower lip a little to keep herself from speaking too harshly. "Lady Rose," she said, voice even. "She–"

"Athena, if you are about to bring up the ungodly," Lady Elizabeth cut Athena off, but stopped short. She swallowed hard, held her hand to her jewel-studded throat, making a show of her false nausea. "That *science...* she says she conducts there, I'll not hear of it. It is a stain on our family, and I cannot tolerate such talk in my own home."

Athena leaned forward in her chair, her fingers curled.

"No," Giuseppe said quickly, cutting in before Athena could start a fight. "No one is insinuating anything of that ungodly nature."

Coward.

Athena wanted to hit him over the head like when they were kids. Back when she would get a good first hit in and wrestle him to the ground before anyone could stop either of them from getting their clothes dusty. That always put him in his place.

Instead, she cast him a quick glower and tried to sigh out her annoyance. It didn't work.

"You will go get Poppy and bring her back for the wedding," Lady Elizabeth commanded. "We do not want to be the talk of the town. The announcements have already gone out. People will soon be inquiring as to her whereabouts and starting rumors."

A slight knock at the door made Seppi jump.

Lady Elizabeth remained still, eyes lazily drifting to the other side of the room as a young maid's face appeared in the crack in the door. "Lady Elizabeth, Lord Artis is here."

Lady Elizabeth nodded calmly, but Athena's blood suddenly chilled. Their grandfather? What was he doing here?

The door opened wider, and Lord Artis stepped through the door with a surprising swiftness for his age. He shot a narrowed glance at Giuseppe.

Athena elbowed him, subtly, she hoped, in the ribs.

Giuseppe cleared his throat and rose from his seat. He gave the older man a quick nod, and Athena knew that he, too, was starting to understand the severity of the situation they had found themselves in.

"Ah, good," Lady Elizabeth said. She gestured to the loveseat for Lord Artis to sit.

He gave her a bow, then sat, hands resting on the silver-tipped cane as though he was about to use it like a sword. "Forgive my tardiness," their grandfather said to Lady Elizabeth. "Have you had the opportunity to discuss the situation with the two of them?" he asked, as though Athena and Seppi weren't in the room at all.

Lady Elizabeth nodded. She turned her gaze back to the two of them.

Athena hoped her stare matched the older woman's intensity. She wasn't about to be bullied. Not by her. Not by her grandfather. Especially not by both of them thinking they had the upper hand.

"I have," Lady Elizabeth said. "I was about to tell them that they are the ones to do it, what with our advancing age. Seafaring is unbecoming, and there are only merchant ships that sail those waters."

Lord Artis hummed. "Indeed, though, I am happy to travel, if need be," he said. "You mustn't leave a man's work to women. Or weak men." There was a jovialness to his tone, as though he was telling the lady a good joke. But Athena knew better. He was making a threat.

Get her. Or I will.

Sure, Poppy was stubborn, but her grandfather never took 'no' for an answer. He would tie her up and bring her home in a trunk if that's what it took. The thought made Athena's back prickle.

"I am curious to see what about that island has kept her there for so long," Lord Artis said slowly. He cast a sideways look at Lady Elizabeth. A sign, Athena figured, that he had at least somewhat acknowledged that Poppy may very well be involved in one of her aunt's mysterious experiments. "And, I look forward to seeing the shipments of honey improving."

Lady Elizabeth's eyes narrowed, and she flinched. "You have nothing to worry about, Lord Artis," she nearly barked back. "I assure you, this is a calculated marketing strategy to drive up exclusive sales."

Athena watched the two older aristocrats carefully. She had seen enough standoffs between barn cats and elderly, wealthy folks to know that whoever moved first was doomed.

"We'll be on the first ship out," Giuseppe promised quickly. The tension in the room dissipated, though a coil lingered in the base of Athena's neck.

"Good," Lord Artis said with a curt nod. "I look forward to your success. Though Athena, is a ship really a place for you?"

"I've traveled before, grandfather." She grunted a little as she pushed herself up with her hands on her knees.

Lady Elizabeth backed into her chair, mouth slightly agape at Athena's unladylike sound.

She had to admit, even when her grandfather was belittling her, she did enjoy watching Lady Elizabeth break her statuesque nature.

It was the little things.

ATHENA IS BAD AT COMFORTING PEOPLE AND THAT PROBABLY WILL COME BACK TO BITE HER

Giuseppe was throwing up into a bucket, and despite all Athena's bravado, there she was, eyes squinted shut, fingertips pressing down into her temples, utterly avoiding the situation. She had a steel stomach. She had been on ships before. However, being in close quarters with someone else, dry heaving was making her queasy despite everything.

When she opened her eyes at last, she focused them steadily on the wood-paneled walls, examining the grain of the dark wood and trying to follow each line until its endpoint.

She wondered what kind of wood it was, and how human hands had been able to design and build such a thing. She studied living things, as best she could, at least. Any engineering may as well have been magic to her.

Her thoughts were interrupted by her cousin spitting loudly into the bucket. He groaned even louder, like he had just been hit in the gut.

They had been aboard the boat for three days. And for three days, Giuseppe was clinging to the bucket or the wall, or lying in bed, griping about his lack of appetite.

To make matters worse, the room was smaller than she had hoped. It had no windows. Their bodies jostled about with every bumpy wave, and Athena was sure that another day of this and she would be tossed overboard for murder.

Every time Giuseppe made another gagging sound, she contemplated picking him up over her shoulder, hauling him up the stairs to the deck, and just throwing both of them into the sea to finally end it.

"I'm sorry," Giuseppe gasped at last, lifting his head from the bucket. "I was not created for travel, I'm afraid."

"Now you tell me," Athena said before she could help it. It came out too harsh. She could already imagine how long Seppi would be carrying those words with him. She'd probably hear about it in five years over dinner one random night. She could imagine it now. She'd be on her way to take a bite of some delicious meal, probably ravenous as usual, when a little cough would come from down the table, and then, he'd complain the rest of the evening about that one time she scolded him for something he couldn't help.

Knowing the family, they'd probably all agree with him, and she'd never hear the end of it. She wondered for a moment if Poppy would be there, sitting beside him. And, if she would agree that Athena was too harsh. She probably would.

Athena shook her head as the thoughts spiraled rapidly. No time for that. She had to remedy the situation before he, too, spiraled out of control.

Her eyes softened as she turned toward him at last. It wasn't his fault that he had a weak stomach. Logically, she knew that. She also knew it wasn't his fault that three days without seeing sunlight made her feel trapped.

It was her fault she was feeling this way. She had agreed, or rather, insisted on coming along, after all.

"Seppi," she said at last, placing a heavy hand on his back. She rubbed a circle twice, satisfied the small gesture had undone some of her previous damage. "Come now, you... You will get used to this. At least on the way back, you will know what you're getting into."

Giuseppe looked up at her from the bucket with weepy eyes. "Theni, tell me something good. Distract me. I don't want to hear about the return voyage." He turned back to the wooden bucket and sputtered a little.

A lock of dark waves fell over Athena's shoulder as she turned away. Her hand rubbed his back again slowly. "Well, Seppi, I think that we are almost there. Then you will be on an island so unlike London that... Well, realistically, you'll get a sunburn." She laughed before he had a chance to start pouting. "No, really, I'm sure there will be all kinds of incredible flora and fauna for you to draw on this island.

You can harness your artistic skills away from all the snobby city folks."

He was silent.

"Come on, this is kind of exciting. We're aboard a vessel almost exclusively reserved for letters and shipments. This isn't meant to be a pleasant trip. It's an adventure."

Giuseppe nodded. "An adventure."

"At least we're traveling cabin-class," Athena said, tapping his shoulder gently. "It could certainly be worse, especially on a ship of this kind."

Giuseppe shrugged her off, though not without a little smile. "Ah, yes," he said with no hint of sarcasm or irony. He straightened his back at last. "Do tell me more about your travels in the steerage. That will certainly put this voyage in perspective."

"Well, first of all, women cannot disrobe, so I could not wash either my clothes or myself for the four weeks," Athena said with a shiver.

Giuseppe was silent. It seemed, for now, that he had nothing left in his stomach to give. The color was slowly returning to his cheeks and lips. He looked sullen but happier than she had seen him in days. He always enjoyed hearing about her various exploits or latest secret experiments.

She went on, "And being the only woman aboard, I would say it would have been better to just masquerade as a man. The crew got a little superstitious anytime the waves got too big."

Giuseppe gagged again.

"Oh, don't cast up one's again." Athena quickly changed the subject, "I mostly slept the whole time, Seppi. The bunk was the only private place. There wasn't much to do but read by day in the ship's dark candlelight and eat dinner with the group at night, talking about nothing."

"Doesn't actually sound too bad," Giuseppe said. "I would like to read all day. Draw all day. Be alone all day..." He looked wistfully at the ceiling. "Though, I wouldn't want to feel like this ever again. Or smell *you* and your clothes unwashed for weeks in close quarters."

"Well, start harnessing your inner Athena now and sleep it off," she said, letting out a little grunt as she stood at last. "I'm going to the deck to have a breath of fresh air. When you're ready, come on up. We'll play some chess."

"I don't want to play. You always beat me," Giuseppe grumbled. He made his way to the bed and flopped down so hard he bounced a little.

"Get better," Athena said, though if it was for him to feel better or practice his chess skills, even she was unsure. She shrugged to herself and slipped out into the ship's large hall.

Athena swayed with the ship as she climbed the stairs to the deck. She was grateful to be out of the dark, dingy cabin at last. Ocean air blew gently around her face, and she squinted into the sunlight as she made her way to the edge of the bow.

The calm blue water shimmered in the sunlight. White bubbles from gentle waves hitting the boat burst into bright rainbows as the ship pushed through the water at great speed. Above, the sky was clear and calm, light blue in the mid-afternoon, contrasting with the ocean below.

The same warm blue as Poppy's eyes. The same depth and terror of the ocean... Athena bit her lip and wondered what the hell she was doing and how exactly she was going to pull this off.

She'd been on ships before, traveled to strange new lands before. She'd searched across the ocean for a place to feel at home—a place where she wouldn't be laughed at for her interest in natural *science*.

But no matter where she went, people said it like it was a crude word. Their scowls only deepened when they realized that it was *she* who wanted to practice. For all the places she had been, there was only Seppi and Poppy who had ever encouraged her to keep trying to study, to keep trying her hand at meddling with biology and medicine. To keep her mind sharp.

She had heard stories over the years about Poppy's aunt. She was kindly known in public as 'eccentric'. Behind closed doors, she was more commonly referred to as 'mad'. Athena liked to think of her as simply a knowledgeable woman who, after the death of her husband, seemed to vow to answer to no one ever again, much to the disgust of most of the Fletcher family.

Athena remembered her moving away to the remote island years ago and the absolute scandal it caused at the time. The lady had told the family that she was going to work on creating 'the optimal bee' for their honey empire. At least, that was the rumor that circulated shortly after her swift departure.

When the first shipments of honey came ashore, any scandalous drivel about her dried up. All anyone could talk about instead was the quality and uniqueness of the honey she sent back home. As soon as Athena tasted the honey, she knew that Poppy's aunt had either discovered or created something entirely new.

She used to tell Poppy that she should be happy for her aunt. The family business was doing well because of the 'eccentric' old woman.

Poppy had only folded her arms and said that Athena was frustrating her.

She often did. She couldn't help it. Athena was a frustrating person, especially to Poppy.

Now, she propped an elbow on the wood and held her chin in her open palm. The ship dipped up and down slowly, and she followed the moving horizon with her gaze. Seeing Poppy again was going to be... well, awkward. But convincing Giuseppe that he should leave her on the island was going to be heartbreaking.

That is, if this mysterious aunt would let her stay.

Athena's hands clenched into fists.

No, it wasn't a matter of *letting*, it was a matter of *proving*. And Athena was ready to prove her worth.

ATHENA IS IN A RUSH TO NOWHERE

The shore was in sight. Below them, brilliantly clear water shimmered with warm sunlight. Ahead, a white sand beach and tropical trees, lush and green and vibrant, loomed. Huge mountains atop the island jutted out into the sky; a few seemed to touch the fluffy clouds above.

It was one of the most gorgeous things Athena had ever seen. And beside her, Giuseppe was missing it.

He was clinging to the railing like it was a life-saving jacket. His eyes were sealed shut in a pained expression. But worst of all, he was breathing heavily in through his nose and sighing obnoxiously out through his mouth.

Athena cast a look at him with narrowed eyes, then smacked his back. "Look!" she said, all too loudly. "We're here!"

"Here and in a hurry," the captain's voice cut in. His tone was jovial, despite his somewhat ominous wording. "We made this detour to accommodate the Lady's request. But we cannot linger here."

Athena nodded to him, then shook Giuseppe's shoulder. "Make haste, cousin! You heard the captain!"

Giuseppe looked up at her with one eye open. "You seem awfully pleased at my suffering. Or... are you nervous?"

"Aye, this conversation can happen on the island, can it not?" the captain said.

Giuseppe looked back at him, still gripping the bow. "I can see we are indeed in a hurry," he said. "I'll fetch our things. That is," he turned back to Athena, "if you're not helping me?"

"Henry's getting your goods," the captain said. "He'll be taking you ashore."

"I'll double-check that my sketchbook is packed," Giuseppe said as he finally let go of the wood. He hurried below deck, though his legs were unsteady.

"A lovely island, isn't it?" Athena mused in a mumbled whisper.

The captain stood beside her, looking out with a hand over his forehead to shield his eyes from the sun's bright reflection on the water's surface. "I'd be careful on that island, my lady," he said. "Ships only stop here for the honey shipments. And they only pick those up upon request of the dowager there. She's mighty secretive, that one. I'm not sure she'll take kindly to your unannounced arrival."

Athena cringed a little. Her stomach flipped over, but she was careful to keep her expression stoic.

She was certain that at least one lady on the island wouldn't be happy to see her, for numerous reasons. Least of all, she was supposed to convince her to cut her trip short and go back to London to get married to her cousin.

"Thank you for that," Athena said at last. "We'll take that into consideration."

"Just meaning be careful, is all," he said. "The island is a strange one. Something unnatural is going on here."

Athena looked back out onto the sandy shores. She squinted, trying to see into the treeline, but it was too dense, and they were too far. Her heart ached dully in her chest at the sight of all the green, all the living, thriving things. She felt a kind of protectiveness of this island, unnatural or not. Something about it called to her, but she couldn't quite place what it was.

An image flashed through her mind—a shock of golden hair, eyes as blue as the sky... a wide smile.

Or, perhaps, she thought, she was still protective of the woman she'd find there.

Henry left them at the dock in a hurry. As he was paddling away hastily, Giuseppe held his hand high to wave him one last farewell.

Athena huffed as she stacked her trunk on top of his and fastened them together with a thick rope.

When Giuseppe turned back and saw the size of their

luggage, he frowned. "I think it would have been better to warn Lady Rose about our arrival," he said. "It would be nice to have help with this."

Athena's mouth drew into a thin line. She grunted as she lifted the trunks a little to rest vertically on their corners. "You can complain or you can help." She held out one of the ropes and gestured for him to grab it.

Giuseppe looked glum. He slouched but still made his way to the trunks and grabbed the rope. "Athena, do you think we ought to go find where they are first? Any idea where the estate is here?"

Athena shrugged. She looked into the trees. "It won't be far," she said. "It's just Lady Rose and Lady... whatever Poppy's cousin's name is. Henry said they always meet them on the dock when they collect the honey crates. So they must be able to haul it here themselves."

"I can't imagine..." Giuseppe trailed off. He looked up at the sky, watched a cloud pass by, and then rested a hand on his hip while he meekly tugged the rope with the other. "Hard to imagine ladies of their standing out here working the land on their own," he said.

"Well, that's simply offensive," Athena said.

Giuseppe let out a puff of air, exasperated. "You know what I mean, Theni. It's just not common, is all. And Lady Rose must be reaching up in years. I have no idea how her daughter must have the energy to tend to the business and her mother. It must be a lot of work."

"Some people aren't afraid of hard work," Athena said. She began to pull the rope and nodded her head for him to join. "Come now. Your fiancé awaits."

Seppi grumbled something she couldn't hear. And Athena didn't care. For all her courage, her hands still trembled at the thought of seeing Poppy again after all this time.

Chapter Eight

ATHENA AND THE USE OF LANGUAGE

"Giuseppe?" Poppy's voice rang out as soon as the two had set foot into the treeline. "What in the devil are you doing here?"

Athena's body tensed, every muscle tightened in her limbs, and her fingers curled as if ready to fight. She froze, eyes darting to find Poppy. But all she saw were ferns and trees and vines. "That's hardly the language one should use around a lady," Athena said as she pulled the rope up over her shoulder to try to stop her shaking body. She hoped the movement looked effortless and casual.

Poppy emerged from the trees like a ghost from the shadows. Her brows were furrowed, and she looked Seppi up and down before turning to Athena as if she had only just noticed her. Her mouth opened slightly, and Athena's insides twisted up like the vines on the surrounding trees, threatening to make her ill on the spot.

It had been years. Years since she had seen her. Years since their last conversation that had left Athena with a hole in her heart, slowly leaking ever since. But memories of Poppy had been frozen in time; they remained vivid and vibrant. Even now, standing among lush green ferns and below towering trees, she looked just the same. She was bright and beautiful and full of life, from the curve of her expressive brows to the twitch of her playful lips...

Now, as she set a hand on her hips like she was about to scold them, Athena couldn't help but notice the slight tilt in her head, the confusion, and something else close to excitement etching along her face.

Athena thought she saw the tips of Poppy's ears redden. But she couldn't be sure. She continued, feigning offense, "Try using 'merciful heavens' next time lest you upset my delicate sensibilities."

"Athena? I... What are *you* doing here?"

Athena set down her rope, and along with it, the trunks, which crashed down onto the mossy forest floor with a dull *thump*. "Hello, Poppy," was all she said. It was all she could say. The fact that Poppy's name had left her throat without shouting alone was a win she would carry with her the rest of the day.

Giuseppe, who had only narrowly escaped the falling trunks with his toes intact, simply brushed his hands on his vest, then stood taller. "Poppy, your mother has been worried ill–"

"I left a note," Poppy said, as if it explained it all. Both of her hands were on her hips now, a sure sign she was feeling righteous. And righteous Poppy was absolutely insufferable. They would not be hearing the end of the note and how that ought to have solved everything for a while, Athena was sure of it.

Still, Poppy took in a deep breath, then huffed a loud exhale. Her pale blue eyes traced the two of them from head to toe with a single raised brow as though she disapproved of their attire, which, Athena thought rudely, was hypocritical considering her own dress among the wild flora. Besides, both cousins were wearing the latest fashion back home, while Poppy's dress was in a rougher state.

But, as if she were reading Athena's mind, Poppy smoothed out her empire waist dress, clearing away the wrinkles as best she could and said nothing.

"Yes, the note. We read it," Athena said to Giuseppe once Poppy had finished fretting about her dress.

Seppi looked at her with narrowed eyes. She knew he was upset at her for speaking for him, as usual. She rolled her eyes back, but tried to play it off as though she were simply looking around at the impressive tall trees, at the dark, leafy vines growing along their bark and hanging from their branches.

"Poppy," he said, "we'd appreciate telling you all about it over a cup of tea." He looked around them with wide eyes, then sneezed loudly.

Poppy sighed again, this time louder. Traces of her blonde hair fell over her shoulder as she shifted her weight onto her back leg.

Athena's eyes trailed down the lock of hair, landing on Poppy's exposed collarbone. Her face flushed, and she pulled her eyes away, back to the treetops above once again. This was miserable, awkward, and stupid. "Do you mind showing us to your aunt's home? No luck finding a hotel here, I take it," Athena said, trying to get her mind off anything related to Poppy.

Giuseppe held out a hand, as he had done so many times before when they were children. A simple move to ready himself when she was about to spring on someone: he had always been good about putting himself between her and a target. Her tone must have come out more sternly than she thought.

Still, Athena looked down at his hand and pursed her lips. She wasn't about to attack anyone. Probably. Though frustration, at herself, or Poppy, or Seppi, was filling her veins even now.

Giuseppe pulled his hand back quickly. He spoke even faster, "Poppy, my darling." His voice sounded a little strained. "Please, we packed our own teas and could really use the respite. It's been a long and difficult journey."

"Yes, well, attempt making the journey while pretending to be the opposite gender," Poppy said with a grin, clearly pleased with herself.

"So that's how you did it." Athena's chest expanded a little, the anger dissipated, and was replaced by something new. Something light. She was proud, if only for a moment.

Poppy always had been resourceful when it came down to it, but she hadn't expected her to resort to this.

Poppy's smile brightened. "I know, right?"

"Tea and rest, please," Giuseppe interjected.

Poppy folded an arm around her waist. She shrank back a little. "Well," she murmured. "Well, you see the island is... Well, it's unique. My aunt and cousin have been here for some time, as you know."

Giuseppe looked around them as if she actually meant for him to see with his own eyes now. Athena's stare was fixed on Poppy.

"And?" Athena prompted.

"And she's been doing some experiments... on some old bones she found here."

Athena's eyes narrowed slightly. She watched as Poppy's face winced a little as though she had just been stung by something. She waited.

"You will just have to see for yourself, I suppose," Poppy conceded. "That's how I discovered it all. It's probably how you ought to also." She turned her back on them, fixing her long, gold waves into a quick bun at the base of her neck. "Though I doubt Aunt Rose will be pleased," she mumbled just loud enough for them to hear.

Athena and Giuseppe cast each other a quick glance. He shrugged, and the two lifted their trunks again and followed Poppy on the narrow trail.

Athena's body grew warmer in the humid air. Lugging the trunks in the heat she was unaccustomed to, and watching Poppy's movement, her poise even along the jungle path, was too much. She was suffocating.

Poppy looked over her shoulder for a moment. "Just try

to contain yourselves when you meet Reggie," she said ominously.

"Reggie?" Athena hissed under her breath. A bead of sweat dripped down her nose, itching her uncomfortably.

But it was at that moment that a low and rhythmic rumble at the trees beside them sounded.

The group stopped.

Athena listened closely. It was as if deep in the jungle, the trees were being parted by something massive, their steps quaked the ground, vibrating her feet. It sounded huge. It sounded like a monster was approaching.

Poppy turned on her heel suddenly. "Oh, actually, you'll probably meet Francesca first. Actually, right now—"

Giuseppe's shrill scream cut her off as a massive, green, speckled head emerged from above the treetops. The monster's head was the size of their trunks, Athena was sure of it. She could only imagine, however briefly, how giant the rest of it was.

Their luggage fell to the forest floor with a loud bang, and Giuseppe grasped at Athena's forearm, shaking it to do something.

Big, black, doe-like eyes gazed down at them, then blinked slowly with long lashes. A snort blew from her slit nostrils and her face moved down closer to them.

Athena recoiled quickly.

Giuseppe sprang back behind her. "Dragon!" he cried, pulling on Athena's arm harder to move farther away with him.

"Don't fret," Poppy said gently. She moved in front of Athena and held out a delicate hand to the monster before them. The beast closed her eyes and leaned into her open palm, rubbing her scaled cheek into Poppy's hand. The creature emitted an almost purr-like sound, a deep rumble from its throat, still hidden in the trees.

Athena, eyes wide, took a small step closer.

Giuseppe's hand slipped from her sleeve, and with his closeness gone, Athena felt as though she was suddenly untethered to the earth below her feet. Her body was light, her mind was clear and empty, save for an overwhelming awe as her mouth dropped open slightly. A chill prickled down her arms as she made her way to stand by Poppy. "What..." she whispered as she studied the creature's face. "What is she?"

Up close, Athena could see the wrinkled but soft-looking scaled skin, like old leather worn down with time and love. She was a muted sage color with speckles of dark emerald dotting her head. She was all curve and round, but for the large bridges of bone above her thick, lashed eyes.

Poppy turned to Athena, her smile wide and just as dazzling as the creature before them. The corners of her eyes creased with pure joy. "This is Francesca," she said softly. "She's an apatosaurus."

"A... apa..?" Athena struggled, though, from the actual pronunciation, or because her tongue refused to cooperate, she wasn't sure. Her jaw was still slack with wonder. She forced her mouth closed and blinked hard.

"It took me a few tries to pronounce it, too." A giggle broke from Poppy as Francesca nuzzled at the top of her head, fluffing up Poppy's golden hair. "And don't worry. She only eats plants and is actually a bit of a coward. But once you give her affection," her voice lowered as if Francesca couldn't hear her, "I'm afraid she would put even the most desperate of debutantes to shame."

From behind, Athena heard Giuseppe approach slowly, with small, cautious steps. His eyes were just as wide as Athena's. he reached out his hand to her arm again, but this time, it was as if he wanted to be sure she was still real. "Hello, Francesca," he said quietly. "You're actually quite beautiful."

Francesca opened her eyes, head tilting to look at Giuseppe more carefully. She snorted again, blowing his thick hair from his forehead. Then, she lifted, exposing a long, *impossibly long* neck. She was wearing a few pink ribbons around her neck, tied in delicate bows.

Athena's gaze followed her up to the tops of the trees. She looked from her cousin to Poppy, then back at the long neck, hidden partly by the tree branches.

Francesca moved to look behind her once more, and with thunderous steps, she disappeared back into the jungle.

"So, an apatous, not a dragon, then?" she asked Poppy.

"Apatosaurus," Poppy corrected with kindness in her voice. "My aunt insists on giving them names with Greek roots. She's a true bluestocking, if you remember."

"She found her here?" Giuseppe asked.

Poppy shook her head. "I can have her explain it all," she said. "Come on, you have to meet Reggie."

Chapter Nine

POPPY KNOWS THERE'S A VOLCANO AND THAT'S ABOUT THAT

Poppy wanted to scream. From an overwhelming joy, from uncomfortable anger, but mostly from confusion. She had to keep moving forward or else she was certain it would burst from her lungs like a cannon fire, and then, she knew she couldn't stop the damage that would be done.

She was listening to Seppi fuss about the dinosaur and Athena's marked silence. Athena was rarely silent. Poppy knew it meant her mind was racing. She wished she didn't know that about her, though. She wished for many things.

At that current moment, she wished she dared to turn around and shout, "Why are you here!?" Maybe even grab Athena's shoulders and give her a good, hard shake while she was at it.

But she had neither the courage nor the energy, truth be told. Her aunt had been putting her to work since early morning. And she was not an early riser by nature. She was tired.

Between the manual labor, trying to pry information out of her family about their finances, and writing all night about her latest dinosaur run-in, the past few weeks had been exhausting. She wasn't just tired. She was weary to her core, into her very heart. A heart that the woman walking behind her had broken.

There was no time to worry about that now, she told herself. She had her own things to be concerned about. Athena would have to simply fend for herself.

"Did you say you brought your own tea?" she asked instead of the thousand other questions that ran through her mind. "That would not happen to be *the* Antonopoulos Family Teas?"

"Of course," Seppi said, grunting a little as they heaved their trunks over a slightly too large rock in their path. "I never travel without our family's signature blends."

"Which are?" Poppy asked. If anything were going to set her right, it'd be a bohea. She was already imagining wrapping her hands around a warm ceramic teacup. Two spoonfuls of sugar, a splash of milk to transform the black tea to a warm caramel color. The smoky, rainy day aroma...

She would close her eyes and imagine she was home and famous and rich and...

Giuseppe broke her thoughts. He was always doing that. "Of course. We came with a selection. Gifts for Lady Rose and yourself."

"And my cousin," Poppy added. "Willa is here too."

"It'll be plenty," Athena said with a hoarse voice.

Poppy turned her head over her shoulder to catch the other woman's dark eyes. She couldn't, of course. Athena was looking everywhere but for her.

She watched as Athena's eyes darted around the tops of the trees, down to the overgrowth of wide ferns. She looked wild, as if she was seeing things emerge from every corner of her vision.

She was probably trying to see what kind of flora was here, internally cataloging every detail. And, she was probably trying to see if she could spot another dinosaur.

Poppy bit the inside of her cheek. She felt grateful that Athena hadn't been able to make her feel like she was falling again. It had already happened once today, and that was one too many. *Thank you very much*. She turned back.

"Why is it so hot here?" Seppi grunted, still struggling with the trunk. He had made no progress on finding a better way to carry it.

Even Athena wasn't complaining so much, though she didn't seem to be faring any better. Her cheeks were flushed, and Poppy noticed droplets of sweat glide down her temples, following the curve of her cheek and down her long neck.

Poppy turned back to the path ahead. "It's a pocket

climate. The volcano keeps the temperature here warm and humid. A big change from England, is it not?"

She heard Seppi whisper, "Volcano?"

She could just imagine Athena hitting him over the head with her hand. A gentle tap to tell him to be quiet and that whatever he was worried about wasn't a thing to fret over.

From his pained, "Theni!" she assumed she was correct.

She had spent enough time with them to know that Athena was in charge. And that Seppi still wouldn't let her get away with much.

"Not much longer to go," Poppy called brightly. "And, Athena, stop looking around like a frightened deer. You would hear the big ones. They don't tend to sneak up on you."

She heard Athena sigh.

Poppy's smile widened as if her lips had a mind of their own.

The group stopped at a clearing that, even to Poppy, having made the trek several times, felt like it came out of nowhere.

The estate where Poppy had called home for the past few weeks was as impressive, certainly, as it was out of place here. Its stately columns held up a wide wraparound porch that surrounded the entire house like a heavy blanket. Surrounding the property was a white picket fence that enclosed several raised garden beds, where lush vegetables grew in abundance. A sleepy coop with worn and scratched wood rested in the corner of the property. And a few rocking chairs were sprinkled about, each facing a different direction, a little haphazardly.

She remembered being amazed and confused by it when

she first arrived. Who had built this house? With what money? How had they managed to get it all set up like this? She had no idea. Those questions were left largely unanswered, like all the questions that have been asked so far.

Poppy waved her hand and told the two of them to keep following her. They had already gawked at Francesca; they would certainly feel similarly about Reggie, and she didn't want to stand around and listen to them admire the architecture here as well.

Especially not Seppi. He could go on and on about shapes and color for longer than she ever wanted to hear. It was sweet that he liked to share so much. And frustrating. Both could be true, she reminded herself.

They followed along, whispering questions to each other. She had to admit, she had similar concerns too, and no answers yet.

Aunt Rose was elusive about it whenever she pressed her aunt to elaborate. Poppy didn't have the answers they sought. She hardly had any of her own questions answered yet.

But she would. Aunt Rose was stubborn, but she was just as persistent.

"Poppy?"

It was Willa's voice that broke her thoughts. Her cousin was standing on the porch with her eyes wide and mouth open. And why wouldn't she? Poppy was approaching the house with two strangers on their otherwise uninhabited island.

Poppy waved and did her best to smile brightly at her. She hoped it looked authentic, but she was certain it was strained and forced.

From behind, she heard Seppi grunt, struggling with the trunks, and Athena mumble something under her breath.

"Who...?" Willa inquired, approaching the white wood gate with light steps.

Poppy turned back, ignoring her for now. "This is my cousin, Willa," she said quickly, cutting off any other form of verbal grumpiness from either of them. "Aunt Rose should be inside with Reggie. I'm not so sure either of them will be thrilled to see you."

A loud chirping sound trilled in the breeze once Poppy opened the gate for them. Reggie rushed from the porch to the gate with stout legs.

Poppy had fallen in love with Reggie from the moment she saw him. He, on the other hand, wasn't exactly her biggest admirer.

He was something like a cross between a very large, very fat sparrow and a lizard. He had two powerful, scaly legs, a potbelly, and tiny, clawed arms that he liked to wave about wildly. His snout was full of teeth, but he usually only chomped on garden pests, luckily.

Now, he was running at the gate like a guard dog. He only barely reached her knees. He reminded her of her childhood hound. Small, yet always thinking he was so much bigger than he was.

Poppy reached down to rub his head, but he dodged her with surprising grace and speed as his stubby tail swung to keep him upright. He ran to Athena and stomped his feet, chirping at her in a chorus of squeaks.

Athena was staring at him with her mouth open, a look of surprise that Poppy wished she could capture forever.

She had rarely seen her like this, not even when they met the large dinosaur in the jungle. Athena usually seemed bored, or had some quip, never taking anything too seriously, yet always being way too stoic.

"Amazing, right?" Poppy said with a smile.

Athena shook her head, but more in disbelief, she thought, than a 'no'. Her brown eyes locked on Poppy's. "What are these..?"

Poppy waved her hand. "It would be easier for my aunt to explain," she said. She moved past Reggie and guided them inside.

Willa eyed them suspiciously as they passed. But Poppy and Athena, she noticed, held their heads high while Seppi ducked low as he passed Willa, as if worried his stature would be off-putting.

She shook her head slightly.

They entered the home, having left their trunks on the porch, and Poppy took a left to bring them to the kitchen quickly.

"No sitting room?" Seppi asked, caution in his tone as they entered the small kitchen space.

Poppy gestured for them to sit at the table. She had brought them here intentionally. It was where her aunt spent a curious amount of time. Aunt Rose never seemed to care much for tradition, especially not here. Poppy didn't want to make her angrier than she already was by reintroducing the ways of London.

"Island life doesn't exactly follow the same etiquette procedures," Poppy explained. She gestured around at the well-worn kitchen and a little bird-like creature hanging from one clawed talon on the banister.

Athena followed her hand to the bird. She pulled back a little, then leaned in, eyes studying the creature's odd feather pattern, the way they shimmered teal and blue in the light from the stained glass window over the sink. "How peculiar," she whispered.

"It's not a regular bird," Poppy said.

Behind her, Willa entered the kitchen with her arms folded across her body delicately. "I'll get mother," she said quietly.

Chapter Ten

ATHENA WILL DRINK COLD TEA, IF SHE MUST

The tea was cold now, Athena was sure of it. They had been sitting at the table for a long while, and no one but Giuseppe had touched their teacups. She wanted to slap her cousin across the back of the head and tell him he was being rude by drinking it all as he poured himself another cup.

She also wanted to lean across the table and tell Poppy that this was the good stuff. That she had packed it *specifically for her*. And here she was, staring at it like it was poison. What a waste.

But instead, she let out a long exhale and then looked around the group.

"You're here to take my meddling niece home, then?" Lady Rose said at last, once Athena's eyes landed on her.

"But Aunt Rose!" Poppy frowned and crossed her arms.

"Mother!" the other girl, Willa, Athena was pretty sure, scolded her simultaneously.

Lady Rose was a small but fierce woman. She was petite and plump with lines in her face so deep and hair so silver that it seemed unlikely that she could realistically be Willa's mother at all. Unless, of course, either Lady Rose had aged incredibly poorly, or Willa was blessed with a youthful look. Athena's mind scrambled to remember Poppy ever speaking of Willa before... She was sure she hadn't. Or, more likely, Athena hadn't been listening.

"When is the next shipment boat arriving? That's how you are planning to get home, I assume?" Lady Rose seemed unswayed and unbothered by either of them. She scratched the top of Reggie's head with a finger. He was perched on her lap, little arms with silly little claws held close. "You have what you need for your little lady's journal, I'm sure," the older woman said. "The bees are alive and well. Go tell London."

Poppy huffed, and the corner of Athena's mouth twitched up, betraying her. It was always just a little funny when Poppy got all in an agitated state about something.

"Aunt Rose, I do not," Poppy said, her tone was confident and calm despite her previous outburst. "And if you don't mind, it's not *just* a lady's journal. I have aspirations for it to become a serious publication someday. The article about the bees here could be what puts my name in the papers."

Athena smiled. She pulled her mug closer to her and glanced at Giuseppe, who was already looking at her with a puzzled expression. Athena shrugged.

"Our wedding is coming soon," Giuseppe said. Instead, Athena was sure, the million other things he wanted to say. "Your mother was very adamant that we bring you back as soon as possible." He finished his tea with one long gulp and continued, "And not just your mother, I'm sure our families are also eager to get it done."

"How romantic," Lady Rose said, sarcasm heavy in her tone.

Poppy glared at her for just a moment. "Aunt Rose, I absolutely insist on staying just a little longer. And, now that Athena and Seppi know about the dinosaurs, I think it is imperative that they stay a while, too."

There's that spark, Athena thought. She sipped from her teacup. It was, in fact, cold. She thought about spitting it out.

Lady Rose grumbled and set Reggie down. He made a little bird-like chirp, then scampered out of the small kitchen with heavy feet.

"She's right," Willa said. "Mother, they need to experience the island. See for themselves what it's like living here. We're trying to keep this a secret, after all."

"We can keep a secret," Giuseppe said with an uncharacteristically firm nod of his head.

Willa glanced at him, her eyes tracking him up and

down. "Not to be rude, but we don't know you, and this secret isn't like some small piece of gossip."

Athena saw her chance. She took it quickly. "Lady Rose, we can be of service while we're here. At least, until the boat arrives."

Reggie came running back into the room. He cried out, and his little arms clawed at Athena's skirt. She furrowed her brow at him, but a moment later, his distress became apparent. Another little dinosaur, similar in shape to Reggie, though much leaner and more muscular, came chasing after him.

This dinosaur, however, had a bulbous head, with what looked like a thick skull made for ramming into things.

She scooped Reggie up just as the other creature hit her shin.

Athena grimaced, but the pain wasn't much, despite the little monster's brave attempt. She held Reggie closer, peering down at the furious little dinosaur at her feet.

"And how can you be of service?" Lady Rose said, rising from her seat. She plucked Reggie, forcibly, from Athena's arms, and glared at the creature on the floor. "Shoo, Evangeline," she whispered to the helmet-headed creature.

Evangeline made a few protesting peeps, then raced back out of the room just as quickly as she had come.

Lady Rose sat again, an expectant 'Well?' expression etched into her face.

Athena's mind was still trying to process everything that had just happened. But she thought quickly. "I am well read," she said. "A woman of science, as much as I can be. I can help here—"

Lady Rose clicked her tongue to silence her.

Athena suddenly felt a hit in her stomach. Just like everywhere she had been before, she was getting laughed out of the building. Her hands clenched under the table, and her jaw tightened.

Beside her, Poppy caught her gaze. Her blue-green eyes searched Athena's face, and Athena forced her body to soften. She wasn't going to let Poppy see her squirm. She wasn't going to let *any* of them see her squirm. The island was her chance. She had to do whatever it took to make it.

"Let me prove my worth before the next boat arrives," Athena said quickly. "You can decide then."

Willa turned to her mother. "We don't exactly have a choice, they're here. We should show them why this place is worth saving," she nearly whispered.

Lady Rose's expression soured. "So be it," she said. "But I'm drinking your tea."

"Deal," Athena said.

On her other side, she could hear long-suffering Seppi's sigh.

She didn't care. This was going to be good for her. And it was good for him to learn to persevere a little, too.

ATHENA IS IRRESPONSIBLE WITH HER PEN

$\mathcal{I}$t was in the afternoon light that Athena's quill pen tapped on her journal. It was open, but the page was blank. She stared at the bee with narrowed eyes.

She had managed to escape almost as soon as Lady Rose made her own retreat. Athena had left Seppi to clean up the teatime setup under the guise of needing air. But she knew, and he knew, it wasn't really a ruse at all. It had been too much too soon, and she was ready to burst into a million pieces. Seppi had seemed happy enough to make himself useful at home and, she hoped, more accustomed to the dinosaurs.

As she sat in the open field, the bee stared back at her, and if she didn't know any better, she'd think it stared at her *knowingly*. There was a presence about the bee, and not just her size. Which, Athena had to admit, was rather shocking.

The bee was roughly the size of a large housecat. Her black eyes, the length of Athena's fist, gazed like a multifaceted void back at Athena so she could see her faint reflection mirrored back at her in honeycomb darkness. The bee buzzed loudly, her wings flapped so rapidly that Athena lost track of them, and her massive, fuzzy, striped body floated up into the clear cerulean sky.

"You'll ruin your pen if you're not careful," Poppy said, her voice jolting Athena from her awe.

Athena glanced back, trying her best to stifle the feeling of her stomach suddenly turning to rocks. She bit her lip for a moment, swallowing quickly and then readjusting her straight posture. "I hear you're remarkably good at fixing them," she said as she focused her attention on the bee, now dancing away in the light breeze.

"You heard right. But, I don't have any of my tools here," Poppy said quietly. She approached Athena, who, in turn, set her eyes on the landscape ahead of them. She wanted to look at anything but Poppy. And only Poppy. To cry and throw herself into her arms, and tell her she was foolish and reckless and harsh... Her heart beat as rapidly as the bee's wings in her chest. She took in a deep breath and focused on the scene before them, absorbing details to ground herself as best she could.

The wildflowers around them swayed gently in the salty

breeze blowing in from the ocean. The sound of rustling leaves murmuring sweet whispers and the smell of sweet peas surrounded her, wrapping around her like a familiar embrace.

She was used to the hustle and bustle of the city, the sound of horses and people shouting at one another. She has to admit, this was lovely. And, she thought, as she caught a massive bear-like creature with three horns on its head walking in the treeline, it was also terrifying.

The dinosaur in the corner of her vision turned to her, raised its head as if smelling her on the breeze, then shook its armor-plated head, all three horns moving like arrows in an archery target. It lumbered back into the trees, far enough away that Athena was confident it wouldn't return.

"Why did you come?" Poppy asked, so suddenly it jolted Athena from her thoughts.

Athena glanced in her direction as her stomach dropped harshly as though she had just been startled from a dream. She squared her shoulders. "Like we said, your mother sent us," Athena said, her voice low. It came out angrier than she wanted. It tended to.

"Giuseppe, maybe. But you?"

Athena bit her lip. She loosened her jaw as soon as she realized she had done it, but her fingers twitched still. "I didn't think you'd go home if it were just Seppi," she said. "You're stubborn."

Poppy laughed; it sounded genuine. "That and you hoped to study with my aunt here. I know you know the rumors about her."

"Mostly your stubbornness," Athena retorted quickly.

Poppy hummed. Her smile remained. "You're more stubborn than I am, I think."

Athena rested her hands on the wildflowers. She leaned her head back a little and closed her eyes. She wished, so desperately, that she would feel Poppy's lips on hers, or her fingers intertwining with hers, digging into the dirt together.

She hated that she thought that, too. She opened her eyes quickly.

Poppy was still where she had been. Standing beside her, but not too close. Looking at her, but through her. So close, and yet... This was the farthest Athena had felt from her in a very long time.

The two stayed in silence for a long while, watching a few bees bumble by as the sun grew lower in the sky.

Athena didn't know what to say. She didn't know what to ask. Most of all, she didn't know why it would matter. Poppy was going to do what Poppy was going to do. And what she was going to do was marry her cousin. Athena thought, darkly for a moment, that maybe it was best if Poppy left her in the wildflowers to decompose. Her fingertips pushed into the soft earth below her. It was cold.

"They don't know why the bees have stopped producing honey," Poppy said at last, cutting the silence like a hammer cuts paper. It shocked Athena from her thoughts. "Something has been disturbing them."

Athena's brows furrowed. She steadied her hands by holding her journal with both hands, tightly, like fists. "I can help with that," she said. She watched Poppy's expression with narrowed eyes.

Poppy was looking out into the field as though she were all alone.

Typical, Athena thought. Poppy probably hadn't even heard her. Too busy thinking of her next breaking story or next move. Poppy never listened. Poppy only thought of what to say next.

But after a moment, Poppy surprised her. "I think you could," she said with a shrug of one shoulder. "I'd advocate for you if my aunt would listen to me at all."

"Let me step in then."

Both Athena and Poppy turned to see Willa approaching. She was holding her sunhat with her hand as she trudged through the flowers with a fair amount of care. She was silent on her feet, despite her somewhat off-center walk.

Athena had come into the field so carefully, she was sure she hadn't left a trace. Poppy had been quiet as a cat. But Willa? How she had managed to sneak up on them was beyond her. She seemed to be making a show of her trudge through the flowers, Athena thought.

Perhaps she had felt bad for overhearing the conversation, Athena thought. She watched Willa closely. Poppy's cousin was smarter than she let on. More astute. Athena might need to be more careful...

Willa huffed a little, straightening out her skirt once she was standing between them. She tended to her hair, smoothing out the wild red curls as best she could. She held a hand out for Athena to grab.

Athena did, and Willa pulled her up with surprising strength. "You are a lady of science? Like my mother, right?"

Willa asked once she seemed satisfied that Athena was finally on her feet.

Athena nodded. "I'm not formally educated–"

"I understand," Willa said, though she waved her hand somewhat dismissively. "What woman is these days?"

The other two women looked away, following a slow-moving bee in the distance.

"But," Willa went on, "my mother could use the help. Some of this is over her head, brilliant as she is. And she's growing in years. It would be nice for her to have someone to talk about her work with. Someone who understands and can be of service." Willa smiled at Athena, catching her gaze at last. "I will work on getting her to let you stay after the next boat arrives."

"Thank you," Athena said. "I promise I can be helpful."

Poppy grimaced. She looked the other way quickly, and Athena's own expression contorted slightly in response.

Willa went on, seemingly unaware of the tension she had found herself in, that is, if Athena could call it that, "You will still need to prove your worth. No offense. She doesn't tend to listen to me. But you seem up to the task."

"I take it it's not your approval I need to win?" Athena asked, ignoring Poppy for now.

Wila's smile brightened. "Oh, Athena, you won me over with your name alone. I adore Greek mythology! Besides, we'll be family soon, won't we?"

Athena's face reddened. Right. She was Poppy's cousin. And the wedding was soon. "Yes," she said, forcing it out in a way she hoped sounded confident and kind. "Poppy and Seppi are the talk of the town back home." She couldn't help but watch Poppy from the corner of her eye. But she caught nothing but her ex's far-off stare at the passing clouds.

"My mother can be hard to please," Willa said in a jovial tone. Athena caught the warning nonetheless. "But I'd like to think that if you get on well enough with Reggie and the others, you will still win her favor yet."

Athena grumbled a little. She pulled her journal closer to her core. She had never been particularly good with animals. Winning over beasts of legend like this..?

But, she'd have to try.

Chapter Twelve

ATHENA AND THE SURPRISINGLY SMALL HOUSE

The estate was smaller than Athena would suspect from the grandiose outside. Beyond the sprawling garden with raised beds, a coop, and boxes of flowers, the sprawling house soared above as if keeping watch over the clearing. The front of the home had a large wrap-around porch, tall columns, and what looked like an impressive number of rooms, so Athena was surprised that after her short trip to visit the bees, she was finally shown the house, and it was, surprisingly, unimpressive.

Willa led the way with Athena and Seppi close behind and Poppy at the rear. They entered the home as they had before, but this time, with a kind of warmth from Willa like she was showing family around cheerfully, and not some strangers she had only just met without warning. It seemed that, unlike either she or Poppy, Willa was rather content to accept things as they were.

A little twinge of admiration, or perhaps jealousy, rooted in Athena's chest. It seemed peaceful to be so open. She couldn't relate at all. She was a constant coil, a state of discomfort wrapped in apathy.

"You already know the kitchen," Willa said, gesturing to the left to the doorless kitchen.

Willa turned to the right, where, beyond a set of open French doors, was an actual sitting room. Three plush couches in a floral pattern fabric faced one another with a small set of tables in the middle. On the far wall, two large windows let in ample light through sheer curtains, and on the opposite side, a floor-to-ceiling bookshelf was stuffed with textbooks and leatherbound literature.

Athena moved closer to the books, while Seppi inspected the brick fireplace.

"Lovely masonry," he said, one finger grazing the grout.

"A bit delicate, though," Willa said. She stood beside him and eyed his finger, a warning to stop touching if Athena had ever seen one.

He retracted his hand quickly, looking away sheepishly. "I'm just amazed you two live in such a well-crafted home on this island, so isolated. Who did the work?" he asked.

Willa smiled again, her bright face illuminating. "My mother commissioned the work long before we arrived here. I'm afraid that is why some of the home is a little more worn than one would expect. It was left sitting for some time before we moved in."

"I see," Seppi said with a nod.

Athena's eyes narrowed. She went back to inspecting the books, but kept listening to their conversation. She, too, was confused as well as curious about how this impressive structure came to be.

Willa went on, louder now that Athena looked preoccupied. "You may hear little creaks and sounds sometimes," she said. "It's nothing to be alarmed about, but it can take getting used to. It's just a surprisingly old house."

"It's true," Poppy said. "This place sounds haunted. Especially if you're here alone."

Willa's smile softened. "Oh, cousin, you always did have the most vivid imagination. I suppose that's why you're the writer." She moved from the fireplace and gestured for them to follow.

They left the room and followed Poppy up the narrow stairs and into a long hallway that ended at a T. Willa turned. "You're fortunate we have enough rooms," Willa said. "She pointed to the first door on the right. "This is my room. Poppy's been sleeping just across the way."

They moved down the hallway to the next set of doors. "I suppose you two can decide where you want to stay," she said as she opened both doors to let them look.

The first was larger, with a big window facing the jungle and a four-post bed, as well as a dark wardrobe that looked as though it could be its own room once opened. The second was smaller, but it had a comfy feeling about it. A little chestnut wardrobe and a small bed covered in quilts, and a little window was already open to let in a gentle breeze that made the room smell of earth and salt.

Athena and Seppi exchanged glances.

"You can take the larger one," he conceded.

Athena's lips twitch into a mischievous grin. The win was all she needed. "No," she said kindly. "You take the big wardrobe."

Giuseppe smiled and stood tall in the hallway. He looked down to the end where two other halls branched off. He asked, "And down there?"

Poppy was beside Athena before she could track her. She was looking down the end of the hall with fire in her eyes and a chill running from her neck down to her arms and fingers. She had seen this look many times before. It meant Poppy had locked in on something important.

"My mother's wing," Willa explained, cutting Athena free from her rapid thoughts. Willa laughed a little. "I suppose since she paid for the place, she gets a whole wing to herself." She moved back down the hallway, but stopped at the top of the stairs. "Why don't you get settled in? It will be some time before the next boat. You may as well make this place feel as much like home as you can."

Home. The thought made Athena bristle. She had a home, by definition. It felt like anything but homey.

Her eyes moved across the hall to each door. Seppi. Willa. Poppy... and then the wing upstairs is dedicated to Lady Rose. It did seem only fair that the old woman had her privacy, she figured. But a part of her, the part that wanted to think about anything other than where Poppy slept, was curious as to why she needed a whole wing to herself. What was that expression? *Care will kill a cat,* she thought.

She'd better worry about just herself for now. There was enough time to care about everything else later.

Seppi caught her gaze and smiled gently at her. "Let's go get our things," he said.

Athena looked back down the hallway. Poppy and Willa were already gone.

*A*thena's stomach grumbled. But no one had called them down for dinner. She and Seppi had both opened their doors at the same time, given each other sad, hungry expressions, then closed their doors slowly.

She suspected it would be best to eat the last of the bread that she had packed away in her trunk and hope that, in the morning, Lady Rose would be more receptive to their presence. Or, at least, more tolerant. Or, at the very least, let them know where the food was and permit them to help themselves.

She stuffed a big bite into her mouth, resisting the urge to swallow it whole. She chewed slowly, trying to make it last.

At this point, she'd be grateful to have the old woman be less bitter about their unannounced arrival. Though she knew on some logical level that she, too, would be much more hostile if she had escaped to a remote location only for two strangers to appear and eat her food and stay in her space. Lady Rose certainly didn't hold back the way the ladies Athena was accustomed to. She admired it.

She let out a long sigh through her nose, still chewing somewhat mindlessly, as she sat at the edge of the small bed.

She glanced at the wall, wondering how her cousin was fairing. Probably, if she had to guess, either already asleep or pacing up and down the length of his room, worrying about decorum.

Her ear twitched as she heard the faint sound of something rhythmic within the walls. She shook her head.

He was up worrying after all.

POPPY AND THE NEXT CHAPTER

Poppy bit her lip as she stared into the flickering beeswax candle flame. It was dimming lower, battling the shadows more chaotically as the night dragged on. She didn't want to have to rummage around the place looking for a new one. She didn't want anyone to know that she was still awake and working. She didn't want anyone asking her questions.

When this candle went out, it would be her sign to

finally go to bed. For now, she accepted that she could not sleep.

She propped her head on her arm, sinking over the writing desk that faced the window. Papers were strewn across the desk, ink spills, and crossed-out scribbles, run-on sentences that made absolutely no sense at all. The only thing she wanted to do was knock the candle over with cat-like curiosity and watch all the writing go up in flames.

Working on her adventure serial had come easily to her since her arrival on the island. The heroine, who she had to admit was exactly her opposite, had stowed away aboard a ship, been attacked by pirates, seen a mysterious leviathan in the deep, and crash landed on the shore of an isolated island where real, living dinosaurs roamed. It was all thrilling, and she thought it was her best work yet.

Ladies Journal, she thought bitterly, the words in her mind were thick and sour. Her lips puckered, and she sat up again. She could use this for her serial. All the anger and confusion of the day had to go somewhere. She had asked for an adventure, and adventure had come crashing down on her. Just not at all the way she suspected it would.

Her eyes shifted to the wall she shared with Athena, and the taste of lemon filled her mouth again. She could still smell the sharp acid of Athena's words, which she had spoken to her the last time they saw each other. And the fragrance of orange blossoms.

Poppy let out a little grumble, then looked back at her papers.

Athena had left her with words that pierced her body like bee stings and a heart on the verge of collapse. And now she had the audacity to come back. To come back with her betrothed. Even more, she dared to act like she didn't care.

Fine. Poppy wouldn't care either. It was ancient history, just like the damned dinosaurs.

Except. They, too, had risen from the depths of the earth.

Poppy pulled the papers toward her and crumbled them all until she found a fresh page. She dipped her quill and, running the sharp feather tip across her lip, she thought of what kind of villain she could make Athena. Perhaps a two-headed demon from a dark cave, springing forth from the darkness to capture the daring heroine. People would like that, she thought. She could even make her a gorgon. People liked ancient history. It made them feel scholarly and smart when in reality, it was just rehashing the same old trivial things that all humans suffer.

Her chest expanded, and her back straightened. History repeated itself, and she could use that to her advantage, at least in storytelling.

She began to write the next chapter, determined not to sleep until it was finished and determined to find more answers in the coming days. Now that Giuseppe and Athena were here, time was running out. She had to find a way to save her family's business for her sister, for her family, but also herself.

Chapter Fourteen

ATHENA IS NOT TERRIBLY CHARMING

Athena would have sworn that she hadn't slept at all. Her body was stiff, her eyes heavy, and a profound exhaustion radiated throughout her limbs as a dull thud began to beat within her skull.

The knock on her door and the morning light streaming through the window, however, indicated that she had, if anything, overslept.

The knock grew more insistent, a sharp sound that cleared the fog from her mind quickly.

Athena sprang up from the bed and opened the door a crack.

Willa stood in the opening with a wide smile and closed eyes. "I don't want to disturb you," she said, eyes still sealed shut. "Especially if you're indecent."

Athena looked down at her nightdress, which usually covered her entirely, though she had unbuttoned most of it in the night. She held it closed with one hand and mumbled, "Thank you," in a hoarse voice.

Willa nodded. "Breakfast is ready," she said. "It's just toast and honey. And tea, which, thank you for that."

Athena opened the door a little wider but remained quiet.

"It's like we're running a hotel," Willa said, peaking one eye open at last. "Kind of exciting."

"Mhm," Athena said with a half-smile.

Something about Willa's genuine enthusiasm had found its way to Athena's mood. She just seemed so happy, so ready to accept that strangers had arrived here, that Athena had to admire it. She wished she could be so easy in her nature.

"Well," Willa said as she turned on her heel, her red hair spiraling out behind her, "get dressed and get your mind sharp. My mother is down there and she's always more agreeable after honey and toast."

Athena nodded and shut the door gently. She leaned back on the wooden door and blinked into the sun-filled room. Yesterday had gone... well, about as poorly as she expected it to. It was fair for Lady Rose to be disgruntled with them here; she understood that. But she also thought it was fair for her to fight for her chance to learn and study here, too.

The door creaked as she pushed herself off and launched into the middle of the room with light feet. She threw open the trunk and rummaged through for the least wrinkled, and least stained, white blouse she could find. She threw it on and secured a rust colored skirt under her chest. Athena busied her hands, stuffing the blouse into the skirt and smoothing out the sleeves as best she could. She looked around the room for a mirror, but, perhaps thankfully, there was none.

She brushed out her wild waves and shrugged to herself. It would have to do. She could only hope that Lady Rose truly didn't care much about appearances.

Athena had just thrown open the door, one leg already swinging out to fly down the hall, when she stopped suddenly.

A little dinosaur, only the size of a small hound, hissed at her. It had a long body, with a fin-like spine running down its back. Sharp claws dug into the wood floor as it scampered away, down the hall, and toward Lady Rose's quarters.

Athena's body didn't move for a long moment until, at last, she peeked out the door and down the hall, dark hair spilling over her shoulder as she did. Certain that the hallway was clear, she exited her room, closing the door tightly behind her. With careful steps, this time, she made her way down the stairs.

. . .

*S*eppi was charming. At least, he seemed to be charming the table, which included Poppy, much to Athena's discomfort. The table was packed already, with Lady Rose and Reggie taking up nearly half of it, it seemed. Poppy and Willa huddled together, their chairs pushed so close to one another that their knees were pressed into each other.

Neither seemed to mind. Both were looking at Seppi with smiles and kind eyes as he regaled them with the story of their journey. How he was able to articulate the detail of the ship's architecture so well, considering he had spent most of the days with his head either in a bucket or under a thin pillow, she wasn't sure. How he made it sound interesting was simply magic.

"Athena!" he cried joyously, interrupting his own story mid-sentence.

The group turned to her as she loomed in the doorway awkwardly. She was always so awkward. She did her best to smile, not awkwardly, and entered the room with what she hoped looked like confidence.

"Good morning," she said, mainly to Lady Rose.

The older woman snorted back. She reached for another buttered toast and grabbed a knife full of creamed honey like it was a weapon. "Do you usually oversleep?" she asked as she harshly slathered the honey over the toast.

Athena's brows rose. "No, not at all... I'm sorry..." She pulled the only empty chair free and slid into the seat, her shoulders a little slumped.

From across the table, Poppy was eyeing her with an impossible-to-read expression. It could have been amusement or annoyance. Athena couldn't be sure. She ripped her gaze away and settled on Seppi beside her.

"Athena was always the one waking us up anytime we stayed over at your house," Seppi said in her defense. "I've never known you to sleep much. I was certain a dinosaur had smothered you in the night."

"Thank you for checking in on me, then," Athena teased back in a low whisper.

Seppi shrugged with a smile. "I was just telling the lovely ladies that you were taking such good care of me on the ship," he said.

Athena's eyes narrowed slightly. So he hadn't been selling her out for her poor excuse for comfort. She didn't have to wonder at his reasoning for long.

The chair to her left creaked as Willa turned quickly to her. "Athena, I was hopeful that maybe you could help out with some things around the farm today," she said. "I could use some help gathering up some weeds in the garden, perhaps collecting eggs?"

Athena's cheeks warmed as though she had just been slapped harshly across the face. Willa had said she would help her endear Athena to her mother. But she hadn't considered that it meant starting at the bottom rung. She wanted to help, of course, but she wanted to prove her worth more than what she could do with manual labor. "I can help with that," she said slowly, drawing her words out carefully.

Poppy leaned back in her chair slightly, her face a noticeable grimace.

Athena lost her thoughts. She blurted out, "But I can also help with anything else... more intellectual. I have–"

Lady Rose scoffed. She spoke from the side of her mouth, using the half-eaten bread to point at Athena, "You want to help so badly?"

Athena nodded. "I've studied medicine and–"

"Fine." Lady Rose finished chewing and set her bread down on the little pink china plate. "I have a task for you."

Beside her, Seppi's eyes grew wide. Athena glanced at Willa, who was busy shaking her head and staring up at the rafters. A sinking feeling in her stomach began to drag her down slowly. She held her head high despite it. "Yes," she prompted the lady.

Lady Rose smirked. It was a surprisingly wicked look. "One of the stegosaurus has an algae covering her plates. I fear it may cause complications down the line. Are you familiar with flora treatments?"

Athena thought quickly. She wasn't sure, but she had a guess. "I would think I would want to rub the algae off carefully," she said. "I wouldn't want to harm the creature with a solution. Especially if it is something it wouldn't have come in contact with in ancient history. And... stegosaurus, is that the one similar to Dotty?"

Lady Rose's smile grew, though if in amusement or genuine appreciation, Athena wasn't sure. "Clean Theodosia's plates and bring me back a sample of the algae," she said. "If you do this, I will consider letting you help me further in my research here."

Willa leaned across the table. "Mother, you know how Theodosia is about her back plates!"

Lady Rose raised a hand to quiet her daughter. "If the girl wants to try, let her," she said.

Athena nodded. "I won't just try," she said confidently,

though inside, she was sure that the blood in her veins had instantly turned to ice, chilling her to her core. Willa's words echoed in her mind. This wasn't so much an ask for help as it was a challenge.

"Bring Poppy with you," Lady Rose said.

"I can go," Seppi said, rising to his feet.

"Not you," Lady Rose said. "You, I enjoy."

"Gosh, thanks, Aunt Rose." Poppy folded her arms across her chest. She slumped even lower in her chair.

ATHENA IS STILL BETTER THAN NOTHING

They were walking in the vague direction that Willa had said the stegosaurus liked to nap. But it had been a while, judging by the light that filtered down through the canopy, and Athena's aching legs.

"I can't believe I got kicked out of the house," Poppy said with a kick of her feet. She was trailing behind Athena through the ferns in the jungle, huffing and puffing every step of the way.

Athena was just glad she was talking to her. It had been

a long walk in uncomfortable silence. The cadence of Poppy's voice, the way she sounded so effortlessly fun, reminded Athena of old times... She didn't look back, only said, "You didn't *need* to come."

"And what? Let you have all the fun hunting down a dinosaur and... scrubbing algae?" Poppy said with a laugh. "No, I've been here long enough to know that if Aunt Rose wants me out, I'm going to be out. It's either sit in the jungle alone, staring at nothing, or come with you."

"Glad I'm more exciting than staring at nothing," Athena said before she could help it.

"Or maybe I just want to see you try to touch a massive beast that doesn't want anything to do with you," Poppy said.

Athena turned back, one brow raised.

Poppy smiled at her, but it didn't reach her eyes. She trudged through more foliage and nearly pushed Athena on her way past her. "So your whole goal is getting my aunt to let you stay here, then?" she said, her voice low despite their solitude.

Athena rolled her eyes. She followed after Poppy. "Yes."

"And that's the only reason?" Poppy's voice was so quiet that Athena wasn't sure she heard it at first.

"Yes," she breathed back. She moved ahead again. She didn't want to look at Poppy when she lied. Didn't want to hear what sounded like hurt in her voice again. She didn't want any of it. Coming here was a mistake.

She stopped suddenly, before she even truly knew why. Up ahead, resting in the cozy shade of a large tree in a small clearing, rested a huge dragon-like creature.

Athena held a hand out to stop Poppy's trudging

footsteps quickly. She pointed to the dinosaur and then placed a finger over her lips and crouched down low.

Poppy nodded. She leaned in and squinted to get a better look.

The dinosaur had to be Theodosia. She looked just like Dotty—massive, round body, with a triangular head and prominent brow bone over big eyes. Two rows of enormous triangle plates ran down her back. But these were not the same iridescent that Dotty had. No, these, as Theodosia breathed and they caught the sunlight, were dull and mossy green.

Athena followed the plates down her body and to her long tail, curled up alongside her body. It was covered in sword-like spikes, as if it were some medieval weapon.

Poppy shuddered beside her.

It only served to make Athena feel braver. She rose from her squat silently. She waved her hand down for Poppy to stay still. But as soon as she took a single step, Poppy's warm fingers grazed her skin like a lightning strike hitting her arm.

She turned back swiftly, ripping her arm free before she could think about the feeling of Poppy's skin on hers.

Poppy's face soured. She pulled her hand to her chest. "Willa said Theodosia hates having her scales touched. And look at those spikes!" She pointed aggressively at the dinosaur. "My aunt sent you on a fool's errand. Don't do this."

Athena grimaced back. She turned to the dinosaur with her heart already pounding in her ears at Poppy's closeness. She looked at the sleeping dinosaur, then back at Poppy.

Chapter Sixteen

POPPY VERSES THE STEGOSAURUS

"Are you scared?" Athena asked, confidence heavy in her tone.

Poppy's lips drew into a thin line. She waved a hand. "Athena, go do whatever stupid thing you want to do. Get spiked in the gut by a dinosaur for all I care." But she did care. And she hated that she did. More so, she hated how her heart sank in her chest when Athena furrowed her brow and turned to the beast with a kind of determination that reminded her why she had fallen for her years before.

Athena was still looking ahead when she positioned herself between the dinosaur and Poppy. "I'm not reckless like you," she said quietly.

Poppy watched her eyes bounce from one end of the dinosaur to the other. She was thinking. Good. *Finally*.

"Your aunt said that she is worried about the algae," Athena murmured, as if thinking aloud. "And the other one's plates illuminated in the sunlight. Algae feed on sunlight..."

Poppy crept closer to the dinosaur, though she stayed hidden in the ferns.

"She's sleeping because she's tired," Athena whispered. "She needs sunlight."

"She can still kill you," Poppy warned. A spike of fear ran through her. "Tried things might be more likely to hurt first, assess later."

"You would know," Athena said, her words stinging Poppy like a slap.

She wasn't *that* grumpy in the mornings.

Athena crept closer to the dinosaur, unaware or completely uncaring that she had just wounded her.

Still, Poppy's body lurched forward, as if tethered to Athena. She reached a hand out but missed grasping at her skirt by a fraction. She felt the fabric of Athena's skirt pass through her fingers like smoke as the other woman kept moving forward.

Poppy thought Athena had done a good job of pausing to make sure the situation was clear and worth it, but now she was just being downright irresponsible. And Athena used to say *she* was the one who didn't think things through.

"Don't!" Poppy hissed, but Athena only turned back

halfway with one raised brow and a smirk before she kept creeping up toward the dinosaur.

Poppy's eyes darted from the sleeping face of the massive creature to the spikes on its tail and back to Athena. Her mind raced to find a way to help, though a dark thought crept from the back of her mind. If Athena wanted so badly to prove herself, she should go ahead and do it on her own. She shook the horrible thought from her head.

She *hated* Athena. She hated her so much and yet... Poppy stood slowly and quickly unfastened her skirt. It was a thick fabric, heavy enough to block the light if she needed.

Her eyes found Athena again. She had pulled a cloth from her pocket and held a small glass jar in her other hand. Poppy rolled her eyes. Of course. The impossible task of retrieving a sample. For someone so smart, Athena could be really dense.

Athena stood, or more crouched, beside the sleeping dinosaur. She held out a hand, far too confident, Poppy thought, to the first large plate on top of the dinosaur's back.

Poppy waited.

Athena had made it through the first few plates closest to the ground. She was silent and gentle, careful to move as quickly but as delicately as possible to scrub away at the mossy armored plates. But as she moved up the dinosaur's back, it became clear that she would not be able to reach the largest of the plates where the curve of the dinosaur's back was too high. Unless she... She wouldn't.

Poppy stepped forward, one hand holding her skirt up

and the other reaching out. She was just about to whisper, "Don't!" when Athena climbed the dinosaur's huge back, nestling herself between the two rows of plates. Her legs straddled the back as best she could, though she looked unbalanced and terribly unstable.

The dinosaur stirred, and Poppy froze, her blood instantly transforming to molten in her wrists and neck. She pointed frantically to the head that began to move a little, with large black eyes blinking curiously.

But Athena didn't seem to notice. She had the jar open and was scooping a handful of bright green algae into the container with a determined expression. Her brows were knit in concentration, her jaw set, but she wasn't going fast enough and already, her position on the dinosaur's back was unsteady.

Theodosia's eyes grew wide at last. She tossed her head back, a violent movement that shook Athena off balance. Athena remained calm, tucking away the jar quickly, her other hand worked to scrub at the dinosaur's remaining plates, only partly clearing them of the green sludge.

Theodosia roared, a loud and deep grumble as she struggled to get to her feet. Powerful, tree trunk legs untucked from beneath her as she stumbled upward.

Athena grabbed onto one of the massive plates. She yelped a little, her body tossed about the two rows with every movement Theodosia made.

"Devil confound it," Poppy swore under her breath. She slipped free from her skirt and hurried up to the dinosaur before Theodosia could see her.

Theodosia's face was higher than her own. Up close now, Poppy understood just how truly massive she was. But she didn't have time to think about the power the dinosaur held or how small she was by comparison. Not now.

Poppy threw her skirt up high and over Theodosia's head.

"What are you—" Athena started, her words came out in gut punches as the dinosaur continued to thrash, now more violently.

"Be quiet, please," Poppy said back, her words coming out in a sing-song tune. She didn't want to sound frightened or agitated and upset Theodosia anymore than she already was. She held the skirt ends tightly, securing them over Theodosia's eyes quickly. The movement pulled her close to Theodosia's face, and for a moment, she wondered if her jaws could crush her, even if she were a herbivore. Poppy closed her eyes instead, feeling her chest and stomach pressed up against the dinosaur's skull tightly.

Her arms ached as she held the skirt in place despite Theodosia's frantic movements. The harder she held, the closer they got. At last, Poppy's cheek was flattened against Theodosia's rough skin, and the dinosaur calmed.

Theodosia stilled, a sound like defeat rumbled from her throat, and she moved her head back and forth slowly, as if looking for where she was at last.

Poppy pulled the skirt tighter. She opened one eye and glanced up at Athena on the dinosaur's back. "Get it done," she grumbled, her head still resting on the stegosaurus's forehead.

Athena's hair was tousled about her face and shoulders. She had a small cut on her cheek, and wide brown eyes stared at Poppy in utter confusion. "Hurry!" Poppy stressed, though she kept her voice low, her tone kind.

Athena nodded, and it was as if she had come back into herself. Her eyes turned fierce, and her jaw set. She got to work scrubbing, and Theodosia let out a low, almost annoyed moan.

Finished, though perhaps not thoroughly, Athena scrambled off the dinosaur's back quickly. She motioned for Poppy to join her as she retreated into the dense jungle again.

Poppy sighed. Her arms were struggling to keep her hold. She looked down at her skirt. A pinprick of pain blossomed in her chest. It was a good skirt. She would miss it.

Poppy let go, jumping back as far as she could. The skirt fluttered to the forest floor, and Theodosia blinked rapidly in the new sunlight.

But Poppy didn't see any more. She was running into the forest after Athena, swearing the entire way.

POPPY IS OWED A NEW SKIRT

From the silence in the trees, it would seem that Theodosia was too confused to chase after them. The plan had worked, though Poppy was confident it would.

Athena stopped in a sunbeam, finally looking back to see if Poppy was still there. Her dark hair shimmered with threads of golden amber around her face like a halo. Not that Poppy could truly appreciate that now.

Poppy's eyes were fierce. In her white chemise, she was

certain she didn't look too intimidating, but she didn't care. She held out a finger to Athena, pointing at her like it was a sword. "You owe me a new skirt!"

Athena's eyes traced down Poppy's form quickly before landing on her face. Her expression twisted and with it, Poppy's stomach. "You should have stayed out of it!" she shot back.

Poppy's heart thumped loudly in her chest as hot anger surged through her body. She laughed. It burst through her before she could catch it. It was a harsh sound, even to her ears, but she had no idea what to do with any of her emotions.

Athena stomped through the ferns, parting them harshly as she closed the gap between them. "There you go," she growled, her eyes locking on Poppy's with a fiery intensity. "Meddling in things you shouldn't and then playing like the victim."

Poppy's laughter was cut short. Her finger, still in the air, curled into a tight fist. She pulled her hands to her sides but took another step closer. "And there you go, feeling nothing in that shriveled heart," she said as tears stung her eyes. She took one more step so their faces were nearly touching. "You can't be honest with me. You can't even be honest with yourself, can you?"

Athena's eyes narrowed, but her hand reached up to hold Poppy's chin gently, her thumb running along Poppy's jawline like it was made of glass.

Poppy's heart raced in her chest as Athena held her there, brown eyes burrowing into her before she tilted Poppy up, just a little. "You don't know me at all," Athena's voice was low and hoarse, her lips grazed Poppy's as she spoke, sending a storm through Poppy's body. Athena pulled back at last, leaving a cold void where she had been just a moment ago. The place where her hand had held her face, her lips, all shivered in Athena's sudden absence.

Poppy closed her eyes tightly before the tears sprang free. She pushed at her eyes with the backs of her hands. Poppy opened her eyes slowly as the quick rush of the moment finally cleared from her limbs. Her arms and legs ached with a dull tingling numbness, and her fingers trembled. She stared harshly at the jungle floor, trying to ground herself in the green, in the lush ferns that waved gently as a sea salt breeze weaved through the trees. She couldn't look at Athena. Not at her dark brown eyes that turned honey gold when the light hit them, not at the way her jaw clenched when she was deep in thought, not at the little crease that formed between her brows.

She wanted to look at anything but Athena. And take her all in, too.

But Athena was already walking away.

ATHENA IS TOTALLY FINE

$\mathcal{A}$thena wished she were a more skilled inventor so she could build a device to travel back in time and undo what she had just done. She was constantly smacking Seppi upside the head when he did something foolish; now, she wished she could do the same to herself. Instead, she stuffed one hand into her pocket, feeling the cold of the glass jar within.

She gripped it so tightly she worried it might shatter in

her fist as she walked so fast she nearly ran back to the estate.

Poppy was close behind her, from the sound of her panting breath as she gasped out, "Athena!"

Athena didn't turn back. She only narrowed her gaze to the next step ahead of her. She didn't want to say a word. It was a mistake. One she assumed they had made because they were frightened, and fear made people do wild things. They broke up, they had been broken up, for a long time—ancient history. Poppy was marrying Giuseppe. Their families would be happy, and Poppy would live a life of quiet happiness.

Athena let go of the jar as if it were on fire. She couldn't risk breaking her sample.

"Athena!" Poppy called again as her cold hand grabbed Athena's forearm.

Athena ripped her arm away and cast a glare behind her. "What?"

"We—"

"Don't need to ever mention it," Athena said. She pulled her skirt up a little to keep her feet moving quickly as the foliage around them grew dense. "You're leaving this island soon, and I'm staying. And that will be the end of that."

"And that's it?"

Athena huffed as they broke the treeline and came upon the strange estate in the open clearing.

From the porch, Willa stood. Her gasp was audible, her eyes wide.

"What happened?" she cried, racing out from the security of the gate.

Athena and Poppy stood side by side at the fence.

Athena side-eyed Poppy, her hair was wild, she was not, but her white cotton shift had some minor bruising running down the inside of her arms.

Athena's heart sank. Her brows furrowed as she realized just how much Poppy had done to rescue her from the might of the stegosaurus. Her own face began to throb dully. She lifted a hand to her face as sweat beaded down her temples. When she pulled away, her fingers were tinted with blood from the cut on her cheek. It didn't feel deep, but it did hurt.

Willa pulled a silk cloth from her pocket. She reached up to Athena's face gently, but Athena batted her away.

"I'm fine," she said. She lifted the small jar and held it out to Willa. As it caught the sunlight, the bright green algae shimmered beneath the glittering glass. "I got the sample." She glanced at Poppy again, who folded her arms tightly across her chest. "Thanks to Poppy," she added, doing her best to smile nonchalantly. "Her quick thinking saved me."

Beside her, Poppy tossed her head to the side. "Saying that a dinosaur doesn't like her plates touched is an understatement. I'll be suing for damages," she said, her voice light and kind as if she had already put aside their stupidity.

"I'll await the letter from your counsel. For now, I'll loan you a dress." Willa tucked her silk handkerchief away. She raised a single brow. "Come inside. We'll get you cleaned up," she said with a hand wave for them to follow. She glanced back at them as both Athena and Poppy deflated, following behind with their heads low. "I don't think my mother thought you'd manage this," she whispered. "But I never doubted. Though... I didn't think you'd come back this beaten up."

Athena shrugged, holding her head high again. "It was nothing," she said.

It was nothing, she reminded herself.

*A*thena regretted letting Poppy take the first bath. It took her forever to be done, long enough that Athena had started to think she was punishing Athena by making her sit in her sweat.

Athena shook her head. She knew she was being unfair. Poppy was a lot of things, but she wasn't vindictive. Luckily.

By the time Athena was washed and changed into clothes free of any dirt or random leaves, she was starving. And had a headache.

Tea. She needed a huge cup of black tea.

Athena made her way into the kitchen, where Seppi was already sitting, sketching in his book as he stared up at a small dinosaur hanging from the dark wood rafter like a bat.

"Welcome back," Seppi said, his eyes still glued to the creature as his hand moved across the page. "Willa told me you got the moss that Lady Rose was after?"

"Algae," Athena corrected. "And it was... a situation to get it."

Seppi hummed thoughtfully. He finally peeled his eyes from the creature, his eyes falling softly on Athena. "I'm glad you're alright," he said. "You know I worry about you."

Athena's brows furrowed. "You don't need to," she said. "Just maybe take all that energy and use it to brew me a cup?"

Seppi let out a little chuckle. He slid a steaming teacup across the table. "What would you do without me?"

Athena smiled, her heart already warm with affection and gratitude. It had been a long day. "Thank you." She sank into her chair and breathed in the steam. The aroma of wet earth, flowers, and honey filled the air between them.

Seppi cocked his head slowly. "You really intend to stay here, don't you?"

"If she'll have me," Athena said. She blew on the tea and took a small sip. Her eyes fluttered shut, and the stinging in her cheek seemed to heal as she drank in the quiet comfort. "I think my trials are only just beginning," she said at last.

Seppi's lips tightened into a line. He said nothing, but Athena knew. What would she do without him? And he without her? They had been a constant in their lives, even when Athena would travel off to faraway places. She had never been gone too long. At least, she thought, the trip back home was short. She could visit, she almost said. That is, if she could stand to see Seppi and Poppy together...

"Theodosia gives you much trouble?" Lady Rose asked, appearing in the doorway like a specter. Still, her expression was warm, though Athena sensed no apology would come. In her age-speckled hand, she held the jaw of algae.

Athena's eyes flitted down to the sample, then to Lady Rose. She held her teacup closer. "Join us?" she asked, avoiding the question entirely. She was sure that Willa had told her all about the journey while she was busy trying to make herself decent again.

Lady Rose's smile widened. "Another cup of tea for the old woman?" she asked Seppi as she stepped into the room.

Seppi closed his sketchbook quickly and rose from his

seat, the old chair creaking as he did. "You're youth twinkles like the stars," he said sweetly, a little dramatic flair of his arm swept to the sky, and the dinosaur that hung above flapped its wings in protest at the sudden movement.

"Leave the wordsmithing to my niece," Lady Rose teased.

Seppi looked over his shoulder with a smile and a shrug. He busied himself at the stove, lighting a match for the kettle with quick fingers.

Lady Rose sat opposite Athena. She set the jar on the table and flipped through Seppi's sketchbook with a quizzical look.

Seppi turned on his heel. He was laughing lightly, but took the sketchbook from her hands with a swift and decisive motion. "Now, now," he said. "I must insist you let your niece to her words and me to my drawings in peace."

Lady Rose snorted but crossed her arms and leaned back in her chair until Seppi set a cup of black tea in front of her and took his seat with his sketchbook held tightly in his lap.

"Perhaps I can help analyze the sample?" Athena said as Lady Rose took her first drink. "Do you have a lab... or...?"

Lady Rose slurped the tea. "This algae is unlike anything I've seen, but it is not my creation," she said at last. "Perhaps it is just native to this strange island."

Athena shifted in her seat. She wrapped her fingers around the warm cup. It felt like a riddle. "The microclimate, does it last through the winter?"

Lady Rose nodded.

Athena blinked. Her thoughts came slowly, drifting by like clouds in a blank blue sky. "Beside the dinosaurs,"

Athena mused, "there must be many flora and fauna that are unique to here. The unique climate might make things here change to adapt."

Lady Rose's lips twitched up. "You and Darwin would get along," she mumbled through her smile.

Athena looked up and breathed in deeply. She was too tired to ask what dinosaur she was referring to now, sure that eventually she'd meet him. Maybe while she wrestled a scale from it, or some other bizarre and likely deadly task the Lady set her up for.

POPPY AND THE TALE FOR THE BEES

It was mid afternoon and the light from behind a silver outlined cloud burst from every direction into the turquoise sky, drenching the island in a rich golden glow. An easy breeze like light fingertips tickled Poppy's neck gently. She rubbed the back of her neck, freeing herself from the feeling of being touched by a ghostly stranger, and looked out at the few massive bees that flew slow and low in the clearing full of brilliant gem-like wild flowers.

"Is that one... alright?" Athena asked, a small grimace etched into her face, pulling her full lips down to a barely noticeable frown.

Poppy watched her carefully from her peripherals. She didn't want to appear as though she was studying Athena, but she couldn't exactly help that she was doing exactly that. Athena commanded attention, even when they were simply standing in an open field to watch the patterns of bees. It was in the way she stood, back straight like an arrow, shoulders squared, yet relaxed. The easy way one hand found its way to the curve of her hip and the gentle shifting of her feet to lean into her own hand as the other tapped lightly on her abdomen. It was effortless and confident. Cautious, and intense.

Poppy watched as Athena's eyes tracked a large bee that had just bumped into another midflight. It must have been the one she was referring to because something was, in fact, very strange about this particular bee.

It bounced off the other and let out a small *boop* sound that it emitted from someplace unknown in its body. Then, it buzzed loudly to the left, then to the right, then left again as if it had completely disoriented itself and was looking for its way back up into a normal flight pattern.

The other bee simply flew farther away, hovering low again to the field of the flowers. Its black legs grasped at a few of them at a time, searching for the perfect place.

Willa laughed lightly, but crossed her arms over herself as if to stifle it back down. "My mother doesn't like it when we tease him too much," she said through her giggle. "But that's Simon. He's... a sweet bee."

Simon lingered near the other bee, moving about a bit

erratically as though he didn't seem to be able to stay totally still the way the other one did.

Athena leaned forward a little eyeing the bee with a narrowed stare, Then, she side eyed Poppy, her eyes fierce with equal intensity on her as she had for the prehistoric bee.

Poppy smiled and watched the scene before them as a cloud passed by slowly overhead.

Simon had one antenna that didn't seem to quite go the way it should and his eyes were a little too far apart, if that were even possible.

Poppy looked back to wink at Athena as the other woman turned away. "I like him," Poppy said with a certainty that made her feel like she was declaring love. But there was something charming about the bumbling bee that did make her feel that if he was happy here among the flowers and dinosaurs, then perhaps she could be, too.

"My mother thinks the other bees bully him a bit," Willa said with a shake of her head. "I don't think that's how they operate. But I'm no bee expert, truth be told. I just harvest the honey when she tells me to."

Poppy tried to catch Athena's gaze again, but it was fruitless. Athena seemed transfixed on Simon, her scowl now forming a lovely half smile, her eyes were soft as though she was simply enjoying the view for now rather than studying them as she had been before. "Can bees bully, Athena?" Poppy asked.

"Your family are the beekeepers," Athena said, and though her words were gruff, her tone was gentle with the duality only Athena seemed to know how to wield.

"I know a lot of things, Athena. But I fear, I too, am just

a collector of honey *if and when* the occasion calls for it. And you are the naturalist, after all," Poppy said with a simple shrug.

Athena let out a small snort. A most unlady-like sound that would have had the other aristocrats in London grasping at their pearls, Poppy thought. *In the best way.* Truth be told, and as much as she frustrated her sometimes, Poppy genuinely loved the way this place was able to bring out the best in them, it seemed. She knew that here, away from expectations and pretences and all of her 'have to's, this was the place where they could truly be free. All of them.

Athena was always brave, thoughtful, and... Poppy's stomach turned. She was also cold and calculating and risk adverse and–

"Bees are cooperative, and some have been observed having what we may call friends," Athena said, breaking Poppy from her rapidly changing thoughts. Her eyes finally landed back on Poppy.

Poppy's ears burned under her kind stare. A part of her wished she hadn't asked at all.

"I don't know if they would be unkind to each other the way we would think of it, even though they are social," Athena said, turning back to Simon, who was now seemingly gleefully following the other bee along. She stuffed one hand into her skirt pocket, seeming to search for something within. But she let out a small exhale and freed her hand quickly.

"Peculiar how they can be so similar to us, though," Willa said, unaware of all Poppy was seeing. Willa's arms finally freed themselves from around her body. She swung them gently through the air, as though she was trying to catch the breeze that swayed the wildflowers around their skirts. "They are so unlike us, so strange. But they can be the same. They have a queen and rules."

A wrinkle between Poppy's brows formed. She did her best to smooth it out by looking up at the treeline and thinking of something pleasant. But the only thing she could think about was what it would be like to be a bee from ancient history and still be bound by rules so humanlike.

"I like Simon, too," Athena said at last.

The bees moved away, far and up into the sky until the sun blocked them from view.

"My mother will be pleased to hear it," Willa said with a small exhale. "You know things are boring on the island when you have a favorite bee. But, I suppose, that's part of living isn't it?"

"What's that?" Poppy asked, still staring up at the sky waiting for the bees to return.

"Well, there's enough uncertainty in life even if we try to make things orderly. We try to keep things as they are as if that will bring us closer to calm. But when life grows too still, we have a way to create more chaos... to bring us some kind of adventure." She looked up at the sky, too. "We're never really happy, are we? Any of us. I suppose having a favorite bee is no more strange than having a favorite teacup or favorite place by the window when it's sunny. It's about finding the joy when you can, isn't it?" Willa said. She lifted her skirt and turned back toward the path. "Or maybe I'm just spouting nonsense and I've been here far too long with no one but the bees and dinosaurs to talk to." She smiled now, bright as the sunlight. "I better get home and help start dinner. But you've inspired me to make my favorite. Buttered biscuits for dinner." And with that, she made her way down the path back into the jungle.

Poppy and Athena exchanged a long look.

"Buttered biscuits?" Athena asked once the silence grew uncomfortable.

"Where do you suppose they get the butter?" Poppy said with a shudder.

Athena's face went pale. She looked into the forest. "They don't... the dinosaurs don't produce milk, do they?"

Poppy shrugged. "Maybe there's goats around that we just haven't found yet?"

Athena's eyes widened. "I wouldn't be surprised by anything at this point."

Another long pause thinned the air between them. A lock of Poppy's hair blew past her face, scratching at her nose like wool. She brushed it away, turning into the growing breeze as a herd of dinosaurs, each with a large leather saddle full of something bulky she couldn't discern moved near the treeline. "Athena, look!" she said, pointing to them as the group weaved in and out of the trees.

They had duck-like faces, round but long bodies carried by four massive, thick legs. And most striking, a long, bright green crest stretched out from their foreheads. By her eye, it appeared the crest alone was taller than she. At least they were herbivores, she figured, given their lack of claws or teeth that she could see, and their huge size. Still, she was certain they could crush the two of them if they were dedicated enough.

One tilted its head toward them, blew out a large snort

through its nostrils so loud she could hear it clearly from their distance. But, then it moved along as though it were utterly disinterested. Whatever they were carrying seemed more important to them than inspecting the women and bees in the field beside them.

"What's your aunt –"

Poppy narrowed her eyes, trying to catch details of the leather bags attached to the saddles. "It's good leather," she said, cutting Athena off.

She heard Athena sigh out in a quick but heavy breath beside her.

Poppy glanced up at Athena. "I mean, where did she get the nice leather? Here? And with *her* money?"

"How can you tell it's 'good leather'?" Athena said as she folded her arms.

"The stitching."

"You can see the stitching from here?"

Poppy waved her hand as if shooing away Athena like a pest. "Why aren't you taking notes?" she said, switching topics quickly away from the fact that she was mostly lying about the good leather. She was *pretty sure* she was right. But she couldn't really articulate how exactly she knew and didn't feel like being questioned anymore on the matter.

Athena's expression went cold as though she had turned to stone beside her in an instant. "My pen is broken," she grumbled.

Poppy flicked her a sideways look. "I knew it."

"I will borrow one of Seppi's pencils."

"You hate pencils," Poppy said. She didn't wait for Athena to argue or ask her how she remembered that small detail from years ago when they had all sat by the lake and

Athena threw one of Seppi's into the waters after he had stated that they were far superior to ink quills. She started down the narrow path out of the sea of flowers.

Behind her, the swift *swoosh* of Athena's long skirt followed like an echo until they reached the canopy of the jungle where the hum of the breeze and the bees grew fainter and fainter until the darkness of the leaves above extinguished all but the sound of their feet on the ground.

That is, until Poppy heard Athena let out a frustrated grumble.

"Still wondering about the butter?" she asked, turning back.

Athena raised a brow at her and threw her hands up. "Do you think they ship it?"

Poppy laughed. "I would say to ask Aunt Rose, but I doubt she'll be forthcoming, even if the answer is mundane."

Athena frowned.

"I suspect that she milks the dinosaurs here. Maybe Francesca," Poppy said as she shrugged a little. She turned back, tossing a lock of hair behind her shoulder as she did. She didn't really believe it, but she wanted to see if Athena would humor her.

She did not.

The other woman was still silent behind her and though she had been so certain about her thoughts a moment ago, now, it was as though Athena's statue had disintegrated and grains of coarse sand were slipping through Poppy's fingers. She wondered for a moment if she'd ever be able to collect it all again and build her back to what she had once been. If she could ever get back to the understanding they shared–

even when she couldn't study Athena's face. Knowing her and her emotions, even in the dark.

She wondered if she even wanted to at all.

Her stomach dropped as she stumbled over a rock in the path. "Horse feathers!" she swore under her breath as she hopped a little on her other foot, a blooming heat spreading through her big toe. She was *trying* to be lost in her thoughts and aloof as Athena always was but of course, she had to hobble into some kind of predicament. This island was slowly trying to wear her down, she was sure of it.

"Careful, Simon," Athena said, catching up to Poppy now that her steps were shorter and less hurried.

Poppy cast Athena a hateful look.

Athena merely smiled back, though it looked a little wicked. "Should I tell the bees?" she asked.

Poppy wasn't really sure what it meant but it sounded vaguely insulting. She narrowed her eyes and forced her foot back down with a little stomp. "You really needn't always be so strange with me, I don't understand your riddles."

Athena tossed her chin up. "It's not a riddle," she said simply.

"A rude remark then," Poppy corrected quickly.

Athena nodded. "Perhaps that," she said. "I meant it to be funny," she added, nearly so quiet that Poppy was a little unsure she had heard it all.

And, in an instant, Poppy could feel a heaviness in her hands again, the grains of sand forming back to something tangible and solid. Athena did love to tease her once before, and Poppy had loved that about her. Nearly everyone else in her life simply didn't think she was capable enough.

A little jab hit her heart. She missed Ann, the one person who had never dared to tell her she couldn't do something. It was all different kinds of love, she figured. And it hurt to think she was missing out on two kinds now. Her sister was kind and scared of her. Athena was sometimes scary, but had always been kind.

She looked up at the trees as they finished the rest of their walk in silence.

ATHENA IS A SCIENTIST, NOT A DETECTIVE

The quiet of the jungle was beginning to suffocate Athena as they came in sight of the estate. She breathed deeply, though it sounded more like a gasp.

Which elicited a suspicious glance from Poppy.

Athena wanted to furrow her brows back but instead, she only looked past Poppy and continued on their path until they reached the front door and Poppy finally whispered, "Go tell my Aunt that you like Simon. You'll endear yourself to her."

"You mean more than I already have?" Athena said, trying to be as confident as possible to hide the fact that, really, she was certain that Lady Rose at best was neutral about her and at worst was downright hostile.

Poppy rolled her eyes at Athena. She held the door open for her and nodded her to go in. "Well," she said. "After you."

Athena bowed her head. "My lady," she said, her voice a whisper as she passed by Poppy. She caught Poppy's nose and ears turning scarlet from the corner of her eye.

The door nearly slammed behind them as Poppy pushed her way around Athena. She took the stairs two at a time, hiking her skirt up a bit ungracefully as she did.

Athena hated how adorable it was. And also how little time she had to wonder about what her hurry was. Her cousin was already coming from the kitchen with his sketchbook held high.

"Athena!" Seppi said, far too joyfully. "You'll never guess what Lady Willa is making for dinner."

"Buttered–?"

"Biscuits!" Seppi spoke for her. "I'm very much looking forward to it."

"I can see that..." Athena looked him up and down. She leaned forward, peaking in at Willa's back as she busied herself at the counter. "Do you know where they get the butter?"

Seppi opened his mouth, about to answer, then stopped. "I..." He tapped his pencil on his chin, then pointed it at Athena. "Actually, that's a good question. I'll ask." He ducked back into the kitchen before Athena could grab him.

She reluctantly followed him to see Lady Rose was at the other end of the counter, kneading dough. Flour filled the air around her and in the candlelight from the small rafters above, it seemed to shimmer around her as though she were a ghost. Athena shuddered as Seppi asked, "So where does the butter come from, Lady Willa? I cannot imagine they ship it here."

"Oh," Lady Rose answered instead, still working the dough with old hands, "we milk the triceratops, of course."

Willa laughed. "So long as you stay clear of the three horns, it's easy."

Seppi sat down at the table. He opened his sketchbook and began to draw Willa's profile. "Is that so?"

"Are they mammals, these triceratops?" Athena asked.

"Are you daft?" Lady Rose cut in sharply. "I was not being serious."

Seppi glanced at Athena.

She shrugged back. She had tried to warn him. He was just too assuming that people would be forthright and polite no matter how she had tried to tackle it out of him as kids. Now, she wished someone was around to hit her over the head before she could open her own mouth. "I met Simon today," she said before she could stop herself.

She instantly regretted it.

Lady Rose stopped her work and cast a long stare at Athena from over her shoulder. "Oh?" It was a simple sound. And vaguely threatening.

Athena's eyes flicked from Lady Rose to Willa, then back again. She searched either of them for what she was supposed to say next but found no answers in their cold expressions.

It was Poppy who saved her. She swooped into the kitchen with a spin of her skirt and a bright smile. "And he was lovely, Aunt Rose," she said quickly. "I am so excited to learn more about the ancient bee behaviors. But we saw him getting along well enough with another friend out in the field, didn't we Athena?"

Athena breathed in quickly, grateful that Poppy had the social graces to carry her when she stumbled. "Yes," she said at last, kicking herself for not being able to think of anything better or more articulate. "I think that from my understanding of bee behaviors, he was getting along quite well. And, I think is doing his best."

"Which is all any of us can do," Seppi added, still sketching away at his book, though now his eyes were set on a small winged dinosaur that had its long tail wrapped around the rafter above them.

As awkward as Athena was, her addition seemed to ease Lady Rose nonetheless. She turned back to her work with a little huff.

From her place at the other end of the counter, Willa winked at them.

Poppy put the back of her hand to her forehead, feigning that she was about to faint.

Seppi, though still staring above, shook his head with a warm half smile.

At least they were good natured about everything. Athena, meanwhile, had resigned herself to overthinking this interaction all night. If only she could show Lady Rose that she was serious and capable. If only she could show them all that she felt so much more than her cold silence conveyed.

For now, she'd have to be content that she was having a delicious, if not terribly nutritious meal, being made for her even when she had spent the day being a failure.

Athena was full for the first time since she left to get on the boat. Her stomach ached, though now for the opposite reason it had before. There was just no winning.

She sat on the edge of her bed, her toes tracing the grains in the hardwood below. She felt a quick, cold push on her leg and leaned down to see Reggie scrambling out from under her bed.

Once he was fully free, his round belly and back finally escaping the clutches of the covers that had fallen over the edge, he looked up at her and chirped.

In the glow of the beeswax candles, his dark eyes shimmered happily and when he chirped at her again, his row of rounded sharp teeth glistened.

Athena's chest expanded. She picked him up carefully and set him beside her on the bed. "You must have been terrifying back in your time," she said as she gave the top of his broad head a little pet. "Did you know you're supposed to be as big as this house?"

Reggie pushed his forehead into her hand. He trilled back as if acknowledging her words.

Athena smiled, then fell back onto the bed with a light bounce in the mattress. Something light on the pillow fell as her weight hit the bed. She turned to the side to see her quill pen just as Reggie was coming toward it with his jaws already chomping.

"No, no!" Athena hissed and reached for the quill quickly. She scooped it up just before Reggie was able to gather it between his teeth. "It's already broken enough–"

But as the words left her, her eyes narrowed at the pen in her hand. In fact, it wasn't broken at all. It had been mended.

Athena's fingertips traced the long spine of the pen with a delicate reverence. She looked at it from every angle, turning it over gently. The tip had been redone, though a little crudely. It was still far better than she could ever hope to accomplish.

She looked to her closed door, half hoping that Poppy would knock and admit she felt bad for her and fixed it. Half hoping Poppy didn't pity her at all and it was Willa or Lady Rose finally admitting that she, at least somewhat, was welcome here.

She held the pen to her heart.

Reggie chirped at her, stopping one large clawed foot as he did.

She sighed, and held the pen closer. "This is not a toy," she scolded. She looked back to the pillow but there was no note, and no indication about who had mended it or why.

For someone so smart, she really didn't pick on clues very well. Even she had to admit that much.

POPPY DOESN'T UNDERSTAND ONLY CHILDREN

*P*oppy had no idea how Willa grew up on her own.

Poppy had her siblings, well, mostly Ann, who never left her alone and was always ready to jump in and talk to her about the latest gossip or odd thing that had happened that day. Even Athena and Seppi had each other, though cousins, they grew up together and were close. Poppy had watched them having silent conversations with one another using nothing but their micro-expressions over the years. Even now, on the island, they seemed to be able to read each other easily.

So as Poppy flung herself over Willa's quilted bed and already began to complain, she noticed Willa's eyes were wide with what looked like confusion tinted with fear.

Poppy grumbled, rolling over onto her stomach, her feet kicked up behind her. "Willa," she said, her cadence slowing to accommodate her introverted cousin, "If Aunt Rose wants me dead, she needs to try harder."

Willa sat on the edge of the bed gingerly, as though afraid Poppy might strike her. She opened her mouth, but Poppy cut her off.

"And if she wants me gone, she needs to stop sending me on adventures. It's all premium writing material."

"You mustn't!" Willa said with her hands waving. "My mother will kill you if you're writing about the island!"

Poppy flopped her head onto the bed, her blonde waves splayed around her, hiding her face. "Relax, cousin, I write a ladies' journal, remember? Gossip and fashion and whatnot." She opened one eye, watching Willa through the screen of yellow hair. "She won't *actually* kill me, right?" she grumbled.

Willa leaned back, propped on her elbows. She let out a heavy sigh and looked up at the ceiling as if she'd find the answer written there.

"How did she even find the initial dinosaur bones?" Poppy asked. She rolled onto her back, keeping Willa in her peripheral vision. "And the bees? You've heard about the other family hives collapsing, haven't you?"

"What are you getting at, Poppy?"

Poppy shook her head slowly, feeling the soft quilt

beneath cradle her neck gently. "Is it so bad that I wish to talk with you after the agonizing days I have had?"

Willa's eyes narrowed slightly. She stood, watching Poppy with a suspicious look.

Poppy waited, trying to make her face look as sweet as possible. She softened her brows, tilted her lips up ever so delicately.

Willa rolled her neck. She murmured something faintly, then squared her shoulders to stand taller.

Poppy raised her brows a little. She patted the place on the bed beside her. She wanted answers, yes. But she wanted company more. She'd take what her cousin would offer for now.

"Alright, then," Willa said as she fell back onto the bed beside Poppy. "I don't know where she found the bones, or how she managed to turn those into living things," she said.

Poppy couldn't tell if she was lying or not. She wanted to know more, but it was clear she had pushed Willa enough for now.

She'd have to keep hunting for answers the old-fashioned way.

POPPY FLETCHER HAS AN ILLNESS

Poppy didn't know what about her meant that she just couldn't be satisfied. It was a sickness, she was sure of it. One, she didn't know how to cure other than let the fever spike her into a frenzy and either find the truth, or burn trying.

As she sat in her aunt's room, she half hated herself. Half knew she had to try to get some answer to the problem of the bee decline. The previous day had yielded nothing but bruises on her arms from treating a dinosaur like a horse, which had only barely worked. She hadn't even written about the experience yet. She was too tired and too worn down by the time the sun had set, and the cool, crisp air finally relieved the oppressive, humid heat she had been trapped in.

She would have to write it down soon, though. The experience of leaping onto a dinosaur, a massive, angry dinosaur... the kiss... all of it was buzzing through her with such intensity that she was worried she might burst. Her former lover had only been there two days and was already distracting her from what she needed to do and causing all kinds of distress among the creatures of the island.

But she couldn't think about Athena. Not now.

She opened the drawer of a writing desk positioned under the quaint window. She rummaged through it quickly, looking for anything anomalous. Anything out of the ordinary.

It was all blank pages. Stationery with her intricate rose flowered trim and nothing written. She found a ring, the sapphire glittered in the morning light as she held it up. Nothing about it looked strange, and it wasn't a piece she recognized. She set it back down and shut the drawer with a slight grunt.

She crossed her arms, and her eyes inspected the room. Of course, the one opportunity she had to sneak about this room, and it turned out it was immaculate without any hint of answers.

At every turn since her arrival on the island, Poppy had hit a wall in her ventures. She was no closer to where her aunt found the money to afford all this, how she had created dinosaurs, or why the bees were not cooperating—question after question with no solution in sight.

She hissed a breath out as a small stab in her gut threatened to make her frantic. Her heartbeat quickened beneath her shirt. There was nothing here. She'd have to resort to other methods to find the truth.

A little trill from under the bed spooked her from her self-pity. She flinched just as a dinosaur, about the size of a small rabbit, shuffled out from the shadows. It looked like a lizard, long body, short legs, and whiplike tail, but along its back ran a fan-like spine of red and gold. It looked up at her and made a little sound again, then sauntered past her as if it had decided she was not worth its time.

"Well, good day to you, too," Poppy said with a beaming smile. She moved in front of the creature carefully and reached down, holding out a hand in front of the dinosaur. It sniffed at her, eyes blinking a few times, before it nuzzled her open palm and then walked off.

Poppy rose and watched it walk around in a little circle before going back under the bed, deciding, she supposed, that there was nothing out there worth seeing. It was right. This room was a dead end. "Have a good nap," she said quietly.

"What are you doing in here?"

Poppy nearly fell over, the sound of Athena's voice jolting her back to reality.

She backed away from the bed as though she had done something wrong by touching the dinosaur, as though she were a little kid who had been caught stealing cookies.

She stood up, straight and firm. She wasn't going to let Athena worry her. If anything, it was her ex who had some nerve coming in and acting as though she owned the place. Especially after she kissed her. Or, had Poppy been the one to initiate it? It didn't matter. It was a mistake. One, she wasn't going to repeat.

She squared her shoulders and, once she met Athena's dark eyes, a genuine smile slowly betrayed her smooth demeanor. She corrected quickly, "I followed Harrietta in here. I was worried she'd seen a mouse or something. Like how cats do. You know how they leave them in the bed like little gifts…"

Athena's mouth drew into a thin line. She raised a single brow. "Oh, you would clean up a dead mouse?"

"I'd call for someone, of course," Poppy said, hoping she sounded confident. She added quickly, "Seppi, probably."

Athena laughed—dry and fake sounding.

Poppy's cheeks flushed hot. She turned away, looking sternly out the window as her fingers began to quiver like the last little leaf clinging to an empty branch. "He's *your* cousin, you know. He ought to have your support."

"He has my support," Athena said.

"And your grandfather," Poppy went on, her voice sounded rushed, even to her own ears. "He's the one who arranged the whole thing."

"He has my support, too. But it was your mother who pushed it."

"It matters little," Poppy said with a bright, fake smile. She pushed past Athena, her shoulder grazing the other woman as she did. "Seppi would dispose of the dead mouse for me if I wished for it. But there's no dead mouse. Or any other dead thing here."

Athena hummed in response, and Poppy couldn't make

out what kind of noncommittal reaction it was. Could Athena see through her? Or was she dismissing her? Again.

She was just outside the threshold of the room when the sound of Athena clearing her throat stopped her.

She turned to see Athena, a half-smile illuminating her face in the most annoying level of arrogance. Poppy put one hand on her hip, waiting.

Athena pointed to the emerald green dresser beside the bed. "You forgot to close these drawers," she said wryly. "You know, on your search for the dead mouse."

Poppy huffed, then stormed back past Athena. This time, she let her shoulder hit the other woman hard on her way. She closed the dresser drawers, then spun on her heel, about to explain herself with some other fake excuse, but Athena's hard stare made her pause. "I wish..." Poppy started, then stopped. She wanted to say more, but she didn't know what she wished for. That Athena hadn't come? That Athena would help her find what she was looking for? That they hadn't kissed? That she could do it again now?

Athena's eyes narrowed. "I wish, too," she said, though Poppy couldn't read her tone. She stood taller, then said, "I'll see what Seppi is doing." She left the room, and a dull ache in Poppy's heart.

Chapter Twenty-Three

ATHENA THINKS TOO MUCH FOR SOMEONE WHO HASN'T BEEN THINKING MUCH AT ALL

Poppy was up to something, and it wasn't just being stubborn about coming home. No, she was up to something that she didn't want her family to know about. And Athena was going to get to the bottom of it. And the mystery of the bees. And how Lady Rose had been able to bring ancient beasts back from bones...

They had only been on the island for two days, and already, the whole thing had ended up being bigger than a simple rescue mission. She had very nearly died. Kind of.

Athena rubbed the bridge of her nose and shut her eyes tightly.

"Oh my," Seppi said. "Athena is having a thinking moment."

Athena opened her eyes and grimaced at him.

He held his hands up. "It's not a bad thing," he said quickly, a gentle smile on his face. "Honest, I like thinking, cousin. It's when you have your best ideas. So long as they won't get me in trouble."

Athena sighed. She looked down at her tea.

They were sitting in the small kitchen at the little round wooden table. The stained glass window over the water basin let in rainbow light that shimmered off the teacups between them. For such a large estate, the kitchen was almost claustrophobic, especially as they filled the room.

Athena figured if Lady Rose had commissioned its build, knowing that she wouldn't have any help around to work in here, she would have made it at least a little more inviting for herself. But, alas, it was as small and cramped as hers at home.

Athena bit her lip, her mind wandering off now to buildings, of all things.

"This... won't get me in trouble, will it?" Seppi asked, tentatively.

Athena shook her head. She sipped her tea. It was already lukewarm. She set down the little teacup with a slight *clink* on its pink saucer.

"Wondering how you're going to convince Lady Rose to let you stay, even after the whole 'retrieve moss from a monster' thing?" he asked at last.

"Algae." Athena looked up at him, but he was flipping

through his leather-bound sketchbook, seemingly disinterested in her answer. She knew better. And, eventually, she caught him glancing up at her through his thick lashes. "And you? You're always up to something and blaming *me* for getting *you* into trouble," she said at last.

Seppi laughed lightly, a warm sound. "Oh, cousin. I'm just happy to sketch out some of these incredible creatures." He held up his sketchbook for Athena to inspect. It was a rough, but endearing, portrait of Reggie. She smiled, the corners of her eyes crinkling despite the creeping feeling that she was slowly sinking into the floor. "And Willa has been incredibly hospitable. If we must wait for the next boat, at least she's been kind."

Athena's eyes narrowed, just barely. She finished her tea in one big gulp, then said, "Yes, she's lovely. And sweet."

Seppi set his sketchbook down. "Athena, you're not...? Willa–?"

She set her teacup down so hard it almost cracked. "No," she said quickly. "Not." She looked under the cup for any sign of damage, conveniently avoiding his gaze. "I'm just interested in the bees and the dinosaurs. I think I can help."

Seppi let out a quick breath. He closed his sketchbook and tapped the table lightly with his fingertips. "It's quite hot here," he said, blissfully changing the subject. "Perhaps it's too hot for the bees."

"It's too hot for you in all those layers," Athena said, eyeing him up and down. "Must you insist on wearing the waistcoat?"

Seppi flattened the dark purple fabric out across his

chest. "I think it looks rather dapper. Being warm is a small price to pay, I suppose."

"Yes, yes, very dapper," Athena said with a wave of her hand.

"Perhaps the dinosaurs are hunting them?" Seppi suggested.

Athena tilted her teacup in her hand; she inspected the intricate pink rose design along its delicate side. "Willa says she doesn't suspect that as much," she said. "You've seen the bees, they're huge. And the predators on the island are all stunted by design. Apparently, Reggie is supposed to be tall as a tree, if nature had its way."

"None of this is natural," Seppi said, though his voice hinted at his amusement.

Athena always did love to puzzle something out with him. When they were kids, they'd find some mystery afoot and spend hours working together, usually until way past their bedtimes, trying to solve it. Most famously in their household was the summer they spent trying to find out who was stealing strawberries from their garden, based on footprints, bite marks, and sneaking out at night to watch for the perpetrator.

Seppi, ignoring her wistful stare into nothing, cleared his throat. "Then Lady Rose found a way to keep the ones with sharp teeth small? That doesn't mean they aren't harassing the bees, massive though they are," Seppi said. "Interesting..."

"Don't let my mother hear you speak like this," Willa's voice said from the doorway. Her expression was playful as she leaned on the doorframe with her legs crossed at the ankles casually.

Athena couldn't help but notice Seppi's expression mirror hers. She leaned back in her chair a little. "You're as quiet as a cat," she said.

Willa let out a little giggle as she pushed herself from the doorframe. "Quiet as an aquilops, actually," she said, moving into the room.

"Aquilops?" Seppi asked.

Willa set a leather satchel down at the table gently with a sly smile. She reached in and pulled out a little dinosaur the size of a kitten.

But that was where the comparison ended. Athena squinted at the little creature. It was the ugliest thing she had ever seen. And that made it adorable.

Its round, bulbous face nudged into Willa's chest as she cradled it gently. It had dark green skin and electric blue little bumps across its back and a tuft of brown, either fur or feathers, Athena couldn't quite tell, along its short and fat tail. Its head had a crest at the forehead, arching back like a tiny shield.

"She's a quiet little thing," Willa said as she scratched the top of its head carefully. "I take her with me on walks sometimes, and none of the other dinosaurs ever seem to notice her." She positioned the creature so it faced Seppi. "Her name is Beatrice."

Seppi reached forward, then stopped.

"It's alright," Willa said. "She's quiet but friendly."

"Hello Beatrice," Seppi said. His smile grew, and he stroked under Beatrice's chin with one finger.

Athena's brows rose. He was getting awfully comfortable with all of this rather quickly.

"She's beautiful, do you mind if I...?" He held up his sketchbook.

"Now?" Willa asked.

"I can't really draw anything I can't see in front of me, I'm afraid," Seppi said lightheartedly. "I tried to draw a horse once from memory." He cast a glance at Athena. "And, what was it you said it looked like?"

"An abomination?"

Seppi's laugh only grew. "I can't risk doing that to this beauty."

"I'm certain it would be fine," Willa said with a smile.

Seppi shook his head with an exaggerated grimace. "Oh, certainly it would not."

Willa held the dinosaur close to her chest again, angling her body so that Seppi could get a good look as his lead flew across the page quickly. Willa's head tilted to Athena. "Really, Athena, you mustn't compliment my mother too much," she said, returning to her original discussion quickly. "She had a big enough ego as it is."

Athena let out a little chuckle. "I would say she's earned it," she said. "This... all of this. It's amazing. This could change the way the world. Change history and our understanding—"

Willa cut her off, "No, definitely don't let her hear you talk like that." She held Beatrice a little closer. "My mother is very protective of them. I think she might care more for them than me." She was smiling, but Athena thought she might not be joking. There was a way about Willa. An honesty that seemed neither spiteful nor callous. She seemed to see the world as it was and say so.

A faint twinge of envy rooted like an aggressive weed in

Athena's chest. She wished she could be so forthright. "I wouldn't want to do anything to hurt them," Athena said at last.

"I wasn't implying that," Willa said. "Just be careful how you speak in front of my mother, is all. She will sooner throw you to the sea than hear of anyone finding out about them."

Seppi, seemingly in his own world, was sketching away, occasionally looking up to Willa, though his eyes were otherwise fixed on either his page or the dinosaur. He turned the sketchbook around to show Willa.

"Oh, that's lovely!" Willa said, her voice filled with excitement. "You're rather talented!"

Seppi laughed. "Thank you," he said. "I've been practicing a long time."

"It's the one thing you've stuck with," Athena added.

Seppi looked at her with a warm grin. "That's true," he said. "I'd like to say I'm notorious, but I could never be so interesting."

Chapter Twenty-Four

ATHENA IS ONLY SLIGHTLY CONCERNED ABOUT THE TEETH SITUATION

The rest of the day grew longer and less fruitful.

Giuseppe seemed content to wander the property, though he never left the boundary of the white wooden fence. Not that Athena could blame him, really.

Athena eyed him with envy from the window, watching as he sketched and admired, occasionally as he ran screeching from something she couldn't see, chasing him. He looked up at the sun with his eyes closed, then sneezed violently, spooking the group of dinosaurs once again. He took off running again, sneezing the whole way.

All around, he seemed to be living his happiest life without a schedule or tether.

Lady Rose made herself scarce, and Athena had sequestered herself to the sitting room, pulling texts at random and flipping through them on the couch. While her cousin looked blissful, Athena could only see the fence as a cage, trapping her from a great adventure, an incredible discovery, as though that little fence was containing not only her body, but more painfully, her mind.

She stood up and paced the sitting room with her book in hand, doing her best to read while also getting some movement into her body. She had done a good job, hadn't she? Proved her worth in strength and smarts. She had done what was asked. Why didn't it matter?

She heard it again, the tapping on the walls. Her eyes narrowed. They had some kind of infestation. She had to assume it was dinosaur-related. There was no way that there could be many mice on the property. Not with Reggie and the others around.

Willa appeared in the doorway, and the tapping stopped. "Athena," she said brightly. "Just who I was searching for."

Athena shrugged. She closed the book. "This is where I am today, it seems," she said.

Willa only smiled. "I was hoping I could use your help tomorrow. The next boat is scheduled to arrive in two days. Since you're here, it'd be nice to have help staging the crates along the shore."

"Of course. I can help lug honey," Athena said, though her shoulders sank a little, making her smaller. She was strong, sure, but she wanted to use her mind. To help with more.

"Oh, no," Willa said quickly. "I was thinking your cousin might be better suited for that job."

Athena raised a brow. Her excitement blossomed. "How can I help?"

"There's a dinosaur that has been acting strangely," Willa said. "Lethargic and unwell, unfortunately. I was hopeful you might be able to help. You said you studied medicine?"

"A little," Athena said. "But their metabolism would be quite different from our own. I would think they are cold-blooded creatures, like lizards?"

Willa shrugged. "See, this is why you would be helpful. You think of these things." She leaned against the doorframe gently. "It's a flying one, but it hasn't moved much in a few hours. My mother hopes he will recover on his own, but would you mind checking on him tomorrow morning?"

"I can do it now," Athena said.

Willa shook her head. "The sun is setting soon," she said. "My mother thinks morning will be fine."

"Certainly," Athena said with a confident nod. Though the thought crossed her mind that perhaps this was another way that Lady Rose was trying to get her into a dangerous predicament.

Willa didn't seem to notice Athena's mind racing. She tapped the doorframe with her knuckles gently. "Excellent. I'll prepare your bags to bring. Tonics, and the like. Hopefully they won't be necessary at all, but you never know."

Athena's eyes brightened. However, guilt crept up quickly on pride's heels. "What else can you tell me about its condition?"

Willa frowned a little. "Not much," she said. "I haven't been able to get up too close to it. But you have a very calming presence. You handled Theodosia just fine. I'm sure it will be... fine."

Athena's brows twitched. "Is it dangerous?"

"Not really," Willa said. "Just some teeth, but nothing to worry about."

Athena couldn't help but feel more worried now than before. She did her best to hide it behind a mask of confidence. "Thank you for trusting me with this," she said.

Willa nodded and left the room as suddenly as she had come.

Athena hurried back to the bookshelf and pulled every medical book she could find until her arms were full.

POPPY IS MODEST. MOSTLY.

There was a slight knock on Poppy's door. Quiet, almost sneaky. She looked up from her writing and narrowed her eyes in the low candlelight. She waited.

The knock came again, this time a little more insistent.

She rose from her bed and crossed the rugged floor with light steps. The door creaked as she opened it slowly, just a crack to peek through.

Athena was standing in the darkened hallway with a frown already etched on her face.

"Athena!" Poppy cried. She opened the door wider but clutched her robe close to her with a tight fist. "I'm not decent!"

Athena's eyes flitted down to the end of Poppy's nightgown. It reached the floor with a bit of lace trim. Her eyes moved back up, stopping on the collar that frilled about Poppy's neck.

A chill prickled at Poppy's scalp. She was exposed to Athena's stare. She couldn't help but feel that she was being judged. And was also, strangely, naked despite being covered completely.

"Poppy, you're more dressed than in the daytime," Athena whispered. She waved at Poppy's neck where the white collar nearly reached her chin. "I mean, really."

Poppy shrugged, though her cheeks burned under Athena's stare. "It's the principle of the thing." She was grateful that it was too dark for Athena to notice the redness making its way to her nose and ears.

"Mhm," Athena grumbled. She adjusted her night robe around her waist, as if trying to prove a point.

"What are you doing here in the dead of night anyway?" Poppy asked with a little huff.

"It's early morning," Athena said. She leaned to glance around Poppy and into her room. "Your candles are lit, what were you doing up?"

Poppy grumbled, letting out a quick huff. Athena had always been the one who was up before dawn. It was Poppy who came alive at night. She felt a sense of entitlement to her time long after everyone else was asleep. "I couldn't sleep," she said.

"Doing more mouse hunting?" Athena raised a brow.

Poppy crossed her arms over her chest. "Athena, why are you here in the early morning, or whatever time it is?"

Athena gave Poppy another quick look over.

Poppy stirred uneasily under her gaze. Her lips pulled into a line, and she shook her head, her hand on the door about to slam it in Athena's face. She didn't care if she woke the whole household up.

But when her dark eyes made their way back to Poppy's, her anger dissipated like midnight mist meeting the warmth of the sun. Her hand dropped from the door.

Athena went on, "Willa's meeting the shipment boat with the last batch of specialty honey."

And just like that, a sense of excitement radiated through Poppy's body again. She stood a little taller. She wanted to brag, even if it was just a little. She wanted, in that moment, for Athena to see her again. See her, truly as she was. "You know, I was the one who helped with that," Poppy said with a half-smile.

Athena cocked her head. "With the special edition idea?"

Poppy nodded, her smile brightening. "It's good, right?"

Athena crossed her arms. "It's clever," she said. "It will keep people guessing rather than worrying about the supply, and it will drive prices up."

"Exactly," Poppy said as she leaned in. For just that moment, she let herself pretend that nothing else existed beyond the shadows around them. That it was just them, and things were different. That things were as they had been before everything had fallen apart. "It buys us some time to figure out the mystery of the bees, and I think it should keep the business afloat for a little while longer."

"You're worried about it?" Athena prompted.

Poppy looked down.

The world came crashing back into her. Just like that, the shadows were no longer walls of sanctuary but an oppressive darkness drowning her quickly. She had wanted to keep things light and happy. Athena had a way of cutting into that. "Alright, Athena," Poppy said with a cock of her head. "Why are you here?"

The other woman changed the topic as quickly as Poppy had, and she didn't even seem uncomfortable by it. For a reason Poppy couldn't quite find, she was annoyed by it. As if she wanted to watch Athena squirm.

Athena went on, unaware of Poppy's subtle changes. "I was hoping you would come with me to check on a flying dinosaur. I could use the extra hands, since Willa's busy."

"And Seppi?"

"Going to help Willa," she said. "The ship is arriving soon. They want to stage the crates."

"Finally admitting I saved your life with the plate-backed dinosaur?"

Athena rolled her eyes. "I already did, not 'admitting' needed," she said through a clenched jaw.

"Alright, give me a moment to get dressed, then," she said, closing the door.

"You mean less dressed," she thought she heard Athena grumble just as the door clicked shut.

The sun was rising over the crest of the mountaintops. Rays of golden light burst through the tallest tree branches, illuminating the field of wildflowers before them in a warm, ethereal glow. The flowers' bright colors shimmered with morning dew sparkling on their petals. They could have been in a field of jewels, glittering and precious, and it would not be as lovely, Poppy thought.

The air was crisp, but warming quickly. It smelled like fresh salt and honeydew.

It had been weeks since Poppy had first stepped foot on the island, but still, she had to admit, she was grateful that Athena had summoned her early in the morning. This was the first sunrise she watched here. And it was magical.

She turned to Athena. Watched as she moved among wildflowers with her dark curls tied up in a long, loose braid down her back. She was wearing a plain white blouse, the collar hung open around her collarbone, but she still had a shawl, dark burgundy and lovely, draped around her elbows to keep the morning chill at bay.

As the sun continued to rise slowly, golden light hit her skin and hair so that she glowed. She was carrying her journal and a medical bag, looking very official and... Poppy hated to admit as her cheeks began to burn brightly, very beautiful.

Athena turned to her and raised a brow. "Yes?" she asked.

Poppy shook her head and hoisted the larger medical bag up over her shoulder. "Just wondering why I'm carrying the bigger bag," she lied.

"It'd be lighter if you didn't have Beatrice with you," Athena said.

"I don't. I don't want her to catch whatever this other poor creature does."

Athena tilted her head, her mouth pulling to one side as if she was about to give her some medical lesson.

Poppy adjusted the strap quickly. "You never know," she said before Athena could speak. "Anyway, I'm just saying, I am coming here out of my own goodwill and generosity. I don't see why I'm being punished for it."

"You could use the muscle," Athena said. It sounded like teasing.

Poppy smiled, slowly, as though she couldn't help it. And she couldn't. There was just a way that Athena had to get her to feel a strange kind of joy in the face of uncertainty. Still, she refused to look back at Athena. "Ha, ha," she said dryly. "I was able to wrestle a dinosaur just fine the other day."

Athena shrugged.

"Alright, if you're so savvy with the outdoors, why don't you get busy finding this dinosaur so I can get back to my morning tea?"

"As you wish," Athena said. She led the way into the wildflowers as the sun continued its journey into the cerulean sky. "Willa said he's probably at the edge of the clearing." She pointed up ahead at the thick treeline. "He probably didn't go far from yesterday."

Poppy adjusted the bag across her body, still trying to find the best way to carry its cumbersome shape. With quick steps, she caught up to walk beside Athena.

Flowers clung to their long skirts as they moved slowly through the field. Poppy was watching them closely, admiring the way the petals pulled at them, the way the dew speckled the fabric. "Do you think he'll be alright?" she asked at last.

"Seppi is stronger than he looks," Athena said. "I'm sure he'll manage to make himself useful carrying the crates."

"I meant the dinosaur," Poppy said.

Athena nudged her shoulder with her own. "I know," she said with a warm smile. "I'm just trying to make you laugh."

And Poppy did, despite it all.

"I'm sure he'll be alright," Athena said at last.

Though if it was Seppi or the ill dinosaur, Poppy still wasn't sure.

"Wait," Athena said. She stopped in the middle of the field. "Do you hear that?"

Poppy leaned in a little. She heard the rustling of flowers in the wind, the sound of leaves on the trees, and a slight *hiss* just ahead. "A snake?" Poppy asked as she sidestepped closer to Athena.

Ahead of them, the flowers parted, and a little dinosaur, about the size of a small cat, was already violently hissing at them.

Poppy laughed. The little thing was so angry-looking, but its stature reminded Poppy of a little dog barking for treats rather than a real threat. She moved from behind Athena and looked down at the creature. "We mean no harm, little friend," she said.

The dinosaur hissed louder. From its neck, a flare of scales burst out like a parasol, shaking in brilliant red and blue. Its little teeth snapped the air.

"Oh, no," Poppy said, rising. "It's furious."

Athena looked like she was fumbling for her journal, but unable to find it in the depths of the bag. "Usually red and blue mean it's venomous or at least pretends to be. I would stay clear of it, even if it's small."

"Valid point," Poppy said. She snuck back behind Athena. "Shoo!" She waved at the little creature with an aggressive motion.

Athena grumbled to herself, abandoning her quest in her bag. She nodded for Poppy to follow her around the little dinosaur, giving it a wide circle so as not to upset it further. "I wonder if your aunt has made it so that it isn't dangerous?"

"She's thought of almost everything, it seems," Poppy agreed. "But best not to test this one."

They made their way around it, and it scurried off into the field again, the flowers bending wildly in its wake.

Poppy followed its path of disturbed flowers to the other side of the clearing, where a massive creature walked toward them with even and slow steps. Poppy squinted at it, her mind a little lost on what exactly it was. It looked like a bear, only scaly, with armored plates running down its back and a long tail. A set of tusks, or horns, she couldn't tell, jutted out from its head and out wide to the sides. It looked at them, and Poppy grabbed Athena's elbow.

Athena turned to the creature with wide eyes. Poppy watched her face as she, too, seemed to be struggling to comprehend what her eyes saw. Her gaze followed the armor on its body, then landed on the spikes at its sides. "I don't like the look of that one," she said quietly.

"Nor do I," Poppy said. She looked down at the trajectory of the little, flared-neck dinosaur. It was heading right for the larger one. She pointed, slowly raising her hand. "I especially don't like that. The little one might upset it..."

From across the field, Poppy watched as the flowers

shifted before the big dinosaur. It raised its front legs and slammed onto the ground, roaring before taking off like a spooked horse toward them.

"Athena!" Poppy cried.

Athena grabbed her hand and took off before either of them had time to adjust. "Hurry!"

With her free hand, Poppy grabbed her skirt and hoisted it up as she ran. She followed close to Athena as the sounds of the terrified creature behind them grew louder. She propelled herself forward with everything she had, but, for some reason, she was smiling.

Athena's hand was still holding hers when they reached the treeline. Thick jungle leaves blocked the sun here, and it felt like a lifetime away, not mere moments from their silly little escape from a charging beast. Poppy thought Athena squeezed her hand, a subtle, quick motion, but then, it slipped free from her grasp.

Poppy looked at her with a half-smile, still panting from their run. She wanted to reach out and grab Athena's hand again. Bring it to her lips...

"Will you write about that in your ladies' journal?" Athena said between her quick breaths. She leaned down to put her hands on her knees as she looked behind them at the dinosaur that was sauntering away back into the field, clearly content that it had chased them off.

"Only the best parts," Poppy said.

Chapter Twenty-Six

ATHENA HELPS A PTERODACTYL AND BATTLES A GIANT LEAF

Athena's hand was still on fire. She had grabbed onto Poppy instinctively, without any thought at all. Old habit, or protectiveness, or simply because she had wanted to, she wasn't sure. She also wasn't sure it mattered.

Only the best parts, Poppy had said. The best part of a daring escape from a massive herbivore had to be holding on to Poppy's hand and feeling that lightning strike spark again.

"Let us keep going then," Athena said, rising from her

squat. Her breathing was back to normal, even if her stomach still flipped as she made eye contact with Poppy.

"Lead the way," Poppy said, gesturing for her to go on.

Poppy followed close behind, no longer standing beside her, Athena noticed. She berated herself for grabbing onto her hand. What was she thinking? At least it was only one more day. Poppy and Seppi would be on the shipping vessel the next day. And she, hopefully, would be staying. She just had to convince Lady Rose first.

The idea of watching Poppy and Seppi on a ship, their little specks getting smaller and smaller as they sailed away and into their new happy life, made her feel sick.

She pushed aside a large leaf hanging low in her path. Perhaps the dinosaur was love-sick too?

She grimaced at the passing thought. What a horribly unscientific thing to think.

Behind her, Poppy cried, "Mind the leaves!"

Athena glanced back as Poppy dodged the large leaf that swung back once free from Athena's hand. "Sorry," she said honestly.

Of course, she had saved Poppy from a charging dinosaur only to hit her in the face with a giant leaf.

But Poppy's annoyance didn't last long. "I think I hear it," Poppy said, sliding up to stand beside her.

Heat at Athena's shoulder bloomed. She looked down at Poppy, but the other woman had her eyes closed. Golden hair shone as the leaves above swayed in the breeze and concentrated rays of sunlight bounced off her like starlight. She looked ethereal.

Athena forced her eyes forward just as Poppy opened hers.

"This way," Poppy said, pointing left. She grabbed Athena's hand and pulled her along, though she struggled with the medical bag as she did.

"Here," Athena said, pulling her hand, and with it, Poppy, back a little. Painful though it was, she let go of Poppy and held out her hand again. "I'll trade you the bag for my journal."

Poppy looked down at the bulky bag at her hip. She raised a brow. "Why?" she asked, suspicion lacing her voice.

Athena rolled her eyes. "I'm trying to be nice, Poppy," she said. "You have a long trip tomorrow. And let me tell you, the sleeping quarters are nothing if not outrageously uncomfortable." She flexed her hand, indicating for Poppy to remove her bag. "Come on now."

Poppy let out a heavy sigh. She held the leather strap across her chest with both hands tightly. "I came here on a ship. I dressed as a boy and came here with a ticket purchased in the most sordid part of London."

Athena's eyes narrowed slightly. "I wasn't aware of that part–"

"So I think the trip back should feel like luxury to me," Poppy said as she stood taller. "That is, if I were going. I don't have the answers I'm seeking yet, and I'm *not* going on the shipping boat."

"You are–"

"Anyway." Poppy turned quickly, her long skirt flaring out around her like a flower blossoming. "I heard the creature up this way. Let's get going. This is as good a time as any to prove your worth to my aunt once and for all that you're more than an algae wrangler, don't you think?"

Athena shook her head but followed along behind her begrudgingly. "You have to go tomorrow," she growled.

"I don't have to do anything," Poppy asserted.

"The wedding—"

"Can wait."

"Would you *please* stop interrupting me?"

Poppy was impossible when she got like this. Frustration moved up from the pit of her stomach to turn sour in her throat. She was about to let it free from her mouth, spit something angry and contentious at Poppy about how she needed to be more responsible for once.

But a small sound broke her thoughts.

Between two large, interwoven trees, an almost avian creature lay curled up in its bat-like wings.

It raised its angular head, about the size of a large dog's, at them. A long beak and big black eyes blinked. Its body tried to rise, its wings propping it up for a moment before it collapsed again with a loud squeak.

"What kind of creature is this?" Athena gasped.

"I think a pterodactyl...?" Poppy said, though she trailed off at the end, as if unsure she was pronouncing it correctly. "They fly," she said more confidently. "At least, usually."

"And please tell me they eat plants?" Athena pulled her journal out and began writing everything she could about the creature before them. Its size, shape, and golden brown body made it like a bat, an exotic bird, and a lizard... She looked at Poppy. "Plants, or...?"

"Oh," Poppy said with a half-smile. "I thought you were scared for a moment. Just taking notes, of course." She looked down at the journal. "Mostly fish, I think. I've seen them at the riverside, swooping down to catch fish, at least." She laughed a little. "Are you more frightened of this than the giant stegosaurus?"

Athena's brow knitted. "Not frightened. Just curious."

"I was going to say... Because this little creature is the size of a terrier. I doubt he'll do much damage."

"I'm not afraid," Athena reiterated. She was busy adding the diet to her notes. Fish, or at least hunting behavior associated with fish... She tucked it away in a large pocket hidden in her skirt.

Poppy looked down with wide eyes. "It has pockets?" she gasped, delighted, it seemed, at the discovery.

Athena smiled. "It has pockets," she confirmed.

"You must get me the name of your seamstress," Poppy said quietly as they approached the little pterodactyl slowly.

Athena shrugged.

Poppy huffed. "Fine, keep your secrets," she hissed playfully,

The two crouched down low a few yards away from the flying beast. Athena opened her medical bag slowly, quietly. "It doesn't look injured," she whispered.

Poppy shook her head. "Willa said the creature is sick," she said back. She handed her bag over at last to Athena. "Maybe it ate something? A bad fish?"

Athena's eyes slowly found Poppy's.

Poppy was smiling. She cocked her head. "It's a very real possibility."

Athena looked back at the dinosaur.

"Or it's the plague and we're all dead." Poppy's voice was playful.

Athena ignored her. She looked over the two bags. Hers was full of bandages, cloth, a few splints, and water. Poppy's, with vials and tinctures, each labeled carefully in neat writing. She grimaced. "What if it is a bad fish?" she whispered.

Poppy looked at her with a confused expression. "Then... I'm a genius?"

"No, I mean, what can we use to cure it?" She was carefully inspecting a few vials. Her heartbeat thundered in her ears as she read the glass jars. She had almost no idea what she was doing.

"Come on, Athena," Poppy said. "I'm sure you've read about animal physiology? These are just animals. Extinct animals."

Athena suddenly wished she had more friends who were apothecaries. Or, any friend in medicine. Most of her time back home was on her own, studying, or trying to convince scholars that she belonged in their ranks. Now, when she needed it to prove that she did belong, that she could contribute a practical application of any knowledge, she was failing.

She shook her head.

This was not the time to wonder about what could have been.

She laid out a few vials and looked them over carefully. "If it did eat something, it may just need rest and rehydration." She found a vial of laudanum. It was a risky move, but it could work. "I'll attempt to get this into it." She glanced at Poppy. "This should put it out for a while. Long enough for me to carry it back. I'll have to hope that Lady Rose has some materials for me to craft a fluid replacement. If not, I saw coconuts along the shore. We could use their water..." She held the glass close to her chest and peeked out at the dinosaur.

Its breathing was labored, but it was alert, staring at her. Yes, it was the size of a medium dog, but dogs could do a lot of damage. And what this creature was capable of, she had no idea.

Still, she had to try.

"Stay here," Athena whispered and began to creep closer to the dinosaur.

"Absolutely not," Poppy whispered back. She was crawling along the forest floor at Athena's side, a half-smile on her face.

Athena huffed. "Fine. But keep your dress on this time."

Poppy shot her a scowl.

Athena breathed out a quiet laugh. "You go around back then."

Poppy rolled her eyes, but nodded.

Athena's gaze fixed on the pterodactyl.

Its long head and sharp beak turned to follow her movements. It lifted itself a little with its winged arms, only to fall again. It let out a sound like chirping.

"It's alright, little one," Athena said in the most soothing tone she could muster. She held out both hands, as if she were trying to show that she had no weapon. But her gesture didn't seem to have the intended effect.

The dinosaur scooched back until its body bumped the tree.

Athena's eyes shifted to Poppy, who had managed to get behind it silently. She looked ready to pounce.

Athena lowered her hands and shook her head at Poppy. "Not yet," she said in the same calm voice. "We'll see if I can get closer." She looked back at the dinosaur. "I'm not going to harm you. This will taste a little funny, and then... It's a lovely afternoon nap."

When she was on the pterodactyl, she could see its wings shaking. It lifted its head and snapped its long beak at her weakly.

"None of that now," Athena said. She placed a hand on its forehead, far away from its beak, just in case it had a surge of energy and managed to attack. But when her hand reached the pterodactyl's leathery skin, its shaking quieted. She stayed there for a long moment, feeling the rough texture of its skin on her soft hand, watching its body rise and fall as it breathed in slowly.

Athena smiled and removed the cap from the vial quickly. She poured the liquid into its open mouth before she could think twice about getting her hand so close to its sharp beak.

The pterodactyl's head shook, and it grunted as if it hated the taste. It lifted itself again, and its jaws snapped.

Athena and Poppy both scrambled back, but just as they did, the pterodactyl lowered, chirped, and then lay its head down on the soft green earth. Its breathing grew long and deep.

Poppy's eyes were wide, but she was smiling. She hopped up from the ground. "It worked!"

Athena let out a loud breath as relief flooded her. "Ha! Who needs classical training?" She stood up. Triumph made her posture taller.

"Well, I would hope for my medical professional," Poppy said slyly. "But you'll do in a pinch."

Athena slung her bag over her shoulder. "We should get

it back. We may need to gather up some coconuts before it wakes up." She approached the pterodactyl slowly, unsure if she ought to bind its beak together before she lifted it, just in case.

But Poppy was already crouched down beside it, wrapping up its beak gingerly in white cloth.

"You never know," Poppy said when she noticed Athena staring at her.

Athena smiled. She supposed she was right.

Chapter Twenty-Seven

POPPY THINKS THAT DINOSAUR EGGS ARE NOT AT ALL THE SAME

It was midmorning. The dinosaur was secured and hydrated, sleeping off its medicine. Poppy and Athena huddled around the kitchen table, each watching the old woman work at the stove.

Poppy knew that nothing on the island was really as it should be. But to see her aunt crack a dinosaur egg into a cast iron skillet like it was normal was a bit too much, she had to admit. She glanced at Athena, who also stared with what she could only assume was amusement tinged with bewilderment.

"You're eating a dinosaur egg…?" Poppy asked with a grimace.

Aunt Rose turned back to her, wooden spoon raised as if she was about to hit her with it. "And?"

Poppy blinked a few times, leaning back in her chair. "Isn't that…"

"No different than a chicken egg," Aunt Rose grumbled as she turned back to her skillet. "That was smart thinking, Athena," she said, changing the subject.

Athena's brows rose.

A swell of pride, washing over her like a warm wave, rose in Poppy's chest. She leaned forward again. "It was all Athena," she said. "She knew what to use and to gather up the coconuts."

Aunt Rose hummed a little. "Tell me," she said, "how are you with cooking?"

"Baking, I can do. Follow the recipe, follow the order of operations." Athena said. "Lady Rose, I am afraid I am not a skilled cook. I have been known to bake. However, I'm not sure I could create a recipe on my own."

Poppy's smile turned sour. Where was this going? And since when did Athena bake? Her eyes narrowed slightly.

"Good to know. So you follow recipes well?"

"I can take instruction," Athena said.

Poppy raised a brow. Since when? Athena never did anything *she* asked her to do. At least, Poppy's cheeks grew hot at the flashback, not when other people were around. She shook her head, trying to clear the thoughts from her mind of any time Athena had *absolutely* taken her directions well. She coughed loudly and facetiously. "Aunt Rose–"

"And what do you usually read?" Aunt Rose ignored Poppy.

"Natural philosophy, a little astronomy, physiology..." Athena answered.

Aunt Rose scooped the eggs from the cast iron onto a small plate with a wooden spoon. She sprinkled salt from a glass jar on the counter. "Well, Terrance is looking a little better, thanks to your help."

Athena sat up a little straighter.

"You can stay," Aunt Rose said at last.

Poppy leapt from her seat. She clapped her hands once. "Aunt Rose, thank you! This is the greatest news!"

Aunt Rose's eyes lifted to meet Poppy's. They were stern, hard. "Not you," she said. "You and your betrothed are still leaving on the cargo ship tomorrow."

Poppy stumbled on her feet. She gripped the table as she caught herself, the feeling of being submerged in an ice bath suddenly washing over her. She froze. "Aunt Rose, you–"

"Have already decided," the older woman cut her off. "Athena, you should be helpful around here."

"I can be helpful!" Poppy cried.

Athena looked down, and something like guilt flashed across her face.

Poppy wanted to shake her and tell her to speak up for her. But she knew it wouldn't help. It would only jeopardize Athena's stay if she advocated for her. She didn't want to do that to Athena. But she didn't want her to sit there silently, either. She wasn't sure what she wanted...

She took in a long, deep breath through her nose. "Aunt Rose, please."

The older woman waved her hand. She set her plate down at the small round table across from Athena and said, "It wouldn't matter if I let you stay anyway, child. You know your mother. If she says you need to be home right away, that will be the end of that. It's off with you before she sends the constables after you, and the secrets of my work here are exposed."

Poppy folded her arms. "I could write her a letter. Tell her I'm too ill to travel. It's not forever, just a little while longer."

"I've made up my mind," Aunt Rose said.

The bitter sting of tears in Poppy's eyes began to swell, threatening to break free. Her breathing grew quicker, her hands clenched. There was still more she needed to do here. More she needed to uncover. She couldn't come back.

Not yet. Not like this.

The scraping of the wooden chair on the floor broke her spiraling thoughts. Athena was beside her, a gentle hand on her elbow. "Come outside with me," she said in a low, calming tone. Her voice was soft and warm when all around Poppy was surrounded by a cold and hard reality.

She nodded and let Athena guide her out of the room, down the long, darkened hallway, and out onto the porch.

Outside, the air was easier to breathe. A calm breeze swept through the covered porch as Athena led the way into the garden, where a few wooden rocking chairs had been placed among the flowers and vegetables resting in their little raised beds.

It was far enough from the estate that Poppy felt safer

to speak freely. But she looked around at the tall trees surrounding them; she never did feel entirely safe to speak freely anywhere.

"Sit with me," Athena said. She let go of Poppy's elbow, and Poppy watched as her fingers curled into a small fist. The space where Athena had been was suddenly a void, lacking life and warmth in a way Poppy couldn't quite describe.

She searched the other woman's face for any sign that she felt it too, but Athena was already sitting in her rocking chair, her hands interlaced together as she leaned forward with her forearms on her thighs.

Poppy sighed. The pose was so casual, it was almost odd to see. Athena's thick, dark hair cascaded around her shoulders and down her back. Her white shirt was open low, the collar hanging just far enough for Poppy's eyes to trace along her collarbone. She forced her eyes away to the tall sprouting vegetables around them before she sank into her seat, rocking carefully back and forth with the tips of her shoes digging into the soft, still-wet dirt.

"Why do you want to stay so badly?" Athena asked at last.

Poppy closed her eyes. She leaned her head back against the wood. What could she say? She had come here to find out what secrets her aunt was keeping. Where the money was going. And the dinosaurs only felt like part of the puzzle. Would it be enough to save her family from poverty? If she said anything about the dinosaurs, did she even have enough evidence, or would she be committed?

She decided she still didn't quite feel like she could be honest. Not entirely. "I like the dinosaurs," she half lied.

Though her eyes were still shut, she could feel Athena's intense gaze burrowing into her. She turned her face away, as if that would help. "I like the island life," she offered when she still felt the prickle of Athena's stare.

"Even the eating dinosaur egg part?" Athena asked, a lightness in her tone.

Of course, *she* was happy. She had proven her worth and was allowed to stay.

Instead of offering any solace, however, Athena whispered, "Poppy, look!"

Poppy opened her eyes to see a little chubby Reggie running by, bonnet on over his head, pink ribbon trailing behind him. He was chomping at the air happily, round teeth snapping, trying to catch a dragonfly that buzzed ahead.

Behind him, a gaggle of smaller dinosaurs, bird-like but for their strong legs and sharp claws, chased close behind in a V shape. Each wore a matching little straw hat with different color ribbons tied around the base. One chirped, then the group separated, flanking either side of the raised garden bed.

"I think they're working together," Athena said, amused.

Poppy smiled at the sweetness, the stillness of it all. She watched as one of them chirped again, and the group came together quickly. A few tackled others in the air as they sprang up with their small, but powerful legs, small jaws snapping at one another in an attempt to catch the elusive dragonfly.

Poppy squinted and leaned in closer to see that they were actually chasing what appeared to be a cloud of small bugs. The cloud was dwindling rapidly as they continued their attack.

"Smart," Poppy said with a raise of her brows. She looked at Athena from the corner of her eye. "Very smart."

That was it, she decided with a clench of her fist. She was going to show them yet.

Just a *Ladies Journal*, huh?

Chapter Twenty-Eight

POPPY FLETCHER WILL NOT GO

The group waited at the dock, watching the large ship in the distance lower a little wooden boat into the water. The little wooden boat that would carry the honey shipment, and Poppy and Giuseppe to their fates.

Poppy grimaced. What a terrible way of putting that. She was supposed to be a writer, but all she could think of was that this walk across the dock was like walking the plank, a death sentence in the cold, dark depths of the sea.

How original.

Athena caught her eye and mouthed, "Are you alright?"

Poppy could almost laugh. She wasn't. Instead, though, she smiled, all teeth exposed. "I can't wait to get back to the quiet comforts of home," she said through her gritted teeth. "Don't you agree, Giuseppe?"

"I am not looking forward to being on another ship for so long," he said. He was staring at the large ship with wide eyes. "But I am eager to be home."

He would be, of course, she thought bitterly as the rowboat approached the end of the dock.

Two burly men leapt out with ease. Without a word to anyone, they began gathering up the crates that had been placed neatly at the edge for them. They looked like they were in a hurry. And that made sense, given the reputation the island seemed to have, and the rush shipment that, to them, must have seemed incredibly strange.

The man still in the rowboat, a lanky boy who couldn't have been much older than fifteen, perked his head up. "We're taking passengers, too?" he called. "Those were the orders."

One of the men hoisted the last crate aboard, then turned to the group. "Which three are coming?" he asked.

"Just two," Willa said, a boldness in her voice that Poppy had seldom heard.

Poppy did her best to smile with the same confidence, though her body trembled like she had finally reached the end of the plank and the only out was down into the endlessly empty deep. She moved past Willa, approaching the men with her head held high. "I know you just loaded up these boxes, but will one of you be carrying our luggage?" she asked. "It's just so warm out here for a lady."

"Yes, my lady," said the tallest man, already gathering up hers and Seppi's trunks. "It's a short boat ride, but we'll make sure it's comfortable for you."

It had to be more comfortable than pretending to be a boy and buying a dark alley ticket, she figured. But the stone in her stomach remained heavy in her core, dragging her down. "Thank you," was all she said.

She turned to her cousin and Athena, but Willa's expression was marble, still, and impossible to read. Athena's just the same. Poppy held her head high. "I'll see you at the wedding," she said. But it came out as a command.

Athena and Willa both nodded.

"Right," Poppy said. She turned back and hopped into the boat with a surprising amount of grace in her long dress. She guessed it was easy to escape when she had been running from everything her whole life.

Giuseppe followed, a little less gracefully. The boat rocked as his frame squeezed in between her and the water. "Ready?" he asked her.

But it wasn't up to her. The rowboat was moving. She supposed that, like any other cargo ship, they had a schedule to keep. Poppy's blood quickened, racing through her like a brilliant lightning strike just as an incredibly foolish idea planted its seeds within her.

The corners of her lips turned up.

"You seem happy," Seppi said, a smile of his own followed.

"Oh yes," Poppy said, and her own grew, though she knew it must have looked wicked.

. . .

*A*board the main vessel, Poppy looked out at the island behind them. She was gripping the wood so tightly that she was sure it would leave a mark when she lifted her hands.

A man tilted his hat as he came up beside her. "I have made accommodations for your stay," he said. "We don't often get women aboard, but I've made sure it'll be comfortable."

Poppy bit her lower lip. "Thank you."

He went on, "I'm the captain of this ship. Call on me for anything you may need."

Poppy looked up at him, squinting into the sunlight to catch his expression. "Are you on a strict schedule, Captain?" She was grateful that he was in the sunlight. She wouldn't have to hide that she was frightened as much if she were backlit. But she was sure he could smell it on her. He tilted his head, already suspicious.

He nodded. "No need to fret, we'll get you home soon."

"Then, it's not possible to turn around at this point, is it?" she asked sweetly. "I am afraid I've left my locket on my vanity. It's sentimental, you see." Her heart was pounding; she could hear it so loudly in her ears that she was afraid she would miss his answer. Her head began to ache behind her eyes. She gripped the wood tightly.

The captain shook his head. "I'm afraid not, the ship's too far out. I have a cousin in Mayfair, he'll recreate it for you."

"No. Thank you," Poppy said. She let go and walked several paces away from the bow. She stopped about halfway on the deck and closed her eyes tightly.

The chill of the sea breeze battled the burning heat of the harsh sunlight on her skin. She smelled the salt in the air, making her nose tickle. A bead of sweat raced down her back, and she was suddenly aware of the discomfort of her thick hair sticking to her neck like a noose.

She wanted to feel it all, just in case this was the stupidest thing she had ever done. The biggest leap she ever took. The most she had ever given to run away.

Poppy opened her eyes and turned back around with a deep breath. Before she could think twice, she sprinted for the bow.

"Poppy, what—" She thought she heard Giuseppe cry out, but she was already launching herself into the air. Her first foot pushed off the deck, the other propelled her forward on the edge of the bow where her hands had been holding on tightly only a moment ago.

Relief and sheer terror tore through her mind and solidified into every fiber and bone as she flew through the air.

She knew she wasn't flying, even if for that one glorious moment, it seemed she was.

She was falling.

And she knew that once she hit the water, she'd have to give it everything she had to swim to shore.

Chapter Twenty-Nine

ATHENA IS A GOOD SWIMMER (LUCKILY)

Athena gasped.

A speck leapt from the boat and plunged, without a splash, into the ocean. She screamed when she saw the second figure follow. "That idiot! Those idiots!"

Willa, already halfway down the dock, turned with a quizzical look. "Pardon?"

Athena was busy taking off her boots and rolling up her sleeves. "Those fools!" she cried. "They've jumped ship!"

"Jumped?" Willa called back. She hurried to Athena's

side and held her hands over her brow to try to see into the sun-soaked waves. "They've actually jumped?"

Athena growled, her mind feral. She looked around her, as if it mattered, before taking off her long burgundy skirt and throwing it aside with her boots. Her slip would have to do. She could only hope Poppy and Seppi had the forethought to do the same. "Can you swim?" she asked Willa quickly.

"No, I—"

Athena shook her head, curls flying around her shoulders as she did. "Damn it all," she hissed. "Those idiots are going to drown me." Still, she jumped into the water and began to swim out to meet them.

Athena pushed her body into the waves, fighting against the incoming swells to swim out as fast and as far as she could. With every inhale, another wave smashed into her face, knocking her under the water.

She dove under the next wave, fighting the entire ocean to break free from its grasp. She felt small. Smaller than she had been before any massive dinosaur. To the sea, she was but a drop.

Still, once she was past the breakers, it wasn't too far out, meeting them halfway. She was glad that she had spent her summers with Seppi in lakes and ponds, getting into trouble and swimming far out when they weren't allowed to dip a toe.

For Poppy's part, she was impressed that she was a strong enough swimmer not to sink to the ocean floor immediately. But she was struggling, patting at the surface of the water like a puppy, her head bobbing up and down in the waves like a blade of grass in a storm.

"Help her!" Seppi called from the waves. "I can make it to shore!"

Athena spat as salt water sprayed her eyes. "Damn it, Poppy!" She pushed herself to swim faster, stronger, toward the increasingly frantic Poppy. Her arms burned, and her mouth was full of water.

But Athena reached her quickly, wrapping an arm around Poppy's waist.

Poppy's elbow made contact with Athena's forehead. Her head flung back, and her body sank into the waves, dragging Poppy down with her.

Athena pushed water out of her nose as she kicked her feet up quickly. Her fingers dug into Poppy's dress, ripping part of it at the seam as she pulled them both up and out of the water.

"Stop thrashing!" Athena shouted. "I've got you now!"

Poppy was crying, or laughing. Or possibly both. Athena couldn't tell. She pulled her in close and lifted her so her face was above the waves. She squeezed her fingers into the folds of Poppy's dress, weaving them into the ripped seam for a better grip.

"Stop it! You can either kick your feet with me or just let me drag you," Athena said sternly. "Come on, we're closer to shore than you think."

Poppy rested her head into Athena's shoulder. Her body went limp.

"I'll drag you along then," Athena mumbled, still spitting some saltwater from her mouth.

She pulled Poppy in tight and began to swim for the island.

. . .

iuseppe had, finally, removed his waistcoat. He was lying out on the sand when Athena and Poppy made it to shore.

"Don't mind me," Athena grumbled as she and Poppy waded through the low waves in their long skirts.

"Don't mind *me*," he said back with an uncharacteristic snarl. "I leapt from *a boat* today."

Athena exhaled. She threw her body forward one last time and landed on the sand with her feet still in the water. The waves were gentle now, seeping up her calves and back down again slowly.

Beside her, Poppy landed with a loud thud face-first into the sand. Athena rolled over to get a look at her. Poppy was breathing, and... smiling? Athena's brows furrowed.

"That... was..." Poppy said between gasps of breath, "The most... exciting thing... I've ever done."

"That was the *stupidest* thing you've ever done!" Athena scolded. She hit Poppy's back with her arm, but the effect was weak. She was exhausted. Physically and emotionally. Just when she thought she was finally free–

Poppy was laughing now, her enthusiasm infectious despite it all.

Athena glanced up at Seppi and Willa, who were standing close with huge smiles on their faces. She wanted to hit all of them over the head.

"It was worth it!" Poppy said, her usual chipper cadence back again. "Quick! Look! Is the ship still in view?"

"I'm not looking! I'm not doing anything for you ever again! I just saved your life!" Athena tried shouting, but her voice was weak. It came out like a whisper.

"Still haven't passed the horizon," Seppi said as if he hadn't heard Athena's protest at all. "But they're getting smaller."

Athena glared at him. The waves washed up her legs a little higher, each time they passed over her, a little more sand gave way to bury her. Part of her wished it'd cocoon her entirely. "You, cousin! I thought *you* had some sense about you."

"I did," Seppi said, his hands raised in defeat. As though she could still get him from her position on the ground, slowly becoming one with the sand. "I knew Poppy wasn't a strong swimmer."

"How would you know that?" Poppy asked, propping herself up on her forearms.

"Educated guess, actually," Seppi said. "I was right, though. And brave, if anyone's asking."

"Brave, yes. But I must say, I agree with Athena. Also stupid." Willa finally broke in. "What are we going to do now?"

Athena pushed herself up to a seat. She unburied her legs and pulled them up close to her chest. "It will take time for the boat to get back to London," she said. "And then once the family realizes you're not there..."

"I left a note," Poppy said quickly. "I left it in my trunk on top of all my things. It explains that we'll be a few weeks longer due to a *mysterious* illness." She paused, as if expecting applause. "I'm sure the captain will be going through our things. It's right on top, and it's addressed to him, so I'm also certain he'll open it right away and then deliver it to my family. That way, he's also in on the same fake story about the sickness on the island. After all, he wouldn't want to make it look as though a young lady jumped off his boat under his nose, would he?"

"And me?" Seppi asked. "How is he supposed to explain that?"

Poppy laughed loudly over the waves. "I will admit, I wasn't sure you'd come too. But I thought it was a possibility. I snuck a note into your trunk as well. If you came with me, it explains you're staying to tend to me. And if you didn't jump too, well, at least you'd find it soon."

"You shouldn't have doubted I'd jump too," he said. "Though I suppose I do understand."

Poppy fell back into the sand. "You're braver than you appear, that's the truth."

"Stupid," Athena corrected. "You're both much more stupid than you appear."

Seppi put his hands on his hips. He smiled. "Well, I will admit, I am awfully upset about leaving all the tea in the trunk... I could go for a nice cup of breakfast tea right about now."

Athena finally rose so that she could smack him across the back of his head.

Willa stepped closer to the group. "Well, what's done is done," she said. "I don't think my mother is going to be all too pleased by this development, but it's not exactly as if we can send you to sea in a little rowboat..." She looked out into the ocean as if she were imagining it now. She shuddered, but then looked at Poppy with kind eyes. "I do think she'll admire your tenacity, though. Even if she would never admit it."

Poppy squinted into the sunlight, crinkles formed at the corners of her eyes, and her cheeks rounded. She held up a hand to the sky to block the light and glanced up at Athena with a smile.

Athena wished she could feel that kind of joy. But all she felt was the lingering fear in her bones. The image of Poppy, so far away, bobbing in the sea, flashed into her mind. She looked away and rubbed her eyes, trying to clear away the image that had imprinted there.

Chapter Thirty

ATHENA CAN BE USEFUL

Athena was sure that if Lady Rose were anything like the other members of Poppy's family, she would be appalled that Athena was in nothing but her slip and overshirt. It could jeopardize her stay here. But she didn't feel like putting her skirt back on over her soaked, sand-studded clothes.

Lady Rose, entirely unlike Lady Elizabeth, had only looked them all up and down with a hint of amusement on her face. The usual thin line of her lips was turned up, and she crossed her arms like a scolding school teacher when they all arrived back at the estate.

"If you're going to be here until the next shipment, then at least make yourselves useful," Lady Rose had said simply after Willa had guiltily explained the situation they had found themselves in.

They all stood there in front of the door looking pathetic and silly.

Athena couldn't help but hang her head, utterly useless. She knew she ought to be feeling some kind of joy; she was allowed to stay. Or some sort of horror; she was stuck here longer with her cousin, who was marrying her once-girlfriend... but all she felt was tired. At least Lady Rose seemed to have a sense of humor about it.

"Come on, then. After you dry off, I'll make us some tea and eggs," Lady Rose retired into the house, and the rest followed with their heads hanging low.

*A*thena peeled her wet clothes from her body, not bothering to shake out any of the sand that still clung to the fabric. She fell face-first into the bed and curled her legs up into her body. Her eyes closed, and she let out a heavy sigh. She had no idea how she was supposed to be functional in such conditions. The high of being allowed to practice science on the island with a true scholar, and the low of watching Poppy sail away, however briefly, was all replaced with a sense of general discomfort.

She heard a little chirp from the corner of her room and opened one eye to see Reggie standing by the open window.

His feet stomped when she smiled at him, and he ran up to the edge of the bed. His short little arms flailed about wildly as she bounced his body. Despite her feeling of unease, Athena smiled at him.

He looked like he was trying to fly, and she had to admire his tenacity.

She sat up and scooped him quickly into her arms and onto the soft comforter with her. Reggie pressed his wide head into her chin, and her smile brightened with warmth and affection. He was adorable, and yet, as he snapped his jaws a little excitedly, Athena was grateful that Lady Rose had the forethought to make the carnivores tiny.

"I suppose I'd better get dressed and make myself useful," Athena told him gently. She set him down on the bed carefully and stretched herself taller.

Reggie looked up at her with round eyes and chirped as if he agreed.

*A*thena had managed to successfully avoid everyone for the rest of the day. She crept to the edge of the stairs and waited for the voices to retire before she snuck down the stairs and foraged for a little bit of sustenance. She grabbed an armful of bread and wondered, for just a moment, how it was probably moldy, considering she hadn't seen an import shipment yet.

She stole a few long carrots, too, just in case, before she snuck back up the stairs with quiet feet. She even chewed quietly as she could, taking slow and methodical bites of clearly unwashed carrot.

So it was even more frustrating that she had been so

careful, and yet now, the knock on her door in the dead of night managed to find her.

She glared at the closed door.

Whoever it was, she didn't want to talk to them.

The light from the moon beamed in through the open window, illuminating everything in the room in a pale silver glow. She wished she could sprout fire and light the candles in the room quickly, but maybe it was best that whoever this was thought they were waking her up. She didn't want to admit that she had been lying in bed awake and worried all night. She also hoped, wickedly, that when she did open the door, they'd feel guilty.

She opened the door with a deep frown to see Poppy standing in the dark hallway. She was in her nightdress, the collar tied up tight around her long throat, the ruffles down her sleeves to her wrists, and a slight flower hem along the bottom.

She raised a brow. "Aren't you indecent?" she said with an even deeper scowl.

Poppy smiled and rolled her eyes. She pushed past Athena and into the dark room.

"What are you doing?" Athena hissed. She shut the door behind her and turned with her arms crossed over herself.

Poppy went to the open window, and she looked out into the night sky. "I wanted to thank you," she whispered.

Athena crossed the room, but kept her distance from Poppy. Her eyes started to sting.

Poppy was always larger than life. Even now, her presence filled the room as though she were the air itself.

The moment Athena had watched her jump, an overwhelming fear had taken over her mind and body. She was losing Poppy, no matter what. Poppy was marrying her cousin, and there was nothing she could do to stop that. But, to imagine the world losing Poppy? It was too much.

Athena closed her eyes tightly. She drew her lips together and breathed through her nose. "For someone so smart, that was the stupidest thing I've ever seen," she managed to say.

"Oh, so you *do* think I'm smart," Poppy teased. But she was still avoiding Athena's gaze.

"Of course I do," Athena said. "But you could have drowned. You could have gotten Giuseppe killed."

"It was a calculated risk," Poppy said softly. "And Giuseppe is in charge of himself, Athena. I know you think he's your responsibility. But he's not. And I'm not either."

"I liked this conversation better when you were thanking me," Athena said. She folded her arms tighter around her. "You're welcome, by the way."

Poppy smiled again.

In the moonlight, Athena studied her, trying to decipher any indication of what she was really thinking.

But her mind went elsewhere. To the moment she pulled her close to her, the way Poppy rested her head on her.

The way that now, in the darkness, her golden hair looked silver in the half moonlight, and how she had seen it like this before, in the long nights when they lay together, wrapped up in warm blankets, legs tangled, just listening to the other breathe.

A quick turn in her stomach threatened to make her sick. She looked away. "Well," she said, eyes still fixed on the Poppy's pale shadow stretching across the floor, "you said what you needed to. I'm tired."

Poppy's shadow turned. It moved toward Athena, then passed by without a sound. She heard the door open, then shut gently, and it was as though all the air in the room was gone.

POPPY IS AN ADVENTURER NOW

Poppy was fine being put to work. However, she was not fine with being put to work outside, away from anything important that she was determined to discover. She had already seen dinosaurs.

Been there. Done that.

But her aunt had pushed the four of them out into the early morning air, telling them that while Terrance, the pterodactyl, was healing up, they needed to go to the riverbank and see if they could find any issues with the fish.

It seemed like a flimsy excuse to get them out of the estate, though no one argued with Lady Rose about it, or even questioned it. They exited the house with Aunt Rose shooing them the whole way.

Poppy wondered if the fish were also prehistoric. But she didn't ask. She wasn't sure her aunt would give her an explanation, and if she did, if it would matter. This whole thing was a ruse.

The group meandered through the field of flowers in silence until Poppy finally decided she couldn't stand it anymore. "I should learn to swim," she announced with a wry smile. "You never know when I may need to jump off a boat again."

Athena shot her an angry look.

Seppi chuckled. "That was quite the adventure, I will admit. Probably the most thrilling thing I've ever done in my life."

Willa skipped a little to catch up to them. "You're making me wish I could have done it!"

"You're on an island with ancient fantastical creatures, and you wish you could jump off a boat?" Seppi asked. "I'd think that simply living here would be plenty of excitement for a lifetime."

Poppy side-eyed her cousin, watching her reaction.

Willa's shoulder sank in, her eyes moved about the ground as if she was watching for anything sinister to appear. "A lifetime is relative, isn't it?" she said, a bit sadly.

Poppy turned her attention back to the wide open field ahead. They were making their way toward the jungle, heading north where her aunt had explained the freshwater river ran.

Athena, however, stopped suddenly. She held out her arms, preventing the group from moving forward.

A herd of creatures, the size of deer, but so much more bulky, wandered from the treeline. Poppy leaned over Athena's arm to get a better look.

"Put that down," she whispered, swatting her hand away.

The herd of dinosaurs consisted of about twenty, possibly more; it was difficult to tell, as their bodies had a strange way of molding together. Each with a round body like that of a carriage, merging into the next one. Their ability to hide among the group seemed like it'd be an excellent advantage if they were in their own time, when massive predators roamed.

The creatures were lumbering along, and Poppy did her best to squint to see what they looked like on their own. She caught sight of one in the front, away from the herd.

It had a back full of what looked like skeletal armor plated down its body, with protruding spikes jutting out from its sides. As they walked, long tails with a bulbous sphere at the end swayed behind them. They sauntered along, seemingly unaware of the group of humans.

Though they were relatively small, Poppy assumed almost every creature, compared to Francesca, looked like they could do a lot of damage if they needed to.

She lifted Athena's arm back up delicately. "On second thought..." she whispered playfully.

Willa crept in close with silent steps. "Those are ankylosaurus," she said quietly. "They're gentle. Usually."

"Usually?" Athena asked, tilting her head a little to catch Willa's eyes.

Willa smiled sheepishly. "When they don't feel threatened... They're completely harmless. They are surprisingly fast, though."

"And how are they threatened?" Seppi asked, leaning in closer.

Poppy watched Willa's eyes look over the herd. "When they have their young with them," Willa whispered. "Which... merciful heavens, they do."

"Blazes," Seppi swore. He positioned himself to stand by Athena, a move Poppy thought was uncharacteristically brave. Perhaps almost losing her to the waves had given him courage, she thought.

"We should just back away slowly, or stay still," Willa said. "They have a few babies with them."

"And... how fast is 'fast'?" Seppi asked.

Suddenly, one of the dinosaurs, the leader of the group from the looks of the long horns on its head, turned to them slowly. It eyed them for a moment as the rest of the herd stopped.

"Don't move," Willa breathed.

Poppy could feel her heart beating like a drum, faster in her ribs, vibrating out so she thought anyone could hear. Her muscles twitched with anticipation, and her eyes stayed stuck on the beasts.

Seppi breathed in, a painful sound.

"Seppi, don't you dare–" Athena started, but it was too late.

Giuseppe sneezed.

The herd all turned to them—a deep, primal ferocity in their movements. One of the little ones let out a series of quick cries, followed by a long call, then another few short bursts. Poppy couldn't help but think it sounded like speaking...

A few of the dinosaurs quickly formed a circle around the young. They flared their tails out, swinging wildly in defense.

"They're protecting their young," Willa said quickly. "Avoid their tails at all costs, and maybe they'll leave us a—"

The largest dinosaur bellowed again, then charged.

"Never mind! Run!" Willa cried. She took off to the right, racing through the flowers before Poppy could even register the command.

The dinosaur raced toward them with a swiftness unnatural for its bulky size. Each step shook the ground as it trampled over the wildflowers in its path. It roared, freezing Poppy in her place. Its sharp beak-like mouth opened wide as it swung its head with each pounding step.

Poppy shrieked, then grabbed Athena's arm. "Run, run! Run!"

The two women chased after Willa, with Seppi following close behind.

"Maybe if we turn and make ourselves large suddenly?" he gasped between breaths when he caught up. "Like how one stops a charging horse?"

"*One*, not *you*, Seppi!" Athena said. She was at the back now, pushing Poppy forward with every small stumble.

"The concept seems easy!" he cried, as if that defended his position.

Behind them, the dinosaur was gaining on them. It roared again, too close.

"We don't have time for your familial squabbles!" Poppy shrieked. Her foot caught on a rock and she fell. Hard. Her hands scraped on the dirt, red and purple flowers caught in her hair. She looked up, heart pounding.

She was pulled up violently by her elbow. Athena gripped her tight, hoisting her to her feet as fear coursed through her, her blood on fire.

"Go!" she heard Athena yell, but if it was to her or the others, she wasn't sure. She turned back to the dinosaur as she ran forward. This time, she kept one hand on her skirt, lifting it high as she raced alongside Athena.

Ahead, Willa and Seppi had already disappeared into the treeline when suddenly, she heard another great roar. From the trees, another dinosaur with three massive horns protruding from its head stormed into the field.

It raised its head, horns moving in a frenzy of spears toward them. It rushed forward with far less grace than the dinosaurs behind them, but with the same intensity.

The earth shook.

Poppy screamed again as her body was pulled harshly to the left. She stumbled again, but was jerked upright by her arm.

Athena led them away from the other creature, and they zigzagged through the flowers and disappeared into the lush forest.

They kept running until the light grew dimmer under the cover of the leafy canopy. Here, the sounds of their footsteps and breathing were muted. Here, it was still again.

Athena stopped at last, nearly shoving Poppy's arm away like it was a snake. "I would really like to stop being chased by dinosaurs now," Athena managed between gasps.

Poppy nodded, trying and failing to recapture her breath in her struggling lungs. She doubled over, her hands propping her up as she pushed into her knees. She glanced at Athena, about to make some quip when she noticed that the other woman had already pulled out her journal and was busy scribbling madly as she struggled to breathe.

"What in the world are you doing right now?" Poppy gasped.

"Taking notes on their behavior..." she said as she sucked in a deep breath. She kept writing, her eyes fixed on the page. She took another long inhale before she went on, "Didn't it seem to you as though they had a distinct cry for danger? It was different than when the other dinosaur appeared. I don't think they were competitors or saw one another as a threat... Do you remember their name?"

Poppy breathed in, forcing herself to inhale until her lungs stung. She exhaled loudly, rising right at last with her hands on her hips. "Athena, I do not remember the name of the dinosaur that almost killed us."

"Shame," Athena said, not even bothering to look up from her notebook. "Should I add that I saved your life yet again?" she added at last. This time, she looked up at Poppy through her thick lashes with a cat-like stare.

Poppy's stomach flipped as frustration coursed through her blood. She threw her hands up. "Thank you, thank you! Athena is the hero! Are you happy now?"

Athena looked back down at her journal. She continued writing. "Rarely," she grumbled back.

Poppy scoffed. "Come on," she said, grabbing Athena's elbow the same way she had been guided along just moments before.

Athena flinched, but Poppy held firm. "Let us see if we can find the others."

"Yes, we obviously can't investigate the waterfront without your groom."

"And your new best friend," Poppy shot back. She was glad she was still pulling Athena along, so she didn't have to see her face. Her cheeks flushed with embarrassment. What a terrible retort.

"She's *your* cousin," Athena mumbled, shaking her arm free at last.

Poppy's hand clenched.

Neither said anything for a long while as they trudged through the thick ferns in the direction that they had come.

Poppy's heart was still heavy in her chest. Sweat at her hairline and beneath her clothes clung to her, weighing her down and making it harder to perform any movement with ease. She was just as waterlogged as when she had leapt overboard. But at least then her heart was racing because she had been brave. This time, she was just wet, uncomfortable, and with nothing to show for it except scraped-up hands and knees.

Poppy wiped her hands on her skirt as she followed bent foliage and disturbed plants in what she could only hope was their wild and weaving trail back toward the clearing.

When they came to the treeline, however, they both stopped. At first, Poppy waited to see if the dinosaurs were still there, still agitated. But what she saw instead made her pull back.

"Are you seeing this?" Poppy asked. "Look!"

The two leaned in to get a closer look out past a thick leafed bush to see Aunt Rose sitting atop one of the armored dinosaurs. The little baby was bounding beside them, frolicking among the flowers with what Poppy could only describe as a joyousness.

In her hands, Aunt Rose was holding what appeared to be thick knitting needles, working diligently on a long scarf. Beside them, lay the three-horned dinosaur, eyes closed peacefully, and yarn wrapped around its horns, seemingly content to keep the colorful string from tangling.

"Why a scarf in this heat?" Athena asked.

Poppy turned to her slowly with a single raised brow. Her first instinct was to tease Athena about her book knowledge not translating to the practical, but she knew that would be a lie. Athena had, she had to begrudgingly admit to herself, proven capable in almost every practical sense. Almost.

So instead, Poppy held Athena's shoulder gently with one hand. "Always asking the right questions," she said kindly. "So, what do we think? Should we venture back out to the field, or try to find this river?"

"There's the right question," Athena said, almost playfully, though she shrugged Poppy's hand off her shoulder. "Let's try to find this river. I don't want to have to run from another charging horde."

By the time they made it to the river, Poppy was starting to think that this whole escapade had been one extremely elaborate attempted murder plot on the part of her aunt. It made sense when she thought about it. Why else would the dinosaurs have charged at them while they sat docile and calm, letting her knit on their horns? Besides, her letter had already made it sound as if she and

Giuseppe were sick. It would be easy for Aunt Rose to write another letter saying they have succumbed to their illness, and she buried them in the garden.

After all, her aunt *had* led them right into angry mother dinosaur territory. And with the guise that *maybe* something was going on with the fish.

First the bees, then the flying dinosaur, now this? Were *all* her creatures so ill?

It was a murder plot, she was sure of it.

Poppy folded her arms as they stood beside the riverbank, determined to stay in a bad mood. No matter how lovely the scenery.

And it was lovely. The sight before her was unlike anything she had ever seen. A swift-moving, but calm, surfaced river raced over smooth brown and red rock. Clear, clean water shimmered in the sunlight, sparkling like diamonds in the afternoon light. A few trees along the riverbank hung their leaves low over the rushing water, as if dipping their leaves into water to test the temperature.

Still, Poppy couldn't quite appreciate it, given the circumstances. Her hands and knees were throbbing, the pain finally settling in after the burst of energy she had spent running for her life. She looked down at her palms and drew in a sharp breath. It wasn't bad, but it looked a little worse than she would have thought. Her skin was cut open in a few shallow scratches. They were an angry, bright red, radiating out to her fingertips.

"Let me see," Athena said. She was already holding Poppy's hands in her own, carefully looking them over with a furrowed brow. "I'm sorry..." she whispered.

"It was my own maladroit miscalculation," Poppy said.

She was staring intensely at their hands together, trying to avoid Athena's gaze. But the way Athena's hand moved over her own, the gentleness of it, the heat of her skin on hers... Poppy's ribs tighten harshly around her lungs and heart. She closed her eyes, unable to watch their hands part as she pulled her away quickly. "I'm fine," she lied.

Athena sighed, or scoffed. Poppy couldn't tell with her eyes still sealed. She opened them at last to see Athena gesturing for a large rock by the water's edge, under the shadow of a large tree. "We will rest here for a bit," Athena said, her voice warm but sounding like a command. She already had her journal out and was making her way up onto the rock and into the shade. "Come on. Close your eyes, I'll keep an eye out for anything strange."

Poppy moved as if a string was pulling her along against her will. She followed that odd sort of tether that Athena seemed to keep in her hand, wrapped firmly around Poppy's heart.

Chapter Thirty-Two

ATHENA CAN ALSO BE AN ADVENTURER

Athena's back rested on the tree that had found its way to root around the massive boulder where they sat. Poppy was lying beside her, hands behind her head to make a pillow. She had been breathing steadily for a while now, asleep under Athena's watchful eye.

She had to assume that meant whatever tension there was between them, Poppy had put it aside and could, in fact, still trust her. That, or she was exhausted from being chased by dinosaurs.

Hounds' teeth, Athena thought to herself as she folded her legs up closer to her chest. She held her journal in one hand and had been dutifully jotting down anything she saw as if it might be absolutely critical, even though she knew it wasn't.

So far, she had seen a few bees pass by, dance with one another, then buzz away. She was still in awe at her enormous size, and it made their plump bodies all the more adorable.

Modern bumblebees were already quite silly. She had enjoyed watching them dance along the fields of lavender when she was a child, often choosing one to follow as best she could throughout the rows until at last she lost track of which was which. She had learned a lot back then, just by watching.

A dinosaur had appeared, though it was also the size of a small house cat. It approached the other side of the river boldly, though, lapping up water carelessly. It looked similar to the other crested, duck-like dinosaur she had seen wandering about the island before. But this one was small, and its bill resembled more of a shovel than a true duck. It was also purple, a striking difference from any others she had seen on the island so far.

It looked up at her after it was done, then bounded off into the jungle again.

She did her best to record the details.

But time had slowed then. It was late afternoon, by the sun's rays, and she was getting hungry. Maybe instead of a murder plot, this was just a way to keep them from eating all of Lady Rose's food, she mused to herself with a half-smile. That would make the most sense. She could eat a lot when she was thinking, and she had been doing a lot of that recently.

Her eyes found Poppy once again, still asleep peacefully as though she were safe in bed. Athena wanted to reach out and brush away one lock of golden curls that had fallen onto her forehead, but instead she began to write some more, a list of all the things she hated about Poppy.

1. Rude / Aloof
2. Uses too many big words. (Pretentious).
3. Never relents when she wants something, no matter what it is.

She breathed in deeply, letting her head fall back. Things she hated. Things she admired. Things she wished didn't matter because they were petty and small.

She closed her journal and rested her chin on her knees, shrugging away the terrible thoughts and the thick waves from her shoulders.

A boat appeared from down the river. Athena lifted her head higher to see as it bumbled along the current, hitting the shore at almost every bumpy wave.

Athena's stare hardened. She felt her neck prickle, her fists clenched, and she wasn't sure why. Not really. It was empty, which, she hoped, meant that it had simply separated from the dock and not that Seppi and Willa had capsized and were now wet and angry further upstream.

She looked down at the sleeping Poppy, then her

journal, then back to the river. Her breathing grew faster as her heart began to race with worry. She tore the page from her journal and crumbled it up, throwing it into the river with one quick motion.

She hated Poppy sometimes. She loved her, too. How could anyone not?

The boat hit the embankment again, this time, it got stuck on a large rock, wedged in the sand.

Athena unclenched her fists. She looked down at Poppy and nudged her shoulder with her knee. "Wake up," she said, more harshly than she expected.

Poppy stirred. "What?"

"We're going on another adventure."

Chapter Thirty-Three

ATHENA AND THE GIANT TURTLE

Athena and Poppy boarded the boat quickly, scrambling in ungracefully as it rocked back and forth along the rocky shore of the river. Neither said a word as they struggled to regain their balance and sat curled up, each on either side of the double bench.

Athena looked up from her hunched-over pose to catch Poppy, blonde hair, and eyes bright in the sunlight, looking out onto the river with slow blinks as though she was still waking up. She was glowing, light freckles across her nose illuminating like starlight on her skin. Her eyes trailed down her neck and chest, rising and falling…

She peeled his eyes away and down to the bottom of the boat where two oars rested. It struck her as odd that the dock into the sea, the gardens, and not to mention *the vast estate,* were built here and immaculate, while this little boat looked as though Lady Rose had managed to cobble it together with her own old hands.

"Do you think this is water-ready?" Poppy asked, with a single brow raised.

Athena took in one final deep breath and then smiled at her. "Of course, I watched it float down here."

"Even with us in it, you think?" Poppy asked.

Athena looked away, but she let out a small chuckle. "Why are you so suddenly nervous about an adventure?"

"I only leap from seafaring ships," she declared boldly with a wave of her hand.

Athena's laugh only grew. She looked back into the treeline, and her face hardened a little. "Do you suppose Seppi and Willa are alright?"

Poppy's demeanor stayed bright. She rocked one of the boats a little with her body as if testing its water readiness still. "You underestimate the resilience of my cousin," she said. "She's a tenacious one. She'll keep Seppi safe."

Athena's eyes moved across Poppy's face as if she were trying to read a complicated text, noticing Poppy's expression mirror her face. They considered each other in silence, each seemingly waiting to see what the other would do or say first.

She had told Poppy that she didn't know her anymore. But maybe it was simpler than that. Perhaps they knew each other as well as they could, but they were both difficult to read.

"Shall we? "Athena broke the silence that lingered too long between them.

Poppy nodded. "We will see what we can see," she said.

"Any idea if we're looking for anything in particular?" Athena asked.

"Anything out of the ordinary that can be a cause of the illness," Poppy said back with a little shrug. "You're the scientist. You tell me."

"I'm afraid everything here is out of the ordinary..." Athena said. With a splash, she thrust the oar into the water and pushed off the shore.

Poppy's eyes softened. She looked up at the tall trees around them, their massive leaves swaying lightly in the breeze. "I keep thinking I will wake up someplace else," she said quietly. "That this will all be a dream and I'll be back at home."

"A dream or a nightmare?" Athena asked, a boldness rising from her chest.

Poppy glanced at Athena for a moment. "Both.'

Athena let out a snort. She wasn't sure Poppy had meant to be funny, but it was only then that he realized that she felt the same way. This was her dream made reality. She was accepted into a place where she had the chance to work with fantastical, long-dead creatures. She could create, to be part of something amazing, when all other avenues had been closed off to her. And yet... She focused on securing the oars to the sides of the boat when the current quickened. The smooth wood slipped from her hands quickly, the water whisking them away in a single blink.

Poppy stood up halfway; she leaned out of the boat. "The oars!" she cried, trying and failing to grab at them from the water's surface. But they were already so small, and getting smaller and smaller as the quick current pulled them farther away.

Athena watched helplessly as Poppy let out a heavy sigh and then slumped back onto the bench.

They were at the mercy of the river now. Just floating along, trying to find anything out of the ordinary until they washed up closer to shore.

Athena was starting to think this whole plan, minus the oars, was just to get the group away from Lady Rose so she could enjoy her solitude.

No, that was giving her too much credit. She was a scientist, not a nefarious mastermind. Right?

Athena was staring into the water. It was clear and vibrant. "Do you think we'll find schools of prehistoric fish, perhaps?" she thought aloud.

Poppy splashed her hand in the water. "That would certainly be unusual."

Athena grumbled a little to herself. She looked around the boat, searching for something to make this trip fruitful. As she neared the back of the ship, gazing into the bright water, a large turtle approached as if spawning from the river rock. "A turtle!" She pointed to it quickly.

Poppy moved cautiously from her side of the boat to the back. She leaned forward, her body crossing over Athena's to get a clearer view. She was so close that she could feel the heat of her radiating out, warmer than the sunlight on her skin.

Athena's jaw hardened. She leaned back a little to stare

instantly at the turtle to avoid looking at Poppy too closely, or putting a hand on the small of her back to stabilize her. Her nose and ears burned. She coughed a little. "It looks," she started, then swallowed. "It looks a bit large to be a turtle... of this time."

Poppy nodded, then lifted her body off Athena's. She sat beside her, eyes still following the turtle. "Yes, probably one of my aunt's," she said. "Do you think it has sharp teeth?"

Athena took a quick breath in. She held the side of the boat with one hand, hard. "Perhaps," she said, her voice rough like gravel. She tried to focus on the giant turtle, happily swimming now alongside the boat. She was a scholar, damn it. She should think like one.

She examined the creature, the way its body moved lazily under the gleaming water. It was a gorgeous green, speckled with deep moss and dark brown speckles over its massive, slow-moving fins. Its shell breached the water's surface. A hard shell with elegant hexagons layered upon itself like honeycombs glistened as beads of water raced down its back. It looked up at Athena with two black eyes, and she felt she had been discovered. It looked at her knowingly in a way she couldn't describe.

Poppy reached a hand down again into the water. She touched the turtle's front fin delicately, then looked up at Athena with a giggle already bursting from her lips. "It's soft! Do you want to try?"

Athena's throat tightened. She looked at Poppy now, her brilliant smile, the crinkles at the corners of her eyes, the light lashes almost invisible in the sunlight. "Yes," she choked out.

She grabbed Athena's hand quickly, and before she could

even register the fire that ignited at the touch, Poppy plunged their hands into the cold water.

"What–" Athena started, but then her hand reached the turtle fin and she stopped. Its skin was soft as velvet, sleek and cold. As it moved through the water, she could feel the ease with which it glided through the river, how it rode the current.

Poppy's hand was still on hers, holding her to the turtle with a kind gentleness in the cold. Her expression softened kindly, warmly, as though all of her previous worry and pain and heartache had washed away in the river. "This is magical," she whispered at last as Poppy removed her hand. Athena gave the turtle fin one last quick pet, then withdrew her hand from the water.

Pappy sat beside her, her wet hand still dripping diamonds, her nose a little red. Her eyes met Athena's, and the corners of her mouth turned up slightly. Her head lowered. "I thought scientists rejected magic?" she said with a warm smile.

"Well, on an island with dinosaurs, I suppose anything is possible," Athena said. She glanced down at Poppy's hands, noticing how they clenched on her lap. Her fingers wove into her dress as though she were afraid it would crumble on her.

A flutter in her stomach moved through her and out to every limb. Her fingers began to ache.

"Anything is possible," Poppy said with a smile.

As if summoned by a force outside their control, the boat ran ashore, jostling the two of them away from one another.

POPPY AND THE... SOMETHING MORE EXCITING THAN A GIANT TURTLE

They had hiked back to the estate in relative silence with Poppy counting her steps to keep her mind occupied on anything other than the way Athena had tended to her after their latest dinosaur run in. Forget the way it felt to sleep safely beside her in the sunlight and the way they had laughed together at nothing.

She focused on how she might write it down later. How could it be in her adventure serial when she returned home?

Perhaps she would embellish quite a bit. It wouldn't be a turtle. No, she could make it a swimming dinosaur chase sequence. One ending in the most spectacular drama. A capsized canoe. A heart-wrenching kiss shared between the leads.

She shook her head with her brows furrowing tightly. Athena had a way of distracting and igniting her. But now, she was proving just a massive distraction. Poppy needed to focus.

Yes, she had come here to go on an adventure, but she had also come to find answers. Her aunt was certainly up to something more, and she was going to find out. There was no way that this honey business alone was making her the money she seemed to have. No way she wasn't up to something that would ruin the family.

This dream was coming to an end, and Poppy was waking to a nightmare. Whether or not Poppy wanted it to end, the end was coming. She'd be back in London, working on her ladies' journal and married and bored.

Poppy was sure that something weird was going on, and it wasn't just the massive bees, the ancient creatures, or her ex, who had been curiously distant since the boat had deposited them back on solid land.

It was only a matter of time before the next boat came, and she couldn't just leap from that one, too.

As they approached the estate, her determination only grew. Her aunt was sending them on fool's errands, running about the island doing grunt work and getting into trouble. It was clear she wanted them gone, away from her and whatever strange happenings she got up to.

Poppy had a hunch. And she had to follow it.

Athena cast her a curious glance before she parted ways at the front door to sit beside her aunt, who was moving gently in the rocking chair on the patio, watching the small velociraptors chase pests from the garden.

"Finally," Aunt Rose called out from her perch. "Willa and Giuseppe have been back for hours."

Poppy smiled as best she could. "I'm tired," she told the two women. "Athena, can you fill Aunt Rose in on what we discovered?"

"Or didn't," Athena said as she settled into her rocking chair.

Poppy shrugged and slipped inside the house quickly.

She had already searched her aunt's room and Willa's to no avail. Now, it was time to get to the heart of the house, the sitting room. It would make sense, she thought, to hide something incriminating in plain sight...

It was fruitless.

Poppy looked under couch cushions, between the grates of the fireplace – what a silly thing to have in a climate like this–and in every decorative vase. But there was nothing. It was plain, boring, and a complete waste of time.

Poppy peeked out the window at her aunt and Athena. They seemed engrossed in their conversation. That seemed good. It would certainly make finding her workshop easier. She let the sheer curtains fall and sat on one of the couches with a huff.

Where did her aunt do all her ridiculous experiments anyway? She had to have a lab, or something...?

Poppy's eyes darted about the room. She looked over the layout of the estate in her mind's eye, starting by coming in through the front door, the long hallway, the sitting room, the kitchen, the dining room... Up the stairs and down the halls to various rooms. There was no door to a basement, at least, none she saw. And as she imagined the house from the outside, there was no room in the small attic to do work...

Poppy nearly sprang up from the couch; the realization made her feel incredibly stupid. *The outside of the house!* The outside seemed so impressively large, yet when they walked in, it was relatively small. At least, smaller than it would appear. There was a whole other wing of the home. Some sections she had yet to explore. Some part was hidden from her, though it was visible from the outside.

Poppy could scream, or cry. It was obvious now. And the constant barrage of dinosaurs and giant bees and, she had to admit, beautiful views unlike anything she had ever imagined, had undercut her ability to see what was right before her. For a moment, she considered burning all of her ladies' journals. She was a terrible journalist.

Poppy began to inspect the walls on the eastern side of the room. Somewhere here, most likely, would be an entrance to the hidden wing...

Her fingers grazed along the floral wallpaper with light touches, looking and feeling for any irregularity she could. She reached the fireplace and squinted at each brick. One, she thought, seemed out of place. They were all a little different from each other, but this one had a chip in the corner. She pressed on it, and the fireplace swung open.

Poppy gasped, but covered her mouth quickly. She turned around.

The hallway was still empty.

For now.

Poppy leaned into the darkness beyond the fireplace. She took a step in before she could think of anything else to do, and swung the fireplace back into its position.

Poppy was drenched in darkness. She reached out with her right hand, finding a cold wall with a delicate, raised texture like wallpaper. She took a careful step forward. Then another, and another, allowing her hand on the wall to guide her forward.

The hallway ended at a door. Wood, hard, and completely surprising. Poppy rubbed her forehead where she had hit it. She cursed herself for continuously being foolish today, but turned the knob nonetheless.

The door opened smoothly, and Poppy blinked into the light of the large room. Windows here, though covered by semi-sheer curtains, allowed sunlight into the room, illuminating the bizarre space before her.

There were long tables in neat rows throughout the space, which was big enough to be a ballroom. A chandelier hung on the ceiling, glass or crystals beaded down like vines, glittering in the sunlight. Her eyes followed it down to the center of the room, where a round table of test tubes and bottles full of colorful liquid spread about almost haphazardly. She was about to take out her notebook when a little voice from the corner of the room coughed.

Poppy spun to see her cousin standing in the corner with heavy gloves on and holding a basket full of eggs. She was staring at Poppy with wide eyes and her mouth slightly open. "What..." she started, then clutched the basket closer to her chest. "What are you doing here?"

"What are *you* doing here?" Poppy shot back. She stood tall and folded her arms across her chest. It was a bold move to act as though it was Willa who was at fault when she was the one who was meddling about, but it was her only option.

Willa snorted. "I live here. I work here. Poppy. How did you find this?"

Poppy tossed her head to one side. Her hair cascaded. "Why do you have a secret..." She stopped, looking around her quickly before she focused back on Willa. "What is this, exactly?"

Willa set her basket down gently. She pulled the gloves off and shook her head sadly. "This isn't my secret," she said. "It's my mother's laboratory. Where she creates the dinosaurs and the bees."

Poppy's eyes flicked to the eggs. "Are those...?"

Willa nodded. "New dinosaurs," she said. "And, really, Poppy, why am I telling any of this to you? What are you doing, prying around in here?"

Poppy raised a brow. She couldn't tell her the truth, but her lies were coming up empty. She looked around the room again, and Willa's gaze followed, as if she was trying to sort out what exactly Poppy was thinking. If only Poppy knew. "This must cost a fortune," was all she managed.

Willa crossed the room, her hands already shooing Poppy away as if she were a stray kitten. "You really must get out of here," she said. "You can contaminate the space."

Poppy's arms fell to her side. "Willa..."

"Poppy," Willa said, her tone uncharacteristically firm. She held Poppy's elbow and gently guided her to the door.

"You have seen the creatures here. You knew this was how it happened."

Poppy shook her head, but allowed herself to be removed from the space. What other secrets was this house hiding? She was determined to figure it out.

Chapter Thirty-Five

ATHENA IS HARD TO KILL

If Lady Rose had, in fact, tried to get Athena out of her way, Athena was determined to make her work harder. She wasn't just going to look and see what was happening and report back. She was going to observe, hypothesize, test, and retest as long as it took to get results.

After she had given Lady Rose her report of the sheer nothingness of their riverboat trip, the old woman scoffed, then said, "Well, go to the bees now."

And so she did.

Athena sat in the field of flowers by the large bee boxes with her pen tapping at her journal like the buzz of bumblebee wings. She watched a few fly free from the hive and make their way into the sky. She followed their pattern until they disappeared.

What was bothering them? She wrote in her journal, 'Climate? Predators? Parasites? Algae??' and with that, she tossed her journal aside. She had clearly been traumatized by the algae, and she still didn't even know why. What did Lady Rose want to accomplish with it, other than get her killed?

She sighed and pulled her knees up to her chest as a warm breeze blew.

From behind her, she heard the sound of rustling plants and small footsteps. "You're not afraid of the dinosaur herd?" Poppy asked.

Athena didn't look up. She only rested her head on her knees and glared at the hives. "I would think you'd have had enough of open fields for a lifetime," she retorted dryly.

Poppy shrugged and sat beside her. "I needed the fresh air, after being behind the fireplace for a while," she said softly.

Athena raised a brow. She side-eyed Poppy. "You what now?"

Poppy laughed, her head thrown back gently as she stretched her neck. "Oh good," she said. "Here I was, worried you knew about the secret tunnel and didn't tell me."

Athena's forehead creased. "Secret tunnel?"

Poppy rolled her neck. She turned to Athena with a wicked smile. "Secret tunnel," she said. "My aunt has a laboratory on the estate. She's hatching new dinosaurs as we speak."

Athena perked up. She looked behind her as if she could see any of it from there. "I want to see the secret laboratory!"

Poppy shrugged, lifting her head at last to stare into the open field where the massive bee boxes were lined up like houses. "I'll show you," she said. "When no one is looking."

Athena turned back to her. She leaned forward, excited. But a part of her held back. If Lady Rose caught her sneaking about, especially around dinosaur eggs, she was sure it would ruin any goodwill she had built up with her. She sighed, hating herself as she spoke, "Actually, no. She'll show me when she's ready."

Poppy's expression shifted from mischievous to worried. "What? That's not like you."

Athena flinched. "You wouldn't know," she said. "You haven't known me for years." Her heart began to pound as she spoke, her words pouring from her before she could wrestle them back.

"You were the one who left," Poppy said. "*You* left *me*."

Athena breathed out. She stretched her legs out. They itched to move, to flee. "I left to study, it was you who said we should end things."

"Because you refused to hear anything about me coming with you," Poppy said quickly. "Because you—"

"You would have what?" Athena cut her off. "Left your family? Your sister? Your wealth?"

Poppy grimaced. She leaned back like Athena was a dangerous snake. "Yes. Not forever, but yes."

Athena shook her head. "Until you got bored with me, that is."

Poppy closed the space between them. "I could never."

Athena rolled her eyes. She knew it was a childish gesture, a false bravado when the reality was that it hurt. She ached at the old memories of their breakup, the stinging words they had pierced one another with. They had been young and stupid and–

"Look at me," Poppy said, her voice a command that Athena could not help but follow.

Their eyes met, and Poppy's gaze burned into Athena's core. "We were young and foolish then. We're young and foolish now. Just trying our best."

"What is our best?" Athena asked, the pain evident in her voice.

"This," Poppy said softly. She reached a hand to Athena's cheek, cupping it delicately in her palm.

A fire burst from Poppy's fingers, lighting everything in Athena from within. She searched Poppy's blue-green eyes for an answer, but none came. Instead, Poppy leaned forward and pressed her lips to Athena's.

Athena reached for Poppy, her hand wrapping shakily around her waist. As soon as her fingers touched the fabric and traced the curve of Poppy's hips, she heard a low moan escape her. Her whole body was alive, bursting with light. She pulled Poppy in close, hard.

Poppy fell onto Athena, tipping them both into the wildflowers. Poppy's soft lips parted as she found Athena's hands on her hips. She laced her fingers in hers and pressed them over Athena's head and into the cold earth. "Athena," she breathed. "Athena..."

Athena waited, panting and heart pounding. She couldn't find the words; her mind was full of bright sparks and fire. She gripped Poppy's hand tighter as Poppy leaned back down again, her lips finding Athena's again.

She let her hands go, tangling one in her hair and the other around Athena's neck. Poppy cradled the back of her neck in her hand, pulling her closer.

"Wait," Athena breathed. Her voice was rough, strained. The word came out before she could think, before she could even register that she had wanted it to escape. She wanted more than anything to pull it back, bury it within her, and never let it out again. She wanted to say, 'more.' But she couldn't.

This wasn't right. It wasn't fair. And she couldn't hurt Seppi, not like this.

"Giuseppe," she said sadly. She bit her lip as soon as the words came out.

Poppy sat up. Her hands fell to her sides. "I love him, Athena," she whispered.

"I know," Athena said. She pushed herself up to look Poppy in the eyes. "I know—"

"I love him the way I love my brother," Poppy said before Athena could speak another word. "And he loves me. The way he loves you."

A crease formed between Athena's brows. "You what?"

Poppy shook her head. She drew in an uneasy breath through trembling lips. "The engagement? It's fake. A way of buying time from our ridiculous families."

Athena was still; she couldn't understand what she was hearing.

"Does Seppi know about us?" Poppy asked.

Athena shook her head. "No one does... No one did."

Poppy nodded. "I thought as much," she said with a small smile. "When he approached me about this idea, I thought, no matter how close you two were, you must not have told him about us."

"That's the way you wanted it."

"I know," Poppy whispered. "I couldn't tell him. I didn't want to damage your relationship. It seems silly now. When dinosaurs are roaming the Earth. Everything does, doesn't it?"

"You weren't going to get married?" Athena asked, cutting back to the heart of it.

"Not at first," Poppy said. "But... Well, we didn't realize things were so dire in my family's business. Or in yours. Once we announced it, as merely a way to avoid other prospects, the families took over. We haven't had much time together to find a way out. But I know he wants out of it, too."

Athena let out a heavy breath.

A cloud passed by, drenching them in shadow. A chill crept up her arms.

"I love Seppi, I really do. Just not the way I love you. And I know he feels the same for me."

"All this time?"

Poppy looked down at her hands in her lap. Her fingers twitched. "If I could go back and do it all again..." She paused, her eyes closed. "I'd do it again. It was the best choice in a bad situation, for both of us. I do believe that....

But this time, I'd be honest with you right away. When I saw you, it threw my whole world off center. I didn't know what to do."

Athena shook her head slowly. "I just..." She pushed herself up onto unsteady feet. "I need to talk with Seppi."

"I understand," Poppy said. "Please. Just be honest with him."

ATHENA AND SEPPI COME CLEAN

Athena found Seppi in his room. He was sitting on his bed, petting Beatrice, who was curled up on his pillow. His bed was made, his comforter crisp, but for the slight indentation where he had sat. Athena always admired how tidy he managed to be, even here.

She knocked lightly on the door, her knuckles aching as though she had punched the hardwood; the sound was like a heavy drum in her ears. Her heart skipped a beat when Seppi looked up with a warm smile already.

"Can I come in?" Athena asked.

Seppi waved her in, giving Beatrice one final pat before he covered her with a little handkerchief.

Athena slipped into the room, closing the door behind her. It felt like closing the door to a cage. But she knew she had to be brave.

Seppi cocked his head slightly, dark curls spilling into his eyes. He pushed his hair back and waited.

Athena sat beside him on the bed. She avoided his gaze, fixing her stare instead on the window on the opposite wall. She watched the leaves from the trees outside shift slowly and gently in the wind. For a moment, she considered opening the window and jumping out.

Instead, she breathed out her anxiety and said, "Poppy told me about your engagement."

Seppi's hands laced together in his lap, his shoulder slumped, and he followed her stare to the window.

"Do you want to marry her?"

Seppi inhaled deeply, his whole body shifted as he drew in the heavy air between them. "No," he said softly. "Poppy and I became closer after you left for a time. And when it came time for us to consider our prospects. Well, it seemed like an easy understanding." He sighed, his shoulders turning inward as he did. "Are you angry with me?"

Athena shook her head.

The bed shifted slightly as Seppi turned to face Athena at last. He looked lost, his eyes searched her face for any clues.

Athena caught his gaze and in an instant, as though she were a little kid and she had just found him after getting in trouble yet again, tears burst from her eyes. She pushed them away roughly with the back of her hands, taking in a shaking breath to try to combat the overwhelming emotions that raced through her and out of her eyes.

"You love her?" he asked.

Athena nodded.

Seppi smiled, though his eyes looked devastated. "I thought maybe," he said. He reached a hand to Athena and squeezed hers gently. "Poppy never said as much, but I had my suspicions."

Athena smiled back, relief flooded through every muscle. She could sink into him and cry it all out. But instead, she heard a laugh break from her lips. "How?"

Seppi's smile widened. "Oh, Athena, you're not exactly subtle."

Athena squeezed his hand back. "What are we going to do?"

Her cousin shrugged. "We'll call it off," he said. "We'll find a way out."

"Easier said than done with Lady Elizabeth involved."

Seppi cocked his head to Beatrice. "Athena, in a world with dinosaurs, I would like to think anything is possible."

Athena snorted. She had said something similar earlier. She was starting to believe it was true. She wasn't sure how, but things would get better from here.

"I'll talk with Poppy," Seppi said. "Don't underestimate the creativity of an artist and a journalist. We will find a way."

Chapter Thirty-Seven

ATHENA AND THE KNOCK AT THE DOOR AT NIGHT ON AN ABANDONED ISLAND

Athena was sure that there was nothing more terrifying than hearing a knock on the front door at night on an island with only five people, all of whom were accounted for. And she had recently been chased by giant monsters and discovered that her ex and cousin were *not* in love. Both of which were horrifying in their own unique and terrible ways.

Willa looked up from the couch, eyes round. She held Beatrice closer to her chest.

The knock came again, this time more insistent.

"This is going to sound strange, but you weren't expecting anyone, were you?" Athena asked.

Willa shook her head slowly. "The next shipping boat isn't supposed to arrive for a while," she whispered. She looked up at the ceiling. "Everyone is home, right?"

Athena nodded. She rose and held her hand out to indicate for Willa to wait silently. She looked to the darkened hallway and then peeked back at Willa.

Willa tucked Beatrice into her arms, hiding her in the folds of her long dress, and Athena moved into the hallway and toward the front door. Each movement was slow and quiet. From behind her, she heard Seppi's voice from the stairs. "Did you hear that?" he whispered.

Athena narrowed her eyes at him.

The knock came again, and from behind Seppi, Poppy appeared. "Who on all of earth?" she said, louder than any of them. She cringed a little when Athena shot her a stern look.

But it was Lady Rose who pushed past both of them on the narrow staircase, already shouting wildly with her oil lamp held aloft. "What is all this commotion?"

She moved past Athena with a speed the younger woman had not seen in her since they arrived on the island. The old woman threw open the front door just as the tall, old man was raising his fist again to knock on the door.

"Where is your calling card?" Lady Rose asked, hand still on the door as if she was about to slam it in his face.

"My apologies for the uncouth behavior," he said. "But it is dark, and there appears to be a large reptile lurking in the jungle here."

His voice was familiar. Athena raised her chin to get a better look at him in the dim lamp light. Her limbs went almost immediately numb as her blood turned to ice.

She stared at her grandfather in the doorway with what she only assumed was a dumbfounded expression. She blinked, then turned to Seppi, who was staring with the same shocked look on his face.

Lady Rose lifted the lamp to his face, illuminating his deep wrinkles, strong brows, and silver hair in the dim orange light. He smiled at her, but it didn't quite reach his eyes.

"Lord Artis?" Lady Rose said as she moved her lamp back away from his face.

"It's been a long time," he said warmly, despite his ghastly appearance. Their grandfather's dark gaze lifted to them, and he held up a Seppi's sketchbook. "Will you let me in?"

Athena's mind clamored for a quick solution. She envisioned herself moving past Lady Rose and slamming the door, locking it swiftly, and pretending that she had never seen him. He could knock all night. It didn't mean they had to open the door.

She could run past him and take her chances with the dinosaurs outside. It was likely that most of them were asleep anyway. She could climb a tree, perhaps, and camp there overnight.

But what she wanted to do more than anything was grab Seppi's sketchbook and rip it into pieces, then hit him with whatever remained.

Instead of any of that, she and the rest of the group all parted so he could enter. He tipped his head and tucked the sketchbook under his arm. "I will admit," he said, "I was not sure if these drawings of yours, Giuseppe, were an indication of you going mad after being away from societal comforts. But, then again, you never could draw anything you couldn't see. That always was the notes your tutors gave, was it not?"

No one answered. Instead, Lady Rose guided him to the sitting room where Willa waited.

The old man stopped and smiled. "Ah, and this must be your lovely daughter," he said, casting a quick glance at Lady Rose before he entered the room. He smiled at Willa and bowed low. "Good evening, miss," he said. "Forgive the lateness of my arrival. I understand this must be an inconvenience for a young miss such as yourself."

Willa nodded her head to him, though her expression remained one of shock.

Their grandfather went on, seemingly completely unfazed by the confusion he ignited, "I am delighted to meet you. Your beauty exceeds my grandson's drawings."

"I did not get your name," Willa said, her voice striking Athena as more confident than she probably felt. Perhaps she had finally reached her threshold with their family and all their oddities.

"Lord Artis," he said with another slight bow. He turned to Lady Rose and nodded his head carefully. "I am afraid my grandchildren have also inconvenienced you, Lady Rose. They were supposed to return home sooner than this. Along with your niece." His eyes shifted to Poppy, who had just crossed the threshold of the room silently. She held her arms around her waist, though her smile was mischievous.

"Good evening, Lord Artis," she said as her smile grew. "I take it my mother sent you?"

"If you want anything done properly," he said, "you must do it yourself. I never should have left such a task to my grandchildren. They still act like children despite their ages, it would seem."

Athena's wrists flared hot, her heart thudded against her ribs. A child. She would always be a child to him, regardless of her age or accomplishments. He treated every woman like a child and called it chivalry.

"Besides," he went on, "I had to see for myself what kind of beasts lived on this island..."

Lady Rose huffed.

"Should the honey business go under, this island would be an excellent opportunity to keep the family afloat," he said, largely ignoring the increasing tension in the room. His eyes found Lady Rose, his gaze a challenge. "I have heard excellent things about the Ménagerie du Jardin des Plantes in France. So many incredible exotic animals on display. Imagine what we could do here."

"They don't charge," Athena cut in, her voice stern.

Her grandfather's gaze shifted to her.

She squared her shoulders back, standing taller.

"But they don't have ancient beasts, now do they?" he said back with annoying dispassion.

"And the tea business?" Poppy asked quickly, a clear attempt to save Athena from further confrontation.

Athena's jaw tightened, but still, a bit of affection crept up her chest, quieting her racing heart. It was a kind thing Poppy did by refocusing his attention on her. She always was so confident, while Athena, for all her bravado, was all bark.

"Whose capable hands are you entrusting it to in your absence?" Poppy went on, freeing Athena's thoughts back to the present.

Lord Artis chuckled. He gestured for the couch opposite Willa. "May I sit?" he asked, ignoring Poppy. "It was a long and difficult walk from the pier."

Lady Rose indicated for him to sit, though she remained standing. "And your crew?" she asked. Athena noticed her eyes descend onto Seppi's sketchbook. The color in her cheeks faded a little. "I assume you have met Francesca," she said at last.

"And I assume you mean the long-necked lizard?" Lord Artis asked. He settled into the couch in a way almost unbecoming. "Tell me, how do the two ladies such as yourselves live on an island of giant beasts?"

Lady Rose's stare hardened. Her eyes shifted, briefly, to the fireplace. "We manage," she said. "You've come to take the children home, then. Have them." She changed the subject quickly.

"No need for such haste, there is little that can be accomplished tonight," he said. He leaned back further into the couch, a nonchalant gesture that indicated he planned to stay a while. He went on, "The family, as I'm sure you are aware, is ready to have their marriage solidified. Almost too eager, don't you agree? I will admit my curiosity was piqued when I saw the latest honey shipment. Exclusive, is it?"

Lady Rose nodded.

"And limited," the lord said as one of his brows quirked up. "You know, when our tea crop is diseased, or the harvest provides less than we anticipated, we also call our blends 'exclusive'. It is a good marketing strategy in hard times."

"We're not in hard times," Lady Rose said.

Athena took a deep breath. She stood beside Lady Rose. "Grandfather," she said, her voice clear and bold, "Who else is on the island with you?"

He looked at her and smiled the same wolfish grin. "My men are still on the ship, save the melittologist I hired, who should be here any moment," he said.

"I assure you, we have no need for a melittologist here," Lady Rose said quickly.

"I'm afraid I must insist," Lord Artis said. "Excuse my curtness. It was late when we came into sight of the island, though I could not delay my arrival. It would be bad manners to arrive without notifying the esteemed ladies of the house of my presence, of course."

"You've made yourself known. Might I suggest we return to the ship now?" Athena said, trying to walk the line between polite and firm. Her gaze passed over Poppy and Seppi quickly. "It's not as though they have much to pack, and I see you are also with just the clothes on your back."

Poppy's smile faded. She stared back at Athena with an icy stare. A prickling chill crawled up Athena's back. She looked away from her but could not peel the feeling of the cold stare from her.

Her grandfather tapped the arm of the couch. He looked at Willa, then down at Beatrice, whose head appeared below her elbow. "What a curious creature," he said, leaning in slightly to catch a better look in the low firelight.

Poppy scoffed, clearly unable to be ignored any longer

now that Athena had turned away from her. "I am not leaving," she said.

"Yes, I heard about your *little leap*," he said. "A reckless move, Lady Poppy."

Seppi moved to stand closer to her. He looked at Athena with pleading eyes.

Athena didn't meet his gaze.

"Grandfather," he said at last, "I will return with you at once, but I am afraid the engagement is off."

Athena felt as though the floor had suddenly shifted. Her eyes darted from Seppi to Poppy, analyzing every minute change in expression. But both looked at her grandfather with conviction, neither of them seemed surprised at his announcement. She wondered if they had been upstairs, talking about this very subject when he arrived. Her chest expanded for the first time in a long time. She took a deep breath.

Lord Artis held a finger to his strong chin and tapped it carefully as though considering what he was just told. "You and your fiancé made a promise," he said at last, eyes landing on Seppi with that same cold, hard look. "I think marrying for love is quite old-fashioned. It is what those beneath us do. You will grow in affection for each other."

"Grandfather, they are not ready to be married," Athena said. A fire ignited in her heart. She wasn't sure what any of it meant or where she stood, but she knew she could be bold and honest. If anywhere, it would be here, now.

"No," he said carefully. "No, not yet. I plan to stay here, on the island, for a bit longer. I have a vested interest in the production of honey here. And Lady Elizabeth is quite upset that the inventory is in decline." He looked up at

Poppy, who was leaning, rather ungracefully, on the wall by the window. He looked her up and down as if assessing if she was worthy through some unknowable metric. "Anthony and I will determine if the apiary needs to be under alternative management, then we will depart." He looked back at Seppi, whose shoulders slumped in turn. "You will be ready to be married then."

It sounded like a threat.

But their grandfather only smiled back. "It is late. I will return to my quarters aboard the ship," he said, rising from his seat. He bowed politely to Willa, then Lady Rose. "So long as the path is clear. I find it curious that my melittologist has yet to arrive."

Lady Rose nodded back. "The creatures are mostly active at dawn and dusk," she said. "He must have gotten lost."

"Very well," he said. "My group of men is awaiting me. Now that I've found your humble residence, I must not delay my return to them. In the morning, I'll introduce you to Anthony. He should be able to get these failing hives back to adequate production levels."

No one spoke. The air was heavy, and Athena wanted to scream.

Lady Rose showed him out, and as soon as the front door clicked shut, she turned on the group with fury in her eyes. "Lord. Artis." She spat his name like it was poison. "You people have brought me nothing but discomfort since your arrival. Now this? I'm going to bed, and you all better find a way to fix this before dawn!" She stormed up the stairs with surprisingly heavy steps. Each one hit her like a small punch to the chest.

Athena winced when she heard a door slam.

Willa sighed. She held Beatrice closer. "We've worked hard to keep this island safe," she said sadly. "I'm worried."

Seppi crossed the floor to sit beside her. "It's going to be alright," he said. "I'll leave with him first thing in the morning."

Athena let out a sigh. "No, Seppi," she said. "You know grandfather. If he believes something strange is going on this island, especially if it will damage the partnership between the honey and tea businesses, he will stay until he gets to the bottom of it."

"I don't like the sound of this, Anthony," Seppi agreed. "Grandfather always surrounds himself with men who only agree with him. I doubt the man will be able to help prehistoric bees."

Athena nodded. Her body was heavy. "And you heard him talk about making money off this island. In the morning, when he sees all the dinosaurs, I'm afraid it will be nearly impossible to convince him that this isn't something he ought to take... By force, if necessary."

Seppi shook his head. He looked at his feet. "I never should have drawn a thing," he said.

Poppy spoke up, this time, her voice was angry, "This whole thing is a mess. I'm just glad my mother isn't here. Yet."

Athena's eyes caught hers. *At least there was that*, she thought.

POPPY KNOWS A LOT ABOUT A LOT

Poppy was up before everyone else. She threw on a dress and shawl quickly, tying her hair up as best she could with the black ribbon her cousin had loaned her. She blinked out into the pale morning light through her window, determined to come up with a plan to keep herself from being forcibly removed from the island.

She still had work to do. Perhaps even more now that Lord Artis was there. He had Seppi's notebook, he had seen Francesca, yet he seemed peculiarly unaffected by the discovery. He was up to something, and if she knew anything about him from the stories Athena had told, and his reputation as a vicious businessman, she knew it was something terribly... *not good.*

She crept out from her room, carefully closing the door silently behind her. She turned and ran straight into Athena.

Athena held her shoulders with her strong hands as Poppy bounced off her with unsteady feet. She looked down at Poppy with an expression as cold as the morning itself. "What are you doing up so early?" she asked, though it sounded like an accusation.

Poppy smiled brightly. If Athena were a cold morning, Poppy would have to be the sun. "I'm going to go see the ship," she said truthfully. "Want to come?"

Athena grimaced. "I want to be nowhere near that ship," she whispered back. "But I'll go with you."

"My hero," Poppy said with a sweet smile, though her tone was cutting. "Come on, two sets of eyes are better than one."

They left the estate with quiet steps, though small, ungraceful footsteps followed. Reggie chased after them as soon as the gate to the jungle opened.

Poppy turned to the little T-Rex and shooed him away. "Not now, Reggie," she hissed. "Go back and make eggs or whatever it is you do in the mornings."

Athena huffed a little. She turned to Reggie, squatted down, and patted his head twice. "Not this time, my friend," she said. "Go on now." She pointed back to the estate.

A bellow echoed in the trees. Francesca, with long lashes and a scaly face, descended from the treetops. She nudged at Poppy's shoulder with her chin. "All of you have decided to be so needful today," Poppy said as she scratched under Francesca's chin. She watched as Reggie, at least, hustled his plump little body back up the steps of the porch.

Athena was smiling at him, soft and warm. A smile Poppy felt like she hadn't seen in a long, long time. "You have a soft spot for him," she said with a slight giggle. She pushed Francesca's face away as best she could.

The dinosaur snorted, making her curls fly into her face.

Athena turned to her and moved a lock of hair from Poppy's cheek with gentle fingers. The spark of her touch on Poppy's face rushed to every part of her.

She turned away. She was still angry. Angry that Athena had not understood her predicament. Angry that Athena had agreed to let her go.

She decided it was better to say nothing for now. There was no fixing this. The space between them pushed and pulled like tides, and now, it was low. They were far apart, and the only thing to do was focus on the problem ahead of them and wait for the moon to pull them back.

She squared her shoulders and focused on the dense jungle ahead. The best thing she could do was move forward, into the deep unknown, and hope that maybe a giant swimming dinosaur would come up from the sea and swallow the boat.

She sighed, looking up at Francesca as she retreated into the thick leaves. She could hope, right?

"Come along," Poppy said, gesturing with a tilt of her head for Athena to follow her deeper into the trees.

Athena did, and the two walked in silence until they reached the shore and the sun began to crest over the horizon, illuminating the small offshore ship in blinding pastel and golden light.

The two waited, squinting into the sun for a long while.

"What did you hope to accomplish here?" Athena asked as she leaned in closer to Poppy, who was staring at the ship with narrowed eyes.

Poppy glanced at her, and her cheeks immediately flushed hot at their proximity. "I'm willing a sea-beast to rise from the depths and overtake the ship," she said, half-jokingly. She turned her attention back to the ship. "No, Athena, I'm trying to see what kind of vessel it is. I read quite a bit when I was preparing to come here, you know."

Athena hummed. Her body shifted away from Poppy, and her sudden absence left Poppy cold.

Poppy did her best to ignore it. She rummaged through her overpacked saddle bag, pulling out a compacted spyglass she had retrieved from her aunt's desk. She extended it and held it up to her eye in what she hoped looked like a confident motion.

She closed one eye and focused on the ship through the spyglass, examining the boat for any telling features.

At first glance, the ship looked just as any other did, sails were lowered, the dark hull covered in weathered wood as if it wanted to blend into the sea at night. The merchant ships she had read about, however, didn't usually have as many sails. No, this one seemed like it was made for traveling at a higher speed when it caught the wind. Why would it need to go so fast? The extra sails would be a burden under most circumstances.

She moved the spyglass down the ship, and she noticed it also appeared strangely well armed for the shorter journey. It was only a week or so, winds allowing, trip. These waters weren't known for their dangers. Still, rows of cannons were visible along its side.

Poppy handed the instrument to Athena quickly. She nodded for her to have a look.

Athena drew the spyglass to one eye with a swift movement, and her shoulders moved forward a little, giving her a better view.

Poppy put a hand to her abdomen as a little twist in her stomach, like a creature squirming within, made her jittery. Athena always seemed so confident. Decisive. Even the simple movement, the way her body leaned into it, the tilt of her chin, it all looked practiced as though she had been on this shore doing this exact thing a thousand times.

The sun rose quickly now, basking Athena in the golden glow. Her dark hair waved around her shoulders like water. In the sunlight, it was tinted just a little red. Her skin was warm, and even her clothes, an open muslin top moving down to her fitted skirt, shone flawlessly in the morning light.

Poppy forced her eyes away just as Athena lowered the spyglass. The other woman handed it back to her, and she took it while avoiding eye contact.

"I would like to think I'm intelligent," Athena said, an earnestness to her tone. "But I have to admit, I have no idea what I'm looking at there."

Despite herself, Poppy smiled. She side-eyed Athena, then folded the spyglass back into her bag. "The ship has more sails than most of its size," Poppy explained.

Athena nodded. "Which means it can go faster."

"And the hull is a very dark wood."

Athena's head tilted. Her eyes flicked upward, thinking. "So it can blend into dark waters?"

"Did you see a flag raised?" Poppy asked with a raise of her brow.

Athena shook her head. "No," she said slowly as though it just occurred to her to look. She snapped her fingers. "Pirates!"

"Pirates," Poppy parroted.

"Poppy, you're brilliant!"

Poppy laughed. She hadn't seen Athena this excited about something in what felt like a very long while. The woman's usually stern face was bright, crinkles formed at the corners of her eyes, and her large smile was genuine. She really did think Poppy had done good work.

Poppy beamed back just as the realization that the ship just offshore was potentially incredibly dangerous truly sank in. "Your grandfather," she said quietly. Though it broke Poppy's heart to see Athena's face turn to stone once again, she had to ask. Her words left her. What was there to say? *Would your grandfather really hire pirates? What kind of people does he do business with? Do you think your grandfather was once a pirate?* Each question that raced through her mind sounded more ludicrous and offensive than the last. Finally, she began, "Do you think he would...?"

Athena's mouth curled to a snarl. "He would," she said through gritted teeth. "I can't say he knows the extent of the trouble he might get himself into. But he would hire the fastest ship that consented to bring him. And... probably not ask too many inconvenient questions."

"What do we do?" Poppy asked.

Athena shook her head. "We tell him the truth. That

your engagement to Seppi was false, and you have changed your mind. We find a way to make him leave."

Poppy's brows furrowed. All she wanted to do was throw herself into Athena's arms and beg her not to let her leave. To ask that they chain themselves to a column of the estate, and vow never to be parted again.

But though Athena's conviction brought her some peace, she didn't know how much of it was loyalty to her aunt, the dinosaurs, or just being vindictive against her trifling grandparent. She bit her bottom lip as she tried to puzzle it out.

It was no use.

Athena was going to do what she wanted to do for the reasons she wanted to. There was no sense in trying to decipher her intentions. Not now, at least. Now, they needed to be on high alert. And focused.

"Should we tell my aunt?" Poppy asked at last.

Athena turned back toward the forest. She glanced at Poppy from over her shoulder. "I'm tired of hiding things, Poppy. I think we should tell everyone everything. When the opportunity arises."

Poppy's frown deepened. She wasn't quite sure what that meant. And a stab of guilt hit her in the chest. Poppy knew she was tired of hiding, too. But she also knew she'd keep some of her secrets close all the same.

ATHENA WILL PROTECT THE DINOSAURS

Athena liked to consider herself an honest person. And perhaps that was the problem. She had found in her travels that most people did not like honesty. People especially disliked an honest woman.

Would it be the same here? She knew Seppi could handle it, but she still felt as though Willa was a stranger and Lady Rose was really more of a boss than a friend.

When they arrived back at the estate, Lady Rose was already giving her orders about tending to the bees, checking on the pterodactyl population, and fetching eggs from the velociraptor coop as a boss would.

Athena held up her hands to quiet the lady, but the old woman was too busy putting on a shawl and a large hat to notice. "Lady Rose," Athena began.

"Auntie," Poppy pleaded over her.

Lady Rose huffed at them. "You people got us into this mess," she said sternly from the steps of the porch. "Now I have to go and tidy it up. Unreasonable."

"We are attempting to elaborate on our explanation. There are new developments," Poppy said quickly. "Lord Artis, he's—"

"I do not care what he is doing or what he wants, so long as it's not my dinosaurs. I'm going to take an inventory. Make sure they're all safe." Lady Rose glared at Poppy.

Athena felt the sting as if it were directed at her.

And just like that, Lady Rose's hard stare found Athena's. "Bees, first," she ordered. "Once you leave, I'll not have any other scientist to talk to on the matter."

A mixture of pride and pain welled up in Athena's chest. A scientist? She had never heard that term directed at her. But she also wanted to grab Lady Rose by the shoulders and shake her until she was ready to listen. She knew it wouldn't help, but it would probably feel good.

Poppy threw her hands up, nearly growling in frustration.

Athena glanced at her, a sadness etched into her face.

People didn't tend to like honesty. In this case, Lady Rose simply didn't seem to care, and Poppy seemed like she hadn't learned the hard lesson yet.

Lady Rose moved past them, the white wooden gate

swinging wildly behind her with a few loud bangs as she disappeared into the trees.

Poppy looked at Athena. "Can you believe that?" she scoffed and folded her arms across her chest. "Why wouldn't she listen?"

"She's in distress," Athena said. She led the way to the house just as a group of tiny velociraptors in their matching hats ran by. She stepped over them. They didn't seem to mind or notice her. "Her priority is her creations; you can't exactly fault her for that." It was the truth, or a part of the truth. But the harsher one was that she knew Lady Rose didn't respect either of them all that much. Especially not Poppy. "Come on, let's tell the rest of them what's going on."

*A*thena stared at Seppi as they all sat in the drawing room. He was in a state of undress, his usual jacket and vest removed. As if that was not shocking enough, he had purple half-moons under his eyes, and his hair was slightly disheveled, as if he had only run some fingers through it and decided that was good enough to be presentable.

Beside him, Willa seemed to watch him carefully from the corner of her eyes.

Poppy started, luckily, so Athena didn't have to. "Athena and I spotted Lord Artis' ship just offshore. We can't be positive, but it does look like it may be a pirate ship."

"Pirates?" Willa gasped.

"Indeed," Poppy said, tilting her chin up.

"Certainly not." Willa turned to Seppi. "Lord Artis is a

reputable man, the founder of one of the biggest tea empires in London. Surely he wouldn't risk all that to consort with pirates?"

Seppi hung his head. He looked at Athena like a dog that had been badly neglected. "Athena, is this true?"

Athena nodded. She addressed Willa, mostly, "Our grandfather is a respectable man, certainly. However, that standard varies depending on who you ask. There's a reason the family business has been a success despite the heavy and longstanding competition. He's a ruthless businessman. And I am afraid to say that it's something we've benefited from."

Willa and Seppi both sighed.

"It's possible that the intent is not as nefarious as the pirates would indicate," Athena said quickly. "He may be focused on his business success, but I genuinely don't think he would, knowingly, agree to travel with pirates. He may have wanted to travel quickly, to get the marriage underway, especially if Lady Elizabeth is so set on it. I hypothesize that he didn't ask the right questions."

Seppi shook his head. "Two businesses on the brink of disaster. Of course, they want us to partner quickly."

Willa dotted one eye with her fingertip. Though to clear away the sleep or a tear, Athena wasn't quite sure. "What will we do?" she asked, her voice quivering.

A knock on the door alerted them to the man's presence. He was quick for an old man; Athena had to give him that. She looked each of them in the eye for a moment before she turned to the hallway. "We tell the truth," she said.

. . .

*H*er grandfather, in the morning light, was much less sinister-looking. Athena noticed that he was rather handsome, in a stern kind of way. He moved with ease despite his years and was polite, though his eyes always seemed like those of a fox looking for its next opportunity, even when he smiled.

And if he was a fox, then on this side cowered a shaking rabbit. The melittologist, Athena assumed, was a small man. At least, he slumped his shoulders and tilted his neck down so he looked smaller, as though he was camouflaging himself. His hands were hidden in his pockets, and he looked at Athena with a difficult-to-read expression.

"Good morning," Athena said with a tilt of her head. She tried to appear confident and capable.

Lord Artis gestured to the man beside him. "This is Anthony. He has come to assess the hives."

Athena looked him up and down. But under her stare, he straightened and stood broader. So he shrank in the presence of men but was emboldened near her? She grimaced in return. "The bee expert," she said with a dismissive hand wave.

"Athena, where are your manners?" her grandfather said. "He is here to do what everyone on this island has failed to do."

A prickle ran down Athena's back just as Seppi stood beside her in the doorway.

"Grandfather, welcome," he said, far too cheerfully for Athena's taste. She could sense the falseness dripping from his mouth, and it made her bristle all the more. "We will take you to the hives. Won't we, Athena?"

Athena drew in a deep breath through her nose. "Of course," she said through gritted teeth. Her eyes narrowed as she side-eyed him. He had a plan. Right? She pushed past both her grandfather and the so-called bee expert with Seppi's quick footsteps following close behind her.

"It'll be fine," Seppi whispered when he caught up to her.

Athena glanced back to see her grandfather and Anthony trailing behind at a distance. Anthony's head was on a swivel, moving all around as they entered the jungle path. She almost felt a bit sorry for him. Almost.

She turned back to Seppi and glared at him. "I can figure this out myself," she hissed back. "I don't need anyone else."

"Even if it would be a help?" Seppi asked.

Athena thrust her head up and quickened her pace.

Seppi was quick to match her speed. "Athena, all I'm saying is that this buys us all some time. If he's worried about the bees and honey, he will not be bothersome about the dinosaurs."

"He *can* multitask," Athena said as the path narrowed. She looked back to see the two figures coming closer. Her grandfather was surprisingly fast for his age. "Enough of this. They're catching up."

The group entered a clearing where the giant beehives were lined in rows.

As far as Athena knew, her grandfather, though scholarly in his own right, knew nothing about bees. So to watch him inspecting the box hives as though he knew what he was actually looking at almost made her laugh. If she wasn't so upset by nearly every development since his arrival, that is.

His posture straightened as a bee flew by. He looked at it with marvel, though, if it was from the large bee itself or the realization that this was what set the Fletcher honey apart, Athena wasn't sure. He turned to Athena and said, "What an odd island it is here."

"Yes," Athena said. She kept her answers short with him, as she always had.

"And does Lady Rose have any reason to believe these strange bees will continue to decline in their honey production?" he asked.

Athena's eyes narrowed slightly. "I am working with Lady Rose on a solution. As of now, we have yet to uncover the mystery behind the decline."

Her grandfather nodded. "Yes, I highly doubt women would be able to determine the cause," he said. It came out effortlessly. Simply. He believed it, and always had. "Anthony, what are your initial impressions?"

Anthony hurried to his side. He has been busy gawking at the massive hives. "It's difficult to say," he said. "These bees are... unlike anything I have ever experienced. Do we know how they came to be so massive?"

Athena's left hand clenched.

"It's beyond me," Seppi answered for both of them.

Her grandfather's eyes shifted down to her fist. "You need a true scholar to understand the situation and make the necessary recommendations. This honey is one of a kind, and I see why now." His eyes moved back to Athena's stern face. "Good thing I am here. Anthony, too," he added as an afterthought.

Athena sucked in a bit of breath. She had to try not to yell at him. It would make her feel better, but only in the short term. She had gotten into verbal spars with him and never prevailed.

Instead, she released her fingers and said, "Grandfather, I have done a lot of good on this island already. And Lady Rose is brilliant. We can solve this ourselves."

"I am sorry," he said, though he didn't sound sorry at all. "But you are not learned enough to solve this mystery."

"And you are?" she asked. It came out quickly, before she could hold it back. She winced at her own boldness. She wasn't even sure who she was speaking to. To her grandfather, to Anthony, to both? She pushed her shoulders back and lifted her chin slightly. She had said what she said. She may as well own it. "I have studied more than most men I know," she said. "I am well read and–"

"Athena," he cut her off as he made his way to her. "Being well read and having practical experience are not the same. I'm afraid this is beyond you." He passed her slowly, and Anthony moved swiftly to stay by his side. "I will have some of the crew dock. We will set up camp here, and these bees, strange as they are, will produce. Will they not, Anthony?"

Anthony nodded quickly. "Yes, yes, I will figure out the cause of the lack of production quickly."

"I do not think Lady Rose would appreciate that," she said back.

"I do not care what Lady Rose thinks," he said without turning back.

ATHENA IS MANY THINGS – SHE'S ONLY PROUD OF A FEW OF THEM

Perhaps in another life, Athena would be a pirate. Bold and brash and full of bravado. She'd be a good pirate, though, like Robin Hood. She had always enjoyed that story... She could rob merchant ships that got their gold through questionable ethics and disburse the money through an underground system in London. Maybe she could adopt an entire orphanage.

Athena hung her head as she sat on the edge of her borrowed bed. She was always trying to prove herself, and in the face of everything, she had stood her ground, worked hard, and fought for her place. It had never been given, despite her best efforts. Even with another woman in charge, she still had to battle a stegosaurus and cure a flying dinosaur to even have a chance to show she could be of use.

She knew that ultimately, she was simply a spoiled aristocrat who, despite her privilege and station, didn't get much say in the matter of what she could do and what she could be.

She thought of her cousin and Poppy and their fake engagement with a sore heart beating dully under her ribs. It was the same for them, she thought. It must have been why she had agreed to marry Seppi, and why he had agreed to marry her as well. They didn't get much say in what they were able to do, just the same as her. Their marriage was probably the best that either of them was going to do, given the circumstances.

Her time on the island, however, had left her changed, even if only slightly. Sure, she wasn't going to run off with the pirates. But she was not going to let Poppy or Seppi be married off like cattle. And she was not going to let anyone tell her she wasn't capable enough.

Athena stood and took a long, deep breath. All through their childhood, Athena had to save Seppi. She'd have to do it again now.

She set down the stairs with a newfound stride, one of confidence.

It came crumbling down almost immediately upon seeing her grandfather sitting in the drawing room with a book in his hand, casually reading as if nothing else on the island was all that interesting to him.

He looked up at Athena with his dark eyes and said, "Ah, Athena, have a seat."

Athena did as she was told, but she squared his shoulders as soon as she was seated. She wasn't going to get bullied into this. Not when she had Poppy and Seppi to fight for. "Grandfather," she said as assertively as she could, "I understand that the partnership between the two families is important to you."

"And to Lady Elizabeth," Lord Artis noted. "Both of our businesses are scraping by. This could solidify us to true wealth."

Athena shook her head slightly. What did it matter? They already had enough. She wanted to gesture at this massive estate, this island, and ask what else his grandfather could possibly want. But instead, she sighed and said, "Seppi will not marry Poppy. Sign a contract with Lady Elizabeth if you are so inclined. I am sure she would be agreeable to it."

"Generational wealth, the kind you are privileged to enjoy, does not come from contracts," his grandfather leaned back swiftly.

"Neither of them want it. The wealth or the marriage," she said. "Look around, Willa and—"

"Willa and her mother are the reason we are in this predicament in the first place," his grandfather said. "And Willa was born of wedlock. She is not a Fletcher, merely raised by one. Her claim to this estate and the business could threaten the family even more."

Athena's expression twitched; she felt like his whole face stung from a hard slap. She looked into the hallway. "Willa..?"

"It's not a Fletcher," his grandfather repeated. "I hope

you understand that should she try to claim the honey business, it would be a legal nightmare."

"I do not understand," Athena said. Her hands gripped her knees tightly. "And I do not care where she comes from. She is more than a scandal. She's a good person. A friend. She deserves–"

Her grandfather waved her away as though she were nothing but an annoying fly. "Leave this room, Athena, and understand your place in this family. If you want to remain in it, I suggest you think about your next move very carefully."

Athena rose swiftly and left the room before she could say anything that she would regret.

She passed Lady Rose in the hallway on her way out the door. She could not tell in their brief moment in passing if she had heard any of their conversation, or if she cared at all. All she knew was that he had to break free of the house.

POPPY IS STILL A WRITER

Poppy liked to believe she was a good journalist. She had a way of peeling back the layers people wore like armor, of decoding the truths they buried beneath practiced smiles, their expertly polished lies.

But when it came to Athena, none of her instincts seemed to matter. Athena had never been subtle. But she was also closed. Her face was either made of stone, unrecognizable in its apathy, or her emotions thrummed just beneath the surface of her body, wild and unmistakable. It was always all or nothing with Athena.

Now, as Poppy stepped into the field of wildflowers where Athena paced, it was unmistakable how Athena felt. Her boots tore into the earth, kicking up wildflowers in her wake. Her movements were sharp and restless, like a caged tiger.

Poppy approached her the way she might approach a dinosaur on the island. One that was wounded and scared. One with teeth. She kept her distance, circling slowly, making sure Athena saw her, giving her the space to process her.

Athena looked up from her pacing, and she froze.

But the expression that met Poppy's gaze wasn't anger.

It was something far more fragile. Something that threatened to shatter them both.

Athena had tears in her eyes. Her mouth was pulled into a tight line, and her expression was pained. Poppy hurried to her side, grabbing her elbows with her hands firmly.

Athena looked away, and Poppy moved her body to catch her gaze. "Athena, what happened?" she asked quietly. She pulled her closer and held her stare, though Athena's dark eyes looked through her, to something far away. "Athena, please!" Her voice grew urgent.

Athena's vision seemed to focus; she looked at Poppy, truly looking at her at last. She took in a shaking breath, then pulled her arms from Poppy's grasp. Her face hardened. "I can do this," she said.

"Of course you can. You're Athena," Poppy said with a small smile. "But, do what, exactly?"

Athena's posture straightened. She picked up her

burgundy shawl from the ground and wrapped it around her shoulders. "I can find out why the bees have stopped making honey," she said firmly.

"Who said you couldn't?" Poppy asked with a raised brow. "I thought my aunt—" she stopped, the realization hitting her at last. "Your grandfather?"

Athena nodded and blinked away the last of her tears. She looked up at the sky, her eyes seemed to follow a slow-moving cloud above. But her thoughts were hidden from Poppy.

It felt strange.

They had said they were going to be honest. And if everything was falling around her, she might as well try it. "Athena, let's get out of this place," she said quickly. "Let's run away. From the island. From London. Let's go. Just us." The words poured out of her like water, and the more she spoke, the more honest she became. "Since you've arrived, I've savored every moment with you, but it's not enough. I know you feel that too. Let's leave. Together."

Athena snorted. "There you go. Running away again."

Poppy's mouth opened, but for all her words, she was suddenly empty. Athena's words cut into her core. The ground beneath her feet shifted.

Athena looked her in the eyes. "That's the first thing you do, isn't it? Run away when things get hard."

Poppy shook her head. "That's not true!" Her mind sped through her life, all the choices she had made, her time with Athena, and she knew, horribly, painfully, that Athena was right. "That's unfair," she said quietly, though to herself or Athena, she wasn't sure.

Athena looked away. Around her, wildflowers danced as

the wind began to blow. Her curls moved over her face like waves around a rock, steady, slow, and ethereal. Overhead, a cloud passed over the sun, drenching them in sudden shadows. If Poppy didn't know better, she would think she was standing in front of a goddess. Great and terrible and judging. Athena spoke, her voice soft on the breeze as the blossoms rustled, "Do you trust my family?"

Poppy eyes analyzed Athena's face, she looked her over, searching for the meaning behind the question. She answered at last, "No."

"Do you trust yours?" Athena asked.

"No," Poppy answered.

"Then we can't leave," Athena said. "Not yet."

Poppy wanted to kick and scream like Athena had been before. It looked like it would be cathartic. But instead, she hummed a little under her breath before she said, "I'm not running now. What are we waiting for?"

Athena smiled at her, and a warm feeling washed over her despite everything. "I just need a little more time to figure this out," Athena said. "And I suspect your aunt will be putting my grandfather in his place sooner rather than later."

"If she hasn't already," Poppy said. "If you need time, I will buy you time. I'll jump off a ship for you."

Chapter Forty-Two

ATHENA NOTICES THINGS

Once, when Athena and Seppi were children, he told her that when she was angry, her eyes glowed red. She had to admit, her face did look scary sometimes, though his embellishment seemed far-fetched, even to her young mind. But looking at Lady Rose's expression now, Athena was suddenly sure that eyes could glow red.

Athena and Poppy stopped in their tracks, just outside the gate. All of Poppy's things had been stacked surprisingly neatly outside, and Lady Rose stood beside the heap with a furious gaze.

Poppy wore her usual half smile, despite the obvious danger ahead. Athena had to wonder where she got the confidence, or if she was just incredibly, deeply nervous.

Her stomach turned a little at the sight. Her eyes landed on the gate, a few scuff marks along the top of the posts looked as though Lady Rose had already thrown Poppy's trunk out of the property, only, Athena suspected, to haul it back in at her daughter's request.

"A serial?" Lady Rose spat as Poppy took another step closer. "Lord Artis says your latest serial has been published in London. One that details the dinosaurs here."

Poppy's grin faded. "I..." she started, quietly, as if just to Athena. "I can explain."

Lady Rose held up one bony hand. "I do not care for more lies, niece," she said, her voice carried through the garden as if she were addressing a huge group of people. It was powerful and strong despite her small stature.

From behind her, the front door swung open. Willa moved to stand beside her mother, her arms crossed.

"Explain what?" Athena asked.

Poppy breathed in deeply through her nose. She closed her eyes, a long, slow blink. "Aunt Rose," she said, louder this time, "I know what it sounds like. But I'm not just a journalist. I... I want to write fiction. I wrote that thinking no one would think it was real, you have to believe me. I didn't even know that my sister would actually publish it. I mean—"

"It's not just the serial, Poppy! We found your other

writings, too," Willa called back. "You were doing investigative work here? All those times together, trying to get to know me. It was just for some exposé?"

Athena's brows furrowed. She opened the gate and urged Poppy forward, following close behind. The gate closed with a loud crack of the wood hitting the wood.

Poppy flinched.

Athena's heart ached. Despite everything they had just said to each other, despite their time apart, it pained her to see Poppy frightened, even for a moment.

Poppy approached her family with her hands held open. She glanced back at Athena. "We said we were going to just be honest. So I will," she said, turning back to her family. "I won't lie and say I wasn't going to publish that exposé. I was set on it. There was a moment when I would have done anything to publish it."

Willa's shoulders dropped. Her expression looked so betrayed. "Why?"

Poppy shook her head. "Fame? Money? Prestige? I've wanted for so long to break out of just writing boring ladies' journals. I wanted to be taken seriously, and I didn't want our family's fortune to disappear."

Athena stepped back from Poppy's side.

She was writing an exposé? And a serial? Athena had known she was up to something, but this? It felt so... so unlike Poppy. Her eyes searched Poppy's face for any sign to help ground her, any direction to turn. But her face only conveyed a simple, bitter sadness.

What did it mean?

Lady Rose's eyes narrowed.

Poppy put her hands down at last. "None of that

matters now. What does matter is that I decided I wasn't going to publish it. I've seen the goodness on this island, the wild and beautiful creatures, and the love and care you have for them. I was going to go home and publish it, until I wasn't."

"And the serial?" Willa demanded.

Poppy shook her head. "I came here to get answers. I came here to get experience. I... I wrote those stories down. I won't lie to you. Those I was going to publish anyway. I didn't think anyone would believe that they were based on reality. I really didn't. I wouldn't do anything to harm this island. To harm you."

The painful bite of the betrayal tore slowly through Athena's chest. If she had published writings about the island, it would not only put the dinosaurs in jeopardy, but also her own dreams as well. For so long, she had yearned for the chance to learn the way she could here. And Poppy had encouraged it. Was it all just for her own gain? She couldn't be sure, but she felt as though every interaction, every word they shared, was tainted.

"And why should we believe any of what you have to say?" Lady Rose asked, breaking Athena's spiraling thoughts.

"I understand if you don't," Poppy said. "I should have burned those pages as soon as I determined not to publish them."

"You never should have written them at all," Willa jumped in.

Poppy nodded. "You're right. I have no excuse, only my word now, though it's not good for much." She looked to Athena, and, as though seeing the hurt there, she held out her hand to her. "Athena, I'm sorry. You're right. When I am afraid, I run. And this time, I know I shouldn't be asking for forgiveness, but... I am anyway." She turned back to her family. "I am sorry. Truly."

Needle pricks ran down her neck as though a cold wind had just blown by. But the wind was still. She looked around, and the voices of Poppy and Lady Rose faded. Something wasn't right, and when she realized it, the color drained from her face as her anxiety spiked.

"Where is Reggie?" she asked, cutting through the din of the Fletcher women's argument.

Lady Rose and Poppy both stopped. Each looked to Athena for a moment, then at the garden.

"When did you last see him?" Athena asked, her worry creeping into her voice.

Lady Rose blinked. She looked at Willa.

Willa's brows drew together. "Not since last night," she said.

Lady Rose gripped Willa's hand quickly. "I did not see him this morning," she said quietly. "Oh, merciful heavens! Reginald!"

Athena turned back to the gate, her eyes narrowing on the slight smudge on the top point of the picket. "Damn pirates," Athena hissed. She hiked her skirt up a little as she marched to the gate. She leaned down to look at it carefully. The mark was a few finger-sized, dark, and haunting in the late afternoon light.

She turned, noticing now the deep indents in the walkway. Booted feet. None of their shoes, surely. "Where is Seppi?" she asked quickly.

Willa looked as though she was on the brink of tears. "I

haven't seen him since this morning," she choked. "Is he in danger?"

Athena squared her shoulders. She gazed into the jungle. Her fists clenched.

Not if she had anything to do with it.

POPPY AND THE PRIORITIES OF PACKING

The sun's rays were growing redder as it began its descent behind the tall mountain and into the west. It would get dark soon. And the jungle was full of massive, sometimes protective, dinosaurs. And quite possibly dinosaur thieving pirates. But after they had searched the house and the property, it was clear that something had happened to Reggie, and Poppy was no coward. If Reggie was in trouble, she knew she had to help.

Athena was busy preparing her bag to set out into the

night while Lady Rose fretted rather uncharacteristically in the kitchen. She seemed to be baking something, cooking something, and cleaning all at once in a flurry of movement and stress. And while she knew her aunt had far from forgiven her, her worries were elsewhere now, for which Poppy was slightly grateful, even though she cringed at the reasoning behind it.

Poppy tried to get her mind onto more productive things. She leaned closer to Athena, analyzing the contents of her bag with the same puzzled look Athena wore.

There was a small dagger, cloth for bandages, a few vials of pain relief, a rope, and flint and steel.

"Water, too," Poppy suggested. "And bread."

"I'll fetch water," Willa said as though she had been waiting for someone to give her directions. She hurried out of the kitchen.

"Bread?" Athena asked with a raised brow.

Poppy leaned in even closer. "In case we're out all night. We might get hungry. *Reggie* might be hungry."

Athena rolled her eyes, but Lady Rose had already stuffed a loaf of bread into her bag.

"I'll be right back," Poppy said quickly. She spun on her heel and bounded up the stairs two at a time. She went to her room and found it still empty of her things. With a sad sigh, she looked around slowly. Everything she had in here was gone, left still on the front porch, probably being munched on by the little velociraptors. She deserved this reaction. She'd behave similarly if their situations were reversed.

She almost shut the door when she heard a small scurry across the floor. Beatrice, small and sweet, made her way from under the bed to her feet. She looked at Poppy with expectant eyes. "I'm sorry," Poppy whispered. Her heart broke for the dinosaur. Beatrice seemed so calm, yet aware. Her eyes were bright and alert. She must know, Poppy thought, on some level, that her friend was missing. She reached down to pat her head gently. "I know," she said. "But it's too dangerous for a little one like you. We'll find him." She set her jaw and marched into the room. She'd take a pillowcase if that's what it took.

Poppy entered the kitchen with her empty pillowcase in hand. She scooched in beside Athena, almost elbowing her out of the way as she reached into the other woman's bag and pulled out the bread, glass jar of water, and rope. She stuffed the items in the pillowcase before Athena could protest.

"You don't want the glass making sounds against the medicine," she said sternly. "It'll give away your location. And we have to be sneaky."

Athena sighed. "You're not coming with me," she said.

"I have the rope," Poppy said with a smile. "And you'd have to tie me up to keep me from going with you." She held her pillowcase closer to her body just in case Athena tried to snatch it.

She made no effort to remove it from Poppy's hands, but her eyes narrowed fiercely.

Willa watched the standoff from her position in the doorway. Poppy glanced at her and thought she saw admiration, or maybe annoyance, in her eyes. "I'll get you another bag," Willa said softly. "So you can have your hands free."

"Thank you, cousin," Poppy said kindly. She looked back at Athena slyly. "See? She agrees that I will be helpful."

Athena huffed a little. She slung the bag over her shoulder. "Fine," she said. "But this time, if we run into something giant, you're saving me."

"Deal," Poppy said as her smile grew.

POPPY IS A JOURNALIST. KIND OF

Poppy's smile did not last. They were trekking through the jungle silently, and all Poppy wanted to do was talk to Athena. She knew they couldn't, not really. But it seemed like the last opportunity they might get for a while. Or ever. Maybe they'd be murdered by pirates, and that would be the end of Poppy's long and silly saga.

Poppy cocked her head. She supposed that if they were, at least it would make an excellent article.

Athena raised a brow at her as if reading her demented thoughts.

Poppy glanced her way briefly. Athena was always too observant. It was annoying. Sure, Poppy wanted to talk, but she didn't want to explain that if they were about to be murdered, at least it would be an interesting end that people back home would get morbid enjoyment reading about. "It's nothing," she whispered.

Athena didn't look convinced, but she turned and followed the footpath silently nonetheless.

The light was diminishing rapidly, and Poppy knew they'd soon find themselves fumbling around in darkness. They needed to be more intentional about their hike. And so, she decided she was done following Athena around.

She stopped.

As if they were tethered together, Athena stopped beside her.

"Look," Poppy said, softly but firmly, "I understand that you may not trust me right now."

Athena opened her mouth like she was about to protest, but Poppy held her hand up to silence her. "I have read about a lot of journalists. Those who got to go on adventures the likes of which I never thought I would."

Athena waved her hand in a circle, urging her to go on quickly, though there was a sincerity in her gaze that made Poppy's heart skip.

"Safaris, rescue missions, and the like," Poppy explained. "I know some basics in tracking. Not practically necessarily, but I know what to look for."

"We're going in the general direction Lady Rose said

they're likely to be hiding," Athena said, pointing ahead of them. "Up on the hill."

"Right, but Athena, these hills are massive. We need to be intentional while we still have a little light."

Athena wrapped one arm around herself. She looked out into the leaves with narrowed eyes. "Alright," she said at last. "What are we looking for?"

Poppy beamed. She stood a little taller. "Any disturbance in the leaves, any snapped branches, bent foliage. It could be subtle, so while you do that, I'll keep my eyes on the ground. I'll look for any footprints or..." She stopped before she said 'blood'. Her reading about tracking had been about tracking large, wounded animals. Reggie was little, and she hoped beyond anything that he was very much safe.

Athena seemed to notice her hesitation, but gracefully nodded and continued their journey toward the hills.

The sun descended behind the horizon, and the jungle fell into darkness. Poppy moved closer to Athena, squinting at the dark soil in the low moonlight that shimmered down through the treetops. It was just as she started to give up that she spotted it. A faint press in the damp earth, an imprint of a booted heel. Poppy grabbed Athena's arm. She pointed at the spot, then held a finger to her lips. She pointed left, the direction of the print. "This way," she mouthed.

Athena followed her as Poppy continued finding footprint after footprint. They were far apart from one another, but finding the next one proved easier as she continued the trail.

The ground grew steeper beneath her feet. She reached

back for Athena's hand to steady one another as they began their journey up, and the jungle grew darker and darker still.

Athena held her hand carefully, as though afraid she'd break it. But Poppy's hold was confident and strong until they crested the hill, and the light was suddenly warm and flickering from a large campfire.

ATHENA IS A LITTLE STUPID

thena's breath hitched in her throat. She squeezed Poppy's hand and pulled her back a little. She motioned for Poppy to follow her as she crouched down low and eased her way back into the cover of the large jungle leaves.

They huddled together closely. Athena kept her hand securely wrapped around Poppy's as her eyes surveyed the scene before them.

The camp was small and brightly lit by the large

campfire. Three canvas tents in a semicircle were erected in a way that looked hasty and somewhat inexperienced. Her eyes narrowed at what appeared to be well-constructed knots made of the thick rope holding together long sticks and tying the canvas together. She almost snorted. *Pirates.* She guessed they rarely made it to the landslide, where they were held up in someone's hideaway home. She couldn't make a better tent, but it would be closer than it should be.

Among the camp were a few rucksacks, a barrel that they seemed to be using as a table, and... a metal cage.

Athena's pulse quickened. She leaned a little closer to see Reggie inside the cage. He was asleep, or at least lying down, curled up as best his fat little body could, into the corner of the cage.

Athena suddenly wished she had tried harder to keep Poppy safe at the estate. She hated that she was here, with her, in such a dangerous situation. The pirates were gone, it seemed, for now. But she had no idea how long that would last.

She looked at Poppy, studying her face in the flickering firelight. She couldn't lose her. She wouldn't. "Go back," she whispered, finally letting her hand go. "Go back and tell them where this place is. I'll go get Reggie."

Poppy shook her head. "Athena, you're the smartest person I know. How can you *also* be so stupid?"

Athena pulled back a little, but Poppy was smiling.

"Come on," Poppy murmured, rising to standing quickly. She brushed out her long, dainty skirt, then tilted her head for Athena to follow. "The pirates could be back at any moment."

Athena bit her lip, but she nodded anyway. There was no changing Poppy's mind. Not then, and not now.

The two entered the camp with light footsteps, careful not to make more sound than necessary until they reached the cage where little Reggie lay. Athena crouched down and scooted closer to him in the corner where he bundled himself, one little clawed hand attached to his stubby arm clung to a bar on the cage. His eyes were closed, but he was breathing.

"He's alive," Athena said to Poppy, relief filled her chest, expanding her lungs. She could breathe, truly breathe in deeply, for the first time since they set out into the jungle. She thought she might start crying. It felt so blissful for the moment, but then Poppy stood beside her and turned, looking around.

"Is he hurt?" Poppy asked. She set her bag down beside Athena carefully.

Athena shook her head. She eyed his body closely. "He might be sedated. Though he is also a hefty sleeper." She looked up at Poppy. "I think he's safe."

Poppy shot her a frown.

"Relatively," Athena corrected.

"It's locked, though," Poppy said. "Can we carry the whole cage out?"

Athena tried pulling on the cage—it lifted, barely. She strained, and it raised a bit higher, but not by much. "It's heavy," she said.

"We could get it out if we worked together," Poppy suggested.

"No," Athena whispered at the end of a heavy sigh. "It would be too cumbersome. If they get back, they'll catch up to us quickly, and we won't have much of a chance."

"I'll look for a key," Poppy said. She hurried to open up the closest rucksack.

Athena stood. She looked around the camp for anything heavy. A crowbar, or metal pole... Where relief once was, anxiousness began to take its place, twisting her insides and suffocating any lightness. She was heavy, weighed down by the fear.

Poppy turned to her, holding Seppi's sketchbook. "These thieves!" she hissed, then tucked the sketchbook under her arm to continue to dig through the bag. "Oh, Athena," she said, rising again, this time holding up a wooden duck. "What kind of pirate...?" She was laughing a little, and Athena couldn't help but smile back.

How Poppy was able to get her to smile at a time like this was some magic that only she seemed to possess. Still, she felt slightly nauseous.

Athena moved closer to the treeline as Poppy began her search in the second bag. She searched the ground for a fallen stick or rock heavy enough to do damage. A rock might be primitive, it might make too much sound, but it would do the trick. She kicked around with her foot, hoping she would stub her toe on the solution.

"And look!" Poppy whispered, albeit a little too enthusiastically. She was holding up a glittering glass jar that appeared to be full of earth and sprouted seeds. Though especially in the dim light, and her attention drawn elsewhere, she couldn't quite decipher what it was. "I feel like we would all be friends, if they weren't you know... animal stealing pirates." She turned it over in her hands carefully, looking at it from all sides. "It's good quality glass. And the seeds look healthy."

"They probably stole it. Maybe even from your aunt," Athena said quickly. Her eyes landed on a large branch deeper in the jungle, just within the firelight. It looked like it had snapped off clean from the trunk of the tree. Thank goodness for massive dinosaurs, she thought as she grabbed the end of the branch and hauled it into the camp.

"Good find," Poppy said. "When we can't use our brains, we must resort to brawn!"

"Not exactly one or the other," Athena grunted as she moved the branch close to the cage. She set it down beside the lock and pointed to it so Poppy could get a better look at the detail. "It's a padlock, but it looks flimsy. It should have a weakness," she pointed again, "here, and here."

Poppy nodded. "I never doubted you," she said brightly. She went back to searching the last bag.

"I mean, you did say we would have to rely on brawn," Athena mumbled.

Poppy didn't seem to hear her; she was busy pulling various items from the last bag with a curious, almost excited, expression.

Athena heaved the branch so it rested just below the lock. She moved her leg under the branch and cursed her long skirt under her breath. She didn't mind dresses and skirts. In fact, during her childhood, when she chased Seppi around, she found it allowed her greater mobility and ease of movement, except on rare occasions where she had to do something like this. Athena hiked her skirt up to her thigh to get a better angle on the branch and pushed down on the log with all her strength.

The lock busted with a loud metallic *clank*.

Chapter Forty-Six

POPPY AND THE PIRATES

Poppy jumped at the sound of the metal lock breaking. She turned to Athena, a set of paint brushes in her hands. Her eyes moved from the open door of the cage to Athena's triumphant face, and then down to her bare leg.

She was thankful for the low glow of the firelight. Perhaps Athena wouldn't notice her immediate blush. No sign of her heart rate slowing now. First the scare, now memories rushed her mind like a dinosaur stampede.

Athena was already waist-deep in the cage. She pulled Reggie free with some effort, then cradled him in her arms delicately. Her brows knit together as she stroked his snout.

Poppy hurried to her side. "Someone might have heard that," she warned, though her hand also went to Reggie's head. She held his forehead gently in the palm of her hand. He felt the same as he always did. Cold, a little soft despite his scales.

Athena nodded. She rose, then moved Reggie to the crook of one arm, and with her free hand, dug through the bag at her hip. She found a small vial and tilted his head back, adding a few droplets of liquid that looked black in the campfire light.

"What's that?" Poppy asked quietly.

"A waking tonic," Athena said. "I'm not sure it will work on him with his different physiology, but—"

Reggie stirred in her arms, his eyes fluttered open.

"It worked!" Poppy cried, then immediately clasped her hands over her mouth. "Oh, sorry!"

Athena chuckled a little. From relief or Poppy's stupidity, though, Poppy wasn't sure. She also wasn't sure it mattered. Reggie was safe. She grabbed her bag, tucked Seppi's sketchbook into it, and slung it over her chest. They were going to be alright.

The thought crossed her mind easily, a little puffy white cloud in a cerulean sky, but the stomping feet and angry voices of men approaching turned her blood hot as if she had been hit by lightning. She turned toward the sound, arm out to push Athena back if she needed to.

But Athena only swatted her arm away. She had drawn the dagger from the bag and held it raised, dangerously pointed in the direction of the voices. It glittered in the orange glow as if it were lit from within by the same fire in Athena's eyes.

"Hide that," Poppy said as her mind raced through all their options. "They don't need to know we have it. Or that you know how to use it."

Athena grumbled a little, but nodded. She lowered her hand and hid it and the dagger in the folds of her skirt just as three men appeared from the shadows.

The one in the middle, and closest, was a tall, broad man with a thick black beard. It was streaked with silver despite the ease in his movements and the hard cracks in his weathered face. His black curls were tied up on his head in a thick bun, and a pistol was already drawn at his hip. His lips curled up at them with a wicked grin and wide eyes that reminded Poppy of a cat about to pounce.

The other two men were lanky and smaller, at least by comparison. They flared out from behind him quickly and eyed the women with more confusion than anything. "Girls?" one of them asked the group.

Beside her, she felt Athena bristle. She glanced at her briefly, then at Reggie, who was starting to stir more purposefully in her grasp.

"Girls with our beast," the middle man said. He waved the weapon at them, urging them closer. His eyes spotted the cage, then flicked back to them quickly. "You know your locks," he said.

Poppy squared her shoulders despite the pounding in her chest. She nodded quickly and took a step closer. She sensed that Athena did the same, but she held her hand out just enough to stop her. "I do," she said, as boldly as she could.

"Clever girl," the pirate snarled.

Poppy smiled, matching the wild expression on the pirate's face with ease. "And I see you found my sketchbook," she said, her eyes shifting to the open bags on the floor. "Quite the collection of paints, I may add. Did you steal those, too?"

The pirate to the right moved forward. "You went through your thing?"

He sounded so betrayed that Poppy almost laughed. Who was he to be offended by the breach in privacy? Or by anything, for that matter? He had stolen their friend.

Anger surged through her, but she did her best to keep her wry grin. "Oh yes," she said. "And I learned quite a bit about you, *William*."

The man on the left grimaced. "How do you know my name?"

She had been right. Her grin grew. She had really taken an absolute risk with that one, but she hoped it would delay them long enough. How many Williams and Thomases and Johns did she know in her own life? Still, she felt like her luck was going to run out soon. Their options were limited. They could run, but she wasn't sure how far they would get, especially not carrying Reggie. They could fight, but thought Athena was talented, and she didn't doubt her own tenacity; they were still outmatched. Her mind was still spinning, but she thought she'd try her luck again. One of them liked art, one liked gardening; it was likely that they were educated, at least a bit. She tried, "How's Mary?"

The same man's lips tightened.

The man in the middle laughed, and it boomed through the camp like a roar. "Hand over the little monster," he said as he stepped forward. "I don't want to have to take it from you."

Athena pulled Reggie closer to her chest. He squirmed, feet swinging down like he was trying to run. "You'll have to take him," Athena said firmly.

The pirate raised his gun without hesitation, and Athena pulled the knife from her hiding place.

The pirate chuckled again, though amusement and frustration seemed to be mixing in his laugh like a deadly poison. "This wins," he said as he held it aloft.

"Not if you miss," Athena said. Her cold stare was impassive in the dark, a wall of protection despite the danger ahead. A calm fell over Poppy. If this was going to be it, she may as well try her last option while she still had her voice. And if they perished here, at least she'd go knowing she did everything she could, even if she looked like an absolute fool first.

Poppy flashed Athena a quick half smile.

Athena raised a brow back.

Poppy lifted her chin and took a deep breath. Her mouth opened wide, and she let out a series of sharp screams in rapid succession—two high, piercing sounds, then one long, then two again.

The pirates all stopped, confused, it seemed, to the point of paralysis, even if briefly.

Athena's face softened with understanding. She lowered her knife and crouched down quickly, covering Reggie with her body.

Poppy cried out again, but no sound came back. This, she thought sadly, might very well be the end of her story.

The pirates advanced, and Poppy did the only thing she could now. She threw her body over Athena and waited for the shot to fire.

A chaotic pounding sound erupted from the jungle. It started low, so low that Poppy half thought it might be her imagination, a desperate last wish that her mind used to ease her into the afterlife. But then it grew louder. And louder still.

Poppy's muscles tightened. She held onto Athena tightly, turning her head a little now to see the pirates' confused expressions. They looked around the jungle, turning this way and that with large, wild movements.

Good, Poppy thought as a smile found its way to her lips.

The dinosaurs burst into the camp like a flash flood, tearing up the rucksacks and two tents on their way in. Items and bags went flying through the air, landing far and battered.

The dinosaurs' bulbous tails swung wildly, hitting at least one of the pirates as the men scrambled to get away. The pirates ducked and dodged, but Poppy turned her face into Athena's back. She could only hear the roar of dinosaurs, the screams of men, and the shattering of metal and wood.

A shot rang out.

A punch hit Poppy in her ribs as the ground shook around them. She closed her eyes tightly. She held Athena and Reggie closer.

The chaos quieted, retreating into the jungle and slowly away.

ATHENA AND REGGIE

The brawl didn't last long. If the pirates made it out alive, Athena wasn't too concerned. She only cared that they had made it out at all.

She lifted her head, tucked under Poppy's arm, and glanced around the camp with one eye. At her chest, Reggie shifted uncomfortably again, as if he, too, knew the danger had passed. She let him go at last, and he sprang free to stomp his feet on the ground in front of them triumphantly.

Athena laughed from fear, from the sudden drop of happiness that they survived, from the silliness of the little dinosaur, from the feeling of Poppy's arms around her at last. It was all so much.

But then, she remembered the sound of the gunfire. She struggled in Poppy's arms. "Are you alright?" she asked, grabbing Poppy's hands in her own. Her eyes searched the woman for any signs of pain.

Poppy winced, and Athena's heart shattered. "Poppy!" she cried. She dropped her hands and reached into her bag, pulling out bandage wraps quickly. "Oh, Poppy! Where?"

Poppy sat back. She looked down at her own body with shock in her eyes, then she said softly, "Ow..."

Athena's brows furrowed. Her hands traced over Poppy's form, hovering just over her, careful not to make things worse. She stopped at the bag at Poppy's side, where a large hole had been cut through.

Poppy shifted, her eyes following along.

Athena lifted the bag over Poppy's shoulder gingerly with shaking hands.

Poppy looked down at her ribs, clear and free of blood. She looked back at Athena with a smile so bright it lit the space between them. "Oh, look!" she said, squiggling a little to get a better view of herself.

Athena sighed, her body seemed to collapse as if all the tension, and not her skeleton, had been the only thing keeping her up. She fell onto the dark grass, now upturned with fresh mud and sticks, and laughed.

"Look!" Poppy said again, falling back with her. She pulled the sketchbook from the bag and opened it. A single bullet fell between them. "Seppi saved me!"

Athena, still laughing, simply tossed one arm over Poppy. A hit or a hug, or something in between, she wasn't sure. All she knew was that the earth below her was cold, that her arm around Poppy was warm, and that Reggie needed to lose a few stones. He had waddled over to her to lie on her stomach, making her breath shallow.

The fire crackled as the ground below them rumbled faintly at the movement of slow but massive feet sauntering along toward them. They turned in unison, toward the unmistakable sound of Francesca approaching.

*A*thena pushed herself up onto her elbows, squinting into the dark trees.

"Stand back, pirates!" Seppi shouted, seemingly with all his strength.

Francesca blasted through the trees, bellowing loudly. She lowered her head and swayed about the space as though she were roaring in his defense, looking for anything to hit with her massive skull.

Seppi, still one hand raised in a tight fist, looked about the torn-up camp, visible confusion etching into his face. "Ladies?" he asked, his voice lower. "What happened here?"

Despite everything, a loud laugh escaped Athena's throat. Relief made her limbs light and her chest expand. "Dinosaurs and pirates," Athena said back through bouts of laughter. "The usual!"

Seppi's brow furrowed. "I'm here to save the day," he said, though his tone came out as more of a suggestion.

"You already saved the day!" Poppy called. She held his leather-bound sketchbook up for him to see.

Seppi squinted, trying to make it out in the faint firelight. "My drawings?" he asked.

Poppy opened the sketchbook to reveal the hole that had pierced through over half of it.

"My drawings!"

Poppy laughed. "Don't worry," she said, opening to a new page. "The one with Willa and Beatrice is still here."

"And so am I!" a voice, loud and frustrated, hollered from the last tent standing.

All turned to the tent, but it remained motionless.

"Untie me this instant!" the voice said.

Poppy and Athena rose to their feet as Seppi gave Francesca a quick pat, then lowered the rope ladder attached to her back so he could descend. He climbed down as quickly as he could, then tentatively approached the flap of the tent.

Athena moved quickly to his side, her dagger held tightly in her fist again. He may have come in hoping to save the day, but, as usual, Athena was the one who was ready to defend. She nodded to Seppi, who, with a surprisingly steady hand, lifted the opening of the tent in one swift reveal.

Inside, an incredibly disgruntled-looking Lord Artis sat on the wet earth with his hands tied behind him, his body bound by so much rope, Athena half wondered if he could even feel any of his limbs, or if the pirates were really pirates at all. A simple, but effective knot should be much easier than all this.

Their grandfather's hair was wild, sticking up in random places, and he wore a gag around his neck like it was a scarf.

Seppi hurried to him and untied it from his neck quickly while Athena cut his bonds.

"Grandfather? How long have you been like this?" he asked.

Athena helped him to his feet, and he grumbled, rounding his shoulders and tweaking his neck this way and that. "Too long," he said. "I say, did you know that those men were pirates?"

Athena deflated.

Their grandfather rubbed his wrists gently. "Don't you scoff at me, granddaughter."

"Well, what did you think they were?" Athena said with a toss of her head.

Lord Artis shrugged slightly, though he played it off as though it was simply him still warming his shoulders up. "Burly men able to help with the bees as needed, of course. Who in this day and age deals with *pirates*?"

Seppi crossed his arms. "Let's get you home," was all he said.

Athena sighed and left the tent. She secured the blade in her bag and scooped Reggie back up into her arms. With a soft smile at the long-necked dinosaur, she waited for her grandfather and cousin to follow.

The two of them were still complaining to one another about the pirates quietly, and Athena cast a glance at Poppy. "I take it if I ask you to go home with them while I see to it that the pirates don't return, you'll tell me 'no'?"

"Correct." Poppy winked at her.

Athena took in a deep breath with both admiration and frustration. She turned back to the men. "Seppi, can you take Reggie and Grandfather home?" she asked.

"And you will be..?" Seppi prompted.

Athena set Reggie down carefully. She nodded to the broken treeline where the pirates and dinosaurs had run off.

Seppi shook his head. "Oh, Athena..."

"We're just going to go observe the ship offshore," Poppy said quickly. "We just need to confirm that they make it back to the ship. Or... that they don't."

"If you're not back by morning," Seppi said as he bent down to lift Reggie, "I'll send the dinosaurs after you. All of them."

POPPY FLETCHER SAVED THE DAY (WITH HELP)

It was nearly sunrise. The dark sky and the sea below it were beginning to glow in a faint cyan. Off the shore, the pirate ship floated almost peacefully in the still waters. They had been watching it from their vantage point behind the treeline for a while, and Poppy had just started to wonder if Seppi would make good on his promise to send the dinosaur brigade when she felt Athena nudge her.

She cocked her head to the pirate ship and Poppy leaned forward to get a better view.

The ship was lowering a rowboat into the gentle waves.

"Let's get a better view," Poppy whispered. She didn't wait for Athena to protest or agree, but looped her arm under Athena's and began to creep closer down the hill, dragging Athena close behind.

"We could see plenty from there," Athena said quietly. She gave Poppy a little resistance, but followed all the same.

Poppy smiled, her cheeks warmed, and she continued their slow march down the hill. "You never know what you'll overhear," Poppy said. "Come on."

They reached the beach quickly, but stayed huddled in the darkness of the jungle. It was still predawn, and the little boat approached the shore with steady men at the oars. Poppy heard the rustling of leaves far to her left.

She pulled Athena down into the dark as the group of pirates emerged from the trees. The two were carrying the biggest one, heaving him up as though their arms were a throne. He was clutching their shoulders with heavy arms, trying to maintain his balance.

"Steady! Steady!" the captain cried.

The boat landed on the white sand as the first hints of sunlight began to turn the scene in front of them to color slowly.

A man with a wide hat leapt from the boat with the swiftness of a cat. His boots splashed in the low water, and he hurried to the others. "What happened here?" he demanded, his voice steady.

"Quartermaster," the tallest said with a sheepish bow of his head. "The captain–"

The quartermaster cut him off with one hand raised. He was inspecting the captain as a mother would a child who had just been caught lying. "You're drunk!" he said, scolding. "And where is your leg!?"

"That's why he's drunk," the tall one said. "Finished off the last of the rum to keep him calm. We got a good tourniquet on it."

The quartermaster shook his head. "I told you this was a stupid plan from the start," he said to the captain, his finger waving in his face. "You never think these things through! And now look at you. You've lost a leg!"

"We could be rich!" the captain said, ignoring him with a drunken slur in his speech.

The quartermaster tossed his hands. "Who's going to be buying a giant lizard bird thing? Who is the market for that?"

The two other pirates cringed at the words, as they did, the captain slipped a little from their grasp. They both hastily adjusted to keep him aloft.

"Get yourself on the boat," the quartermaster said gruffly. "We're getting off this cursed island before anyone else loses any limbs."

*R*eggie and her aunt had stayed in each other's arms, though Reggie's hold was admittedly with less reach, since they arrived back. As it turned out, Athena had been correct in her measurements on dosage for his revival and had once again proven herself capable in her aunt's eyes.

Whether she was also redeemed remained to be seen.

But for now, she would have to be content to sit in the room among friends and family and dinosaurs... and Lord Artis.

He was looking rather glum and put out, but Poppy thought that ought to be expected. Occasionally, he would grumble something to himself. Otherwise, at least he was quiet as she recounted the events yet again for the group, with Athena making a minor correction here or there.

When they were done and the room fell into a blissful silence again, Lord Artis finally spoke up, this time with his usual force in his voice.

"I have decided to get on the next shipping boat," he said. "And whoever wishes to come with me, may."

Poppy's chest expanded.

On the other side of the room, Seppi sipped his tea in victory, then said, "Does this mean the engagement is off?"

Lord Artis shook his head. "I'm not sure what is happening on this island," he said slowly. "But I no longer wish to have anything to do with it."

Athena looked at Poppy with a nearly imperceptible smile.

Poppy's eyes softened. She smiled back warmly.

"Perhaps the families will join businesses someday after all," Lord Artis said to her, pulling her gaze away from Athena at last. He chuckled a little. "The world is a mysterious place."

Poppy felt color rise to her cheeks. She looked away.

"And you will keep our secret?" Aunt Rose asked. "The dinosaurs cannot fall into the wrong hands."

Lord Artis hummed. "Dinosaur. What an interesting name. Greek?"

"All the dinosaur names have Greek roots," Willa said to her mother. Poppy knew it was before her mother started her rant about the patriarchal naming system.

Lord Artis nodded as if understanding he had better move on. "I think this island, and other people, are best if as few as possible know about it. Safest, at least." He looked at Athena. "I do hope you can solve the mystery of the bees here," he said.

Athena glowered. Her jaw tightened at his words, but she said, "I will."

Poppy beamed with pride. She knew she would.

"Though I still think, should things not improve," Lord Artis said, "you should consider taming these beasts. You really would make a fortune selling tickets to view them."

Aunt Rose held up her hand. "We will find another way to get by, thank you."

"And what of Lady Elizabeth?" Seppi asked, leaning in from his seat on the couch. "She won't take this too well."

"The money being spent on the dinosaurs?" Aunt Rose asked.

Seppi cast her a puzzled look. "All of it," he said, "least of all, the engagement."

Poppy caught his gaze, and she raised a brow. "We could tell him my mysterious illness has taken a turn."

"We cannot tell your mother you're dead!" Seppi cried, clutching his chest.

"Not dead," Poppy gasped, feigning shock. "That I'm incurable and highly contagious and have to stay here forever. She can still write to me."

Lord Artis waved a hand as if dismissing a couple of children bickering. "Leave that to me," he said. "I will explain that the engagement is off. But I will have my lawyer draft a contract nonetheless. That should appease her for a time."

"For a time," Aunt Rose said, a little ominously.

Lord Artis nodded. "For a time."

Chapter Forty-Nine

ATHENA AND THE BEES OF UNUSUAL SIZE

Athena watched the bees. They buzzed loudly about the open field while she tapped her pen against her journal impatiently. The latest shipping boat had come and gone with not but her grandfather and his few items in tow. Athena, Poppy, and Seppi were all permitted to stay on the island for now.

And while she was excited to start working in the secret, well, mostly secret, lab alongside Lady Rose, she still wanted to prove her worth and save the bees for herself and them.

She set her pen down at last and fell back into the wildflowers. She let them sway around her, listening to the gentle hum of giant bees and the rustling of petals in the breeze. She looked up at the clear blue sky and wondered for a moment what it must be like to be a small bug flying up there among monsters. Her eyes tracked one of the prehistoric bees as it floated lazily over her, so fluffy and large it may as well have been a cloud.

Athena's expression shifted from serene to puzzled. The bees were massive. The flowers were not.

She sat up quickly and looked around her. The flowers were small. And, more importantly, not the same flowers that these bees had been used to feeding on in their time.

They were simply hungry. For more food. For comfort food.

Athena ran the whole way back to the lab.

"They're malnourished!" Athena cried as she threw open the door to the lab.

Lady Rose looked up from her desk with a sour expression. "The pterodactyls?"

Athena leaned on the door frame. She held a hand to her chest as she worked to catch her breath. "No," she said quickly. "The bees. They're huge, and the flowers are small. They're just hungry."

Lady Rose huffed. The chair beneath her scraped across the floor as she stood up. "That would explain things..."

"Do you have anything, any matter from ancient flowers? They must have been equally large then." Athena hurried to Rose's side. "We can fix this. Save the bees, and bring back prehistoric flora."

Lady Rose lifted a brow. She looked up at Athena with a mischievous expression. "Yes, we can," she said.

. . .

thena and Poppy's hike to the top of the mountain had taken them nearly the whole morning, though the footpath was surprisingly worn for a deserted island. They sat on the crest, overlooking the island and the sapphire sea with a sense of calm that neither had felt in a very long time.

Athena held Poppy close, savoring the feel of her head resting peacefully on her shoulder, feeling her breath on her neck in a rhythm that mirrored the waves so far below them. From here, it felt as though she was on top of the world, and yet, there was no world other than the one she held.

The sea stretched on until the end of the horizon, where the light nearly blinded her if she looked too closely. Instead, she closed her eyes and pulled Poppy closer.

She felt Poppy smile against her skin, then her head turned a little to look up at her. "Do you think you'll be able to revive ancient flowers?" she asked at last.

Athena kept her eyes closed. "If your aunt can bring back dinosaurs, I think I can bring back flowers. Or, at least create bigger ones from those that already exist."

"Can I have one when you're done?"

Athena laughed. "Poppy," she said quietly. "I'd bring back every flower for you."

Poppy nuzzled closer into Athena's shoulder. "What will we do now? If you plan to stay here?"

Athena's thumb moved down Poppy's arm gently. She closed her eyes, and a feeling of peace washed over her. "Absence makes the heart grow fonder," she said honestly. "You probably need to go back to London, thank your sister for having the courage to publish them, and claim all that fame your serials have garnered ."

"Your nightmare, I'm sure," Poppy said with a small laugh.

"Yes," Athena nodded. She pulled Poppy even closer. "But, you love it. Leave me here sometimes, go back and see your family. Do your tours. I'll be here when you get back."

"Every time?" Poppy looked up at her.

"Every time," Athena said with a small kiss on her forehead. "Who knows," she whispered as her lips grazed the top of Poppy's head. "Maybe I'll even join you from time to time. So long as I can stay off the stage."

"And away from my mother," Poppy teased.

"That was a given," Athena said with a smile.

Poppy's smile grew. "Maybe when you're done with the flowers and the bees are happy again, you and I can go find another exciting adventure?"

"There's nothing I'd like more," Athena said.

ACKNOWLEDGMENTS

First, I'd like to thank the support system around me. If I named you all, it would probably be longer than this book, which makes me incredibly, incredibly lucky. Honestly, every day I wake up in complete awe at all the love, kindness, kick-in-the-pants support I have in all of you.

This idea came to be during a small get together when a friend (hi, John!) asked what I was writing next. My spouse suggested, "What about a cozy Jurassic Park?" and I laughed. For all of two seconds because that was actually the start of a little brain t-rex clawing at my brain until I couldn't think of anything else.

The second half of the idea came on a night with my dear friends (who are all so creative and amazing it makes me mad and also my heart three times as big) and one said, "Can I ask a question?" and that night and through a series of fun but challenging questions, the book was born. Thank you all for helping bring Damsels and Dinosaurs to life.

Thank you to Carly over at Book Light Editorial. I appreciate that you talked to me for so long after you dropped the bombshell on me to cut half this book. You were much more tactful than that, of course. You've been with me from my debut and there's no one else I'd rather kindly tell me that I need to fix a bunch of things. Seriously, I can't overstate how much fun it was fixing plot holes (and discussing pirate hierarchy) with you. You were right about the other two POVs, of course. They needed to be cut. But I never would have caught that on my own. This book shines now because of you.

Thank you to my family who continuously supports me even though I decided to jump into publishing at the oddest time in my life. It's been said I need to get bloody noses before I'm able to learn a lesson, but so far, thanks to you, my nose is bandaged and I'm running back into that wall again. Hopefully, this time, I climb it instead of hitting it head first.

And, if you read this far, please know that I am also thanking you.

Thank you for reading.

For engaging with this story.

For being here, in this brief moment in time, with me.

If I can leave you with anything, for whatever my words are worth, go out there and do something kind for yourself and someone else today.

We're all among dinosaurs.

Ones bigger and more terrifying than in these pages.

But together we can still work to make the world a little more cozy.

About the Author

Wren Jones lives in the Sonoran Desert with her family and two cats. Like most writers, she has been a storyteller for a long time. She is known for doing "the most" at the oddest times. Like deciding to pursue a writing career (finally) while raising two humans and working full time in a public school. She writes what she'd want to read: Stories where things turn out alright in the end.

www.ingramcontent.com/pod-product-compliance
Lightning Source LLC
Chambersburg PA
CBHW032346310726
48973CB00007B/1876